HOMEOPATHIC MEDICINE: FIRST-AID AND EMERGENCY CARE

BY
Lyle W. Morgan II, H.M.D.

HOMEOPATHIC MEDICINE: FIRST-AID AND EMERGENCY CARE

BY
Lyle W. Morgan II, H.M.D.

HEALING ARTS PRESS
Rochester, Vermont

Note to the reader: This book is intended as an informational guide. The remedies, approaches, and techniqus described herein are meant to supplement, and not to be a substitute for, professional medical care or treatment. They should not by used to treat a serious ailment without prior consultation with a qualified healthcare professional.

Healing Arts Press
One Park Street
Rochester, Vermont 05767

LIBRARY OF CONGRESS CATALOGING-IN-PUBLICATION DATA

Morgan, Lyle W.
Homeopathic medicine : first-aid and emergency care
by Lyle W. Morgan
p. cm.
Includes index.
ISBN 0-89281-249-4 (pbk.)
1. Medical emergencies—Homeopathic treatment. 2. Wounds and injuries—Homeopthic treatment. 3. First aid in illness and injury. 4. Self-care, Health. I. Title.
RX390.M67 1989   616'.025—dc19   88—30092

Printed and bound in the United States

10 9 8 7 6 5 4 3 2

Healing Arts Press is a division of Inner Traditions International, Ltd.

Distributed in the United States by American International Distribution Corporation (AIDC)

Distributed to the book trade in Canada by Book Center, Inc., Montreal, Quebec

Distributed to the health food trade in Canada by Alive Books, Toronto and Vancouver

CONTENTS

FOREWORD

This book by Dr. Lyle Morgan should accompany a good homeopathic first-aid kit—a vital addition to every home, office, and outdoorsman's backpack. Backpackers cannot carry excess weight and must therefore pack only the most potentially useful objects. So it should be with every home and office. In discussing the application of homeopathy to first-aid situations, Dr. Morgan suggests treatments for both common and unusual emergencies, remedies that can elicit the quickest natural healing response when time is of the essence.

Dr. Morgan's training in homeopathic medicine is extensive, but formal education alone is not enough. Dr. Morgan has years of valuable experience to supplement his education. An excellent author, he writes with style and enthusiasm; he writes with sufficient depth and explanation to be easily understandable; and his case reports give specific examples of how to apply the principles and practice of homeopathic medicine to individual cases for the lay reader and the professional health care provider.

Pharmaceutical companies' continued existence depends on profits, and profits are highest on sales of new medications protected by patents. With time, patents on medications expire, but some drugs with expired patents do enjoy good sales and provide continuing profits for the pharmaceutical companies. Many valuable medications never reach the market owing to limited use. Others never sell because of competition in strongly established markets. It is difficult to bring out a good drug when another already holds the market.

For many medical conditions the treatments are almost as bad as the disease. For these and other reasons, it is important that on-going studies of current therapy with the "popular" as well as the alternative therapy, be performed. Homeopathic medicine is one such alternative therapy, tested over decades of time and proven successful.

Dr. Lyle Morgan provides a valuable reference text of experiences with homeopathic and naturopathic treatment for many common and uncommon conditions. Dr. Morgan's case studies are particularly instructive, giving graphic evidence of the success of the therapies. Advice given covers the more common situations likely to be encountered, and topics are explained in sufficient detail to be extrapolated to more complex cases. This book is invaluable for medical self-help and first aid, not only in the home but for the outdoors venturer and backpacker, too.

No single methodology provides cures for all conditions, and limitations concerning self-help and first aid are well stated here. Mechanisms of action are provided, and this information helps explain which therapy will likely be the most effective.

Dr. Morgan covers situations with the drama of real life. Rapid improvement with the methods presented is typical; suggestions for enhancing effectiveness are given. Explicit warnings are presented of what to do if the treatment is not rapidly effective. This book, in summary, is one that will be invaluable to anyone called on to give first aid or emergency care.

Harvey Neal Sievers, M.D., F.A.A.F.P.
The Blair Medical Group

ACKNOWLEDGMENTS

I wish to thank everyone who has assisted me in making this book possible, in particular the following individuals:

Jack E. Craig, President, Standard Homeopathic Company, who provided encouragement through his correspondence and graciously granted permission to quote succinct materials from *Homeopathic Miscellany,* which I could not have written any better. Jay P. Borneman, Marketing Director, Standard Homeopathic Company, for his unfailing encouragement and his reading of the final working draft. Dana Ullman, M.P.H., Director, Homeopathic Educational Services and President, Foundation for Homeopathic Education and Research, for his interest in my work. H. Neal Sievers, M.D., F.A.A.F.P., family practitioner and Fellow of the American Academy of Family Physicians. Neal exemplifies the truest definition of *physician*—a humane healer. From editing the manuscript to assisting in other technical matters, Neal provided the boost necessary to complete the task of bringing the clear, sound principles of homeopathic emergency first aid and self-care to the reading public. James F. Bellman, Jr., Ph.D., and Kathryn A. Bellman, J.D., Ph.D., believers in the power and efficacy of homeopathy, for their valued friendship and continued support. My father, Lyle W. Morgan, and my late mother, Ione E. Morgan, for their unflagging belief that I could accomplish whatever goals I set before me, for their love and guidance, always. And certainly not least of all, Paul ("Sarge") and Carol Anglen, Kevin Sean Anglen, and Dr. Michael and Kathy Heffernan, who never let me forget to strive for my *best.* I love you all.

Lyle W. Morgan II, H.M.D., Ph.D.

A READER'S ADVISORY

It is not the purpose of this book to replace the professional services of a physician. The reader should not hesitate to consult a licensed physician or other licensed or certified health care practitioner for any illness or injury that requires professional treatment.

Homeopathic remedies have been used by physicians, licensed or certified health care providers, and lay people for nearly 200 years. Scientific research is now proving that homeopathic remedies have remarkable and valuable healing properties. The United States Food and Drug Administration has recognized the legal status of homeopathic medicines as listed in the *Homeopathic Pharmacopoeia of the United States* as approved medicines, so long as they have not been altered in their formulations or inaccurate claims made regarding their effectiveness. Most homeopathic remedies are available as nonprescription, over-the-counter drugs with the exception of some tinctures, potencies, and special combinations that can be used only by licensed physicians.

The remedy indications and tables in this book have been taken from authoritative sources: the homeopathic *Materia Medica* and the writings of physicians, clinicians, and researchers in scientific laboratory reports, medical documents and journals, and other related sources. No attempt should be made on the part of the reader to use any of this information as a form of treatment for any illness or injury that requires the care of a licensed or certified health care provider.

Principle Sources of Information Used for This Book:
Leaders in Homoeopathic Therapeutics, E. B. Nash, M.D. (Calcutta, India: Sett Dey & Company), 1959.

The Prescriber, 9th ed., John Henry Clarke, M.D. (North Devon, England: Health Science Press), 1972.

Emergency Homoeopathic First-Aid, Paul Chavanon, M.D., and Rene Levannier, M.D. (Wellingborough, Northamptonshire, England: Thorsons Publishers, Ltd.), 1977.

Homoeopathic Medicine, Trevor Smith, M.D. (Rochester, Vermont: Healing Arts Press), 1984.

Practical Homoeopathic Therapeutics, 3rd ed., W. A. Dewey, M.D. (New Delhi, India: Jain Publishing Company), 1981.

A Clinical Repertory to the Dictionary of Materia Medica, John Henry Clarke, M.D. (North Devon, England: Health Science Press), 1979.

An Introduction to the Principles and Practice of Homoeopathy, 3rd ed., Charles E. Wheeler, M.D. (North Devon, England: Health Science Press), 1948.

Homoeopathic Drug Pictures, M. L. Tyler, M.D. (Brux.) (North Devon, England: Health Science Press), 1952.

Pocket Manual of Homoeopathic Materia Medica, 9th ed., William Boericke, M.D. (Calcutta, India: Sett Dey & Company), 1976.

ABOUT THE AUTHOR

Dr. Lyle W. Morgan II has been practicing homeopathic medicine for more than 15 years. Holding a Ph.D. from the University of Nebraska, the Doctor of Homeopathic Medicine from the Université Internationale, and the Doctor of Nutrimedicine from the John F. Kennedy College of Nutrimedical Arts & Sciences, he is currently South-Central Region Director of the American Nutrimedical Association. A Certified Nutrimedicist, Dr. Morgan was recognized as a Fellow of the American Nutrimedical Association in 1986. A health care educator, he is also a professor and academic program director at Pittsburg State University, Pittsburg, Kansas.

PREFACE

MEDICAL SELF-RELIANCE
AND HOMEOPATHY

One of the most rapidly growing movements in America today is holistic health coupled with a surging public interest in medical self-reliance. The term "holism" derives from the Greek *holos,* meaning total. First coined by Jan C. Smuts in 1926, holism, which includes occupational, physical, intellectual, social, emotional, and spiritual health and wellness, is used to "express the idea that a whole organism is greater than the sum of its parts. Since then, the term has been applied to the various groups which promote the 'mind, body, spirit' philosophy."[1]

No right-thinking and intelligent individual would suggest we turn back the clock on some of the great medical discoveries and advances made in the last 30 years. Impressive strides have been made against some of the greatest scourges ever faced by humanity. Doctors Salk and Sabin, through their pioneering research efforts, were able to make poliomyelitis all but extinct. By the end of the decade of the 1980s the World Health Organization predicts that smallpox will have been exterminated worldwide. Considerable efforts are being made against cancers, especially childhood cancers. The rates of remission and the accompanying clinical cure rates have sky-rocketed in the past few years. No one would suggest that the computer-controlled biomechanical devices that permit amputee children and adults to lead more fully useful and comfortable lives be scrapped, or that research be discontinued. And perhaps the fiction writer's concept of a bionic man of television fame is not so much a fiction at all, but will be a reality in the not-too-distant future.

No, no right-thinking individual would ask us to retrogress in medicine.

When some people, with a sparkle in their eyes, speak of "the good old days" when life was simpler and people seemed healthier than today, they ignore the fact that people often died of infection from simple wounds, or were crippled for life by broken bones improperly set. Orthodox medicine had no immunizations against, or effective treatment for, rabies or tetanus or pneumonia. Our ancestors certainly were less exposed to pollution—to the industrial wastes, the pesticides, herbicides, and fertilizer products that seep into our public water supplies, into the foods we eat, and into the very air we breath. But the overall lives of our pioneer forebears were far from idyllic, Adam-and-Eve existences in a Garden of Eden. Our ancestors did, however, accept the bulk of the responsibility for their own health and well-being—something far too many of us "moderns" have abrogated and willingly turned over to the professional purveyors of health: the white-coated doctors and the chrome-and-glass clinics and hospitals.

This latter view may, however, be exaggerated. According to research published by Lowell S. Levin, Ed.D., Professor of Public Health at Yale University School of Medicine, "studies undertaken during the last decade here and in Western Europe form a picture of health care quite contrary to our accustomed view. We are accumulating evidence that perhaps 75 percent or more of *all* health care is provided by lay people to themselves and family without professional intervention."[2] In his article, Vaughn goes on to say that, "Judging from recent studies, up to 90 percent of this self-doctoring is responsible and relevant care."[3]

All too often, medicines and physicians themselves are the *causes* of illness. These diseases, contracted during hospitalization or brought about by patients receiving the wrong medication or the wrong dosages of correct medication, are termed *iatrogenic* (physician-caused) diseases.[4] A recent report from the federal government's General Accounting Office shows that a full 74 percent of deaths attributable to drugs are the result of physician-prescribed drugs and 75 percent of drug emergencies involve prescription drugs.[5]

The major problem with traditional medicine is, as it has always been, a lack of a truly unified theory to support its system of health care delivery. Dana Ullman, M.P.H., President of the Foundation for Homeopathic Education and Research, states that "as valuable as conventional medicine is, it also has its limitations and problems. Because conventional drugs are usually prescribed for their individual capacities to act upon specific parts of the body, it follows that several different drugs might be prescribed to treat the various symptoms of one individual. And, of course, it then follows that additional drugs would be needed to control the side effects of one or more of the other drugs being taken."[6] From its initial inception by Samuel C. F. Hahnemann, M.D., homeopathic medicine (the system of medical self-help, first aid, and emergency care this book presents) has never lacked that unified element. Homeopaths *know* the medicines they employ in health care treatment, are thoroughly aware of what their drugs are, and are intensely knowledgeable of their medications' effects. Unfortunately, the same cannot always be said of traditional physicians.

One of the essential differences between the training of a traditional doctor of medicine and a doctor of homeopathic medicine, or a physician who subspecializes in homeopathy, is in pharmacology. Under current training (which is now undergoing close scrutiny by the medical profession itself), physicians-to-be normally receive only one formal course in pharmacology in 4 years of medical education. The homeopathic physician's training includes both intensive and extensive training in homeopathic pharmacology. In actual practice, the majority of traditional (allopathic) physicians rely heavily for their understanding of drugs on information supplied by drug sales representatives who visit their offices and on the literature that accompanies the samples sent to them by pharmaceutical companies. In homeopathic education, future homeopaths are trained throughout the course of their studies in the history, composition, manufacture, and effect of the medications they employ.

Two prominent examples of *iatrogenic* diseases or severe illnesses directly attributable to traditional drugs have recently received recognition in the medical community. Cortisone and other powerful steroids are routinely prescribed to treat asthma, arthritis, allergies, and various skin diseases, and patients receiving long-term treatment with these drugs frequently experience spontaneous bone fractures owing to calcium loss. Numerous medical studies have demonstrated that it is the steroids themselves, not the natural progress of the diseases, that cause the bone loss. And some children receiving immunizations for diphtheria, pertussis, and tetanus (DPT) or for measles experience severe convulsive seizures following the injection. Hirtz and coworkers, in *The Journal of Pediatrics,* have advised physicians to routinely give heavily sugared drinks, aspirin, or acetaminophen to counteract that side effect.[7]

When traditional medicine, or conventional physicians, complain that homeopathy is "unproven" in a clearly defined and scientific way, they ignore the ever-mounting evidence cited concerning the unknown long-term effects of allopathic medications and the unsubstantiated effectiveness of allopathic health care delivery. A 1978 study on conventional medicine said this: "It has been estimated that only 10 to 20 percent of all procedures currently used in medical practice have been shown to be efficacious by controlled trial."[8]

Newsweek magazine reported a meeting between the American College of Physicians and the United States Food and Drug Administration. At that meeting it was acknowledged that the best drugs often do harm when intended to do good, that there are too many hospital admissions for iatrogenic diseases, and that the average hospitalized patient received 11 different drugs during a course of treatment.[9]

The traditionally trained physicians—the doctors of medicine and the doctors of osteopathy—have at their command some 10,000 pharmaceutical agents that they can prescribe. The majority may, however, use no more than 40 in typical daily use. And some of those drugs are badly misused. Some physicians use drugs to treat conditions for which the drugs were neither tested nor approved. An August 1982 *FDA Bulletin* warned doctors not to give smallpox vaccinations to allay herpes, warts, and other diseases. But some doctors do just that, possibly endangering their trusting patients' health.[10]

The homeopath has a range of nearly 3000 remedies in the *Materia Medica,* of which 140 or more are normally called upon in daily use. The sheer quantity of possible medications ordinarily employed requires the homeopath to be keenly aware of the guiding or Keynote symptoms of these medicines. When confronted with a difficult case or a puzzling compendium of symptoms, the homeopath frequently consults a *Repertory,* which lists literally tens of thousands of guiding (major) and peculiar (odd or minor) symptoms. He or she then double-checks a *Materia Medica* for further confirmation before prescribing, just as the traditional physician may consult the *PDR* (*Physician's Desk Reference*) concerning allopathic medicines.

Time magazine reported that "the failure of doctors in [the 'lack of knowledge and sophistication in the proper use of drugs'] is perhaps the greatest deficiency of the average physician today."[11] The report in the same issue of *Time* continued, stating that "the failure of doctors in this area [drug awareness] traces back to medical schools, most of which give only the one course in drugs and their use. Later, in practice, the physician gets most of his information on drugs from manufacturers' promotional material." This is not, and never has been, true of the homeopath.

In an article in *The Lancet,* a prestigious and official journal of traditional, orthodox British medicine, Frank Brodman, M.D., stated, "Even in orthodox medicine, agents and drugs are employed which benefit although we are still ignorant of their mode of action [while] homeopaths consider that they have a rule of drug selections so clear that, with care and patience, a remedy can be chosen with confidence, even for conditions wherein diagnosis may be doubtful for a time."[12] Additionally, *Prevention Magazine* reported on a highly regarded, prominent British dermatologist who grew so frustrated by the lack of current traditional knowledge, with drug reactions and poor patient results, that he obtained a homeopathic textbook, took a postgraduate course, and now employs homeopathic remedies almost exclusively.[13]

Homeopathy is not a new discovery in medicine. In fact, homeopathy is very old, but in another sense ultramodern. In its declaration entitled *Homeopathy, the Scientific Practice of Medicine,* the American Foundation for Homeopathy states that homeopathy:

> Defines precisely what it is that is to be cured. Through scientific experiment has derived precisely the laws by which life itself, including cure, operates. Is able to reach the entire individual—Vital Force, Mind and Body, with the Single Individual Remedy. Never confuses Symptoms with Disease; has a clear scientific conception of Symptoms, what they mean, and how to use the Totality of Symptoms to find the One Individual Remedy. Realizes the connection between successive maladies. By its treatment strengthens the ability to remain well. Instead of "fighting diseases" treats patients. Makes no experiments on the sick, but has proved every remedy *before* it is used. Goes to work at once, whether the "diagnosis" is known, unknown, or

indeterminate. Goes deeper and further than laboratory findings to facts that are *prior*. Understands the difference between Palliation, Suppression and Cure; understands the consequences of that difference for the Safety and Welfare of the sick. It is not satisfied with Palliation or Suppression. Does not by Suppression drive light maladies to serious ones or the "diseases of youth" into the "diseases of old age." Would, if practiced generally, save the People of the United States, at a conservative estimate, more than $10,000,000,000 every year.[14]

The figure above reads *ten thousand* MILLION dollars.

Every year dozens of books are published concerning popular health care: how to lose weight, how to gain weight, how to remain "ageless," how to age gracefully, how to prevent high blood pressure, how to lower high blood pressure, how to deal with chronic illnesses (such as arthritis and diabetes), even how to die with dignity. These books, published by thoughtful publishers, are bought by millions of people. Why? They are searching for answers to the complexities of modern living, searching for answers to nagging questions about themselves. They ask, "What can we do to prevent illnesses? How can we deal with and take charge of our own bodies?"

Obviously this book cannot provide all the answers to these complex and troubling questions, nor can any one book. But scientific homeopathy, truly a system of health care whose time has come, can take many of the annoyances out of modern living. In the majority of the common accidents and illnesses, in the uncomplicated diseases and disorders each of us faces day to day, homeopathy can help. Homeopathy is not only curative of most of these problems, it is also in instances *preventive* of some. And, because homeopathy has been proved to be absolutely safe, even for treatment of the youngest to the oldest members of our society, it can be well employed to great benefit by the thoughtful and careful lay person. In nearly two centuries of practice on millions of men, women, and children, homeopathic medications have never been proved to cause iatrogenic diseases. The medicines, called "remedies," produce no adverse side effects and cause no unpleasant or dangerous after-effects. The chances are that your family physician has never heard of homeopathic remedies, or perhaps may recall a ten-minute lecture given in medical school in a History of Medicine course. In fact, homeopathy was almost the leading system of medicine practiced in the United States until the early 20th century.

As a major force in medicine, homeopathy rapidly declined following the introduction of antibiotics, and it became nearly extinct due to intense political action taken by the American Medical Association, whose orthodox members did not understand homeopathy and feared its competition.[15] But homeopathy never died. And it never went underground. In the past decade American homeopathy has staged a brilliant comeback. As A. Dwight Smith, M.D., states in his book, *Homeopathy, A Rational and Scientific Method of Treatment,* "When a regular physician investigates homeopathy, he almost invariably adopts it."

Homeopathy, as a major force in the ever-growing holistic health movement, is, albeit slowly, proving itself to be the most rational, thoughtful, and scientific of all healing methods. It is not subject to theories, gimmicks, and half-truths such as may be found in modern medicine today.

This book is dedicated to those men and women who believe they can and should take charge of their own health, who wish to avoid the high cost of medical care in those illnesses and injuries that do not require the immediate attention of a licensed health care professional, and to all those who wish to investigate an alternative to traditional medical self-help, first aid, and emergency care—a homeopathic alternative that *works!*

PART ONE

PRINCIPLES OF
HOMEOPATHY

CHAPTER ONE

INTRODUCTION TO HOMEOPATHY

What are first aid and self-help? First aid is exactly what the name implies: the prompt, initial care of the injured or ill. Medical self-help is also a form of first aid—the assistance that is rendered to one's self, family, or friends at the beginning stages of illness, or immediately following an accident causing physical injury. First aid and medical self-help, even with the use of homeopathic remedies, are no substitute for the skilled attention of a licensed health care professional whenever the injury or illness so indicates. However, when properly administered, first aid or medical self-help often solves the problem and avoids the need to consult a licensed health care practitioner.

What Is Homeopathy?

Homeopathy is a system of medicine practiced by thousands of skilled health care professionals throughout the world. The basic principles of homeopathy date back nearly 200 years, stemming from the research of Samuel Hahnemann, M.D., a German physician and research chemist. Homeopathy is one of the three major systems of medicine currently in practice worldwide: *medicine* (including osteopathy); *naturopathy,* which employs totally natural healing methods: botanical-herbal medicine, nutrition, and homeopathy with emphasis on preventive health care; and *homeopathy,*[16] perhaps the most comprehensive of all healing systems.

Although it is a method of health care delivery most often unheard of, ignored, or misunderstood by the medical profession, homeopathy is gaining a good deal of recognition in the latter part of the 20th century. This recognition develops as people become ever more aware of their innate healing capacities, and desire less invasive and complex approaches to wellness.[17] Homeopathy in practice always recognizes the human being as a totally unique biological and psychological entity; while all humans possess physiological and psychological aspects in common as a race, homeopathy recognizes today, as it always has, the distinct uniqueness of each infant, child, youth, and adult. Accordingly, homeopathy strives for *individualization* of treatment based upon the principle of holism: the healing of Mind, Body, and Spirit.

Homeopathy works by the guiding concept of *personalized treatment.* While modern, orthodox medicine has made gigantic strides in just the past decade, personalized treatment is often lacking. The following is quoted from *American Homeopathy:*

A recent editorial in the *Journal of the American Medical Association* claims that new technology is causing "a serious breach . . . between patients and physicians."

Written by Dr. Lawrence C. Grouse, a contributing editor to *JAMA,* the editorial accuses doctors (specialists in particular) of retreating behind their machines and thereby becoming no more than an extension of those machines.

Dr. Grouse warned that reliance on medical machines creates a rift between practitioner and patient in two ways. First, it contributes to the growing depersonalization of medicine. This trend is a real concern among patients, 62 percent of whom, in a recent AMA survey, responded that doctors are spending too little time with them. The other disadvantage is the inevitable increase in cost to the patient arising from the use of such sophisticated machinery.

Though not suggesting complete avoidance of medical technology, Dr. Grouse stresses that physicians should be careful not to let the machinery create a destructive wedge between themselves and their patients.[18]

Today, as when Hahnemann first introduced his health care system, the modern homeopath is a highly trained and skilled practitioner of the medical arts. The complexity of homeopathic practice requires that the physician spend additional years, normally in formal study and clinical preceptorship, beyond the basic medical training and become adept at the accurate prescribing of some 3000 remedies in the homeopathic *Materia Medica*. However, because the majority of illnesses and accidents leading to physical injury are far less complex than the diagnosis and treatment of major health problems, in the practice of first aid, medical self-help, and emergency care, the careful, nonmedically trained man or woman will have no difficulty in finding and applying the correct homeopathic treatment to bring about *a rapid, safe, and effective cure* for nearly any common problem. Homeopathic medicines, in the context of first aid and medical self-help, *can do no harm, but only good, when used as directed.*

Homeopathy places a strong emphasis on the day-in and day-out responsibility for health and well-being on the public, and seeks to educate and therefore increase the competence of patients.[19] To educate and create competence in applying the principles and practice of homeopathy in medical self-care and emergency first aid is the focus of this book. It is hoped that this text will accomplish the goal of bringing a safe, sane, and effective system of care to the general public.

The Need for First-Aid Training

Because this book is devoted to the application of homeopathic remedies as an adjunct to the practice of competent first aid, it is assumed that the emergency care provider has had the proper training in the basic or advanced first-aid skills through a course in American Red Cross Basic, Multi-Media, or Advanced First Aid, or has taken a recognized course in Emergency Health Care or Medical Self-Help from a community agency or a college, community college, or university. All persons attempting first-aid care of the sick or injured should be trained in the skills necessary to properly handle the primary, on-the-scene care of the sick or injured until more advanced medical assistance can be obtained in those all-important cases when skilled attention is needed.

Homeopathic Remedies Versus Standard Medicine

Homeopathic medicines are called "remedies" because they are not drugs in the commonly used sense. The most common form of medicine today, called *allopathy*, bases its practice on more or less large dosages of drugs. Compared to homeopathic remedies, allopathic drugs are relatively crude and must be given in large dosages to effect a cure.

The traditionally trained (allopathic) physician, either a doctor of medicine or an osteopathic physician, may (for instance) use penicillin for a sore throat, or any of a number of other antibiotic prescription pharmaceuticals. These drugs are given in a total dosage of several hundred milligrams over a period of days or weeks. Allopathic medicines mount a massive direct attack on the disease or disorder itself to overcome the problem. In the case of an infection, for example, an antibiotic will be prescribed for the bacterial infection causing the disease. *Antibiotic* means *anti* (against) *biologic* (life). The antibiotic[20] acts much like an army battling an enemy: it attacks, overwhelms, and overpowers it. This is, in some respects, an oversimplification of a highly complex chemical process. Antibiotics, like any pharmaceutical product, must work in conjunction with the body's immune system. It is the immune system that engulfs the dead and dying bacteria and viruses, and it must as well eliminate the chemical reactions that result from the death of the invading bacteria or viruses and the effects of the dead cells locally and systemically. In essence, no physician and no pharmaceutical product ever "cures" the body of disease. They assist the body's own defensive system to heal itself.

Sometimes one antibiotic will fail to overcome the invading bacteria. This occurs when the wrong antibiotic is prescribed, or the bacteria have developed a resistance to it. When that occurs, the physician will prescribe yet another antibiotic in the hope that it will cure the disease.

Homeopathic remedies, on the other hand, act *with* the body rather than directly against the disease process. This is an important distinction. Homeopathic remedies use the body's own *vital life force*, the natural immunity within the body (that as yet mysterious and not fully understood quality within each living creature), and the body's own defense mechanisms to overcome the disease process.

A parallel can be, and often is, drawn between homeopathic remedies and the injections used to vaccinate individuals against various diseases such as smallpox, tetanus, diphtheria, poliomyelitis, "flu," pertussis, mumps, and measles. The vaccination given to protect the individual from these diseases is a micro-diluted dose of the disease organism itself, either living (but weakened) or dead, which acts by allowing the body to develop its own defenses against the bacteria or virus for which the immunity is being developed. The principle of homeopathy works in much the same, although not an identical, manner. Homeopathy (from the Greek words *homoion pathos,* "similar disease") is based on the Law of Similars, frequently expressed as *Similia similibus curantur*—"Let like be cured by like." It was the guiding principle of the great Greek physician Hippocrates, rediscovered and applied in modern times by Samuel Hahnemann. In homeopathy, a micro-diluted, potentized dose of a substance which, in its rawest and crudest form, would produce symptoms in a healthy person *similar to* those being experienced by the sick individual, is introduced into the body in tablet or liquid form. (The term *potentized* refers to any dilution that has been succussed or triturated, making the medicine highly reactive.) In a homeopathically potentized form the substance given stimulates the body's own natural defense system to react against the disease or physical injury. As homeopathy is based on the *total symptoms* a sick or injured person is experiencing, a homeopathic remedy must be chosen that matches those symptoms.

The essential difference between the allopathic[21] immunological vaccination and the homeopathic remedy is that the homeopathic remedy often works remarkably rapidly, frequently producing a beneficial healing stimulus in a matter of minutes or hours, whereas the vaccination requires days or even weeks before it becomes effective. In addition, *vaccination cannot be used to treat a disease already established.* Homeopathic remedies can often be used as both a preventive and a cure.

Returning to the case of antibiotics used to combat infection, although it is true they can and usually do destroy bacteria and therefore cure an individual of a bacteria-caused[22] illness, the regimen of antibiotic treatment can cause unpleasant side effects.

An example of possible side effects a person might experience with antibiotics is seen in the *Adverse Reactions* statement of a common bacteriostatic drug, Septra or Bactrim, a potent combination of two antiinfectives, sulfamethoxazole and trimethoprim, used in the treatment of urinary infections. Its side effects can include the following:

Blood Dyscrasias: Agranulocytosis, aplastic anemia, megaloblastic anemia, thrombopenia, leukopenia, hemolytic anemia, purpura, hypoprothrombinemia, and methemoglobinemia.

Allergic Reactions: Erythema multiforme, Stevens-Johnson syndrome, generalized skin eruptions, epidermal necrolysis, urticaria, serum sickness, pruritus, exfoliative dermatitis, anaphylactoid reactions, periorbital edema, conjunctival and scleral injection, photosensitization, arthralgia, and allergic myocarditis.

Gastrointestinal Reactions: Glossitis, stomatitis, nausea, emesis, abdominal pains, hepatitis, diarrhea, pseudomembraneous colitis, and pancreatitis.

CNS Reactions: Headache, peripheral neuritis, mental depression, convulsions, ataxia, hallucinations, tinnitus, vertigo, insomnia, apathy, fatigue, muscle weakness, and nervousness.

Miscellaneous Reactions: Drug fever, chills, and toxic nephrosis with oliguria and anuria. Periarteritis and LE phenomenon have occurred.[23]

Not only do antibiotics destroy *disease-producing* bacteria, they can and do destroy millions—or even billions—of beneficial bacteria required for the proper functioning of the system. For this very reason, and because of possible side effects that can occur, oral antibiotics are available in the United States and in most Western countries only on the prescription of a licensed physician.

The use, overuse, or abuse of antibiotics can completely sterilize the intestinal tract of the bacteria necessary for the proper digestion, absorption, and utilization of vital nutrients—vitamins, minerals, and enzymes—leaving the antibiotic-treated individual weakened and susceptible to additional infections and illnesses. Also, modern medical research has proved beyond doubt that the overuse of some antibiotics (such as tetracycline) resulted in establishment of bacteria that are partially or totally resistant to many antibiotics that a few years earlier worked well and were considered "miracles" of medicine. Therefore, the search for new and more effective antibiotics constantly continues throughout the drug-manufacturing industry.

Homeopathic remedies, however, because they work *with* the body's own natural resistance to infection, leave the system strengthened, never weakened. In nearly 200 years of use, homeopathic remedies have never been shown to become ineffective through overuse. As one veterinarian recently lamented, the same amount of penicillin once used to cure a 1500-pound cow of a bacterial infection is now barely sufficient to treat an 8-pound cat with the same infection. The properly selected homeopathic remedy will treat, and cure, that same 1500-pound cow, that same 8-pound cat, or a 200-pound man, *symptoms agreeing*.

Homeopathic Remedies: Not Crude Drugs

Homeopathic remedies are not crude drugs, but carefully prepared medicines, manufactured by highly trained and specialized pharmaceutical chemists. Taken as directed, homeopathic remedies are rapidly absorbed into the circulatory system. Often, these remedies work so quickly and so completely that the body can overcome the physical disorder or disease in minutes or hours, rather than in days or even weeks, as under standard medical treatment. The speed of improvement with homeopathic remedies in the practice of first aid or medical self-help is almost overwhelming— something that must be seen to be believed.

An example of the rapidity of homeopathic remedies in first aid treatment is seen in the use of China or Vipera in the common nosebleed. The reaction is often nearly instantaneous. Usually within 1 minute the bleeding will have ceased. There is no need to tilt the head forward[24] for long minutes, or to place an ice pack on the back of the neck, pinch the nose closed, or pack the affected nostril with a tissue.

> ADVISORY WARNING: A nosebleed can sometimes be a symptom of a serious health problem, such as high blood pressure or a tumor. If a person has frequent nosebleeds, or if what at first appears to be a simple nosebleed lasts longer than 15 or 20 minutes, the person should see a qualified physician.

A case history of homeopathic first aid is illustrative. A retired oil company executive, prior to leaving on vacation, suffered a subconjunctival hemorrhage—a spontaneous "leaking" of blood from the fine vessels in the "white" of the eye. The eye was badly bloodshot. The condition is not serious, but it is always annoying and greatly alarming. The man's physician advised him to place hot compresses over the eye, and to expect the blood to reabsorb in 10 to 14 days.[25] As the man had an important meeting to attend and a speech to deliver two days later, he decided to wear dark glasses to conceal the condition. He also telephoned a homeopathic practitioner, who, on the basis of his symptoms, gave him one dose of Arnica (in its 200 potency) to take before he went to bed. Overnight the Arnica had removed all redness! However, 24 hours later, the blood had "leaked" into the white again. The Arnica had done its job, but had failed to hold. A homeopathic remedy often more specific to a subconjunctival hemorrhage than Arnica is Hamamelis, a homeopathic preparation of the common herb witch hazel. Hamamelis (200 potency) was given, the condition cleared again in about 12 hours, and there was no recurrence. Homeopathic first aid had worked rapidly and permanently, once the *correct* remedy was given!

Other examples of rapidity of homeopathic remedies in first-aid practice will be noted throughout this book.

Can anything be *that* good? Many people, when they first are introduced to homeopathic first-aid principles, are skeptical. They believe that nothing can be that good or every physician and first-aider in the world would be using homeopathic remedies. However, homeopathic remedies do work that rapidly and that completely—symptoms agreeing—and without any ill effects. *There are no side effects, and no unpleasant after-effects, with homeopathic remedies.*

Actually, many thoughtful physicians in the United States and throughout the world are learning about homeopathy and adopting it into their standard medical and even surgical practices. Often the patient is unaware that the tiny tablets or pellets prescribed by the physician are homeopathic remedies. Each year hundreds of new physicians and many veteran doctors in America and across the globe are learning about and acquiring the skills to employ homeopathic remedies in their practice of medicine. Dr. William Tiller, Chairman of Materials Science and Engineering at Stanford University, said: "It is clear that we are going out of the age of chemical and mechanical medicine and into the age of energetic and homeopathic medicine."[26]

American first aid is behind the times. For example, in Great Britain, the two recognized first-aid organizations (the Saint John's Association and the Red Cross Association) incorporate the use of homeopathic remedies into their first-aid instruction. In Great Britain, these organizations have seen what properly applied homeopathic remedies can do to relieve the minor annoyances of everyday living—the cuts, scrapes, and bruises. They have also seen the power of homeopathic remedies in more serious illnesses and injuries. In first aid, the guiding principle is *to do no harm; to assist the sick or injured individual to the most rapid and successful recovery.* It is to this end that homeopathic first-aid principles can best be applied.

Recognition by the United States Government

At the present time no first-aid association in the United States has recognized the use of homeopathic remedies—much to their loss and to the loss of those persons who become ill or injured and are away from immediate, skilled medical assistance. In the case of serious accident or illness, even those individuals who are within rapid access to medical care can be treated on the spot with the proper homeopathic remedy and be greatly assisted in their recovery. After medical attention has been provided, in serious cases, the principles outlined in this book can be used to greatly speed recovery and ease pain. In first-aid applications in the home, the workplace, the school, and numerous other locales, when the illness or injury is not severe enough to require care by a physician, homeopathic first-aid is a godsend.

Remember: Homeopathic remedies used in first-aid care can do no harm and can do only good when used as directed.

Homeopathic remedies are recognized by both the United States Food and Drug Administration, as recorded in the *Homeopathic Pharmacopoeia of the United States,* and the United States Congress under the provisions of Medicare.

Preparation of Homeopathic Remedies

O, mickle is the powerful grace that lies
In plants, herbs, stones, and their true qualities;
For naught so vile that on the earth doth live
But to the earth some special good doth give.
(William Shakespeare, *Romeo and Juliet,* II, iii,15–18)

William Shakespeare lived nearly 200 years before Hahnemann proposed the homeopathic principle. But the great poet was very well aware of the great value of the earth's natural resources to bring healing power to the sick and injured.

Homeopathic remedies are prepared from natural substances, mainly plants and herbs, but also from biological sources and minerals. Of course, modern allopathic pharmaceuticals are also prepared from naturally occurring substances, or from synthetic chemical substitutes, which often are far less expensive and easier to obtain. The difference between allopathic drugs and homeopathic remedies is that homeopathic remedies are *triturated*—diluted—through a complex manufacturing process, under the strictest sanitary and controlled conditions until they become readily assimilable into the system.[27] Homeopathic remedies do not need to be digested; one does not have to wait until the body breaks them down into usable form. They go to work immediately to stimulate the body's vital life force to fight the disease process.

About Potencies

Homeopathy employs two distinctive potency systems. These systems determine the reactivity (or strength) of a homeopathic remedy. The first system is the *decimal* or x; the second is the *centesimal* or c system.

In the decimal system, that most commonly used in the United States, a dilution (and potentization) of a homeopathic remedy is expressed by a number (1, 3, 6, 12, 30) followed by a letter "x." A 1x potency designates the basic homeopathic concentration of the medicinal agent as being 1/10th, 2x–1/100th, 3x–1/1000th. "A simple way to understand is to visualize a zero in the bottom half (denominator) of the fraction for every number preceding the x."[28] A 6x decimal potency would have 6 zeros in the denominator: 1/1,000,000 or *one millionth* of the basic medicinal ingredient in an appropriate diluting medium.

In the centesimal system, that most commonly used in the United Kingdom and Europe, but now also finding more popularity in the United States as well, "each subsequent dilution contains 1/100 of the concentration of the preceding dilution."[29] Therefore, a 1c homeopathic potency would have 1/100th of the basic homeopathic concentration of a medicinal agent. The following table compares the actual dilution ratio of the decimal and centesimal scales used in homeopathy:

DILUTION RATIO	DECIMAL SCALE (x)	CENTESIMAL SCALE (c)
1/10	1x	—
1/100	2x	1c
1/1000	3x	—
1/10,000	4x	2c
1/1,000,000	6x	3c
1/1,000,000,000,000	12x	6c
10^{-24}	24x	12c
10^{-30}	30x	15c
10^{-60}	60x	30c
10^{-2000}	—	M (1000c)
$10^{-20,000}$	—	10M (10,000c)
$10^{-200,000}$	—	CM (100,000c)

For the purposes of this book, and to provide for the ease of application of homeopathic principles in medical self-help and emergency care, tinctures (ø) and the decimal (x) potencies are recommended.

Although it may seem a contradiction, through careful clinical research, study, and actual medical practice, the homeopathic practitioner has found that the *higher* the dilution of the homeopathic remedy, the *more vitally reactive* it is in the body.[30] Homeopathic dilutions may go as high as the 1000 (1M), 10,000 (10M), 50,000 (50M), and 100,000 (CM) potencies.

ADVISORY WARNING: Potencies above the 200c are to be used only by the trained homeopathic physician![31] The first-aider must never use Arsenicum, Belladonna, or Cantharis below the 6x potency. In tincture, 1x, 2x, and 3x potencies, these remedies still contain a high concentration of natural poison. These remedies in low dilution are unavailable to the public.

As one prominent American homeopathic physician[32] once commented, the use of the highest homeopathic dilutions is like balancing on a razor's keen edge; they can stimulate the body's natural defense system so strongly and so quickly, with such violence, that only a skilled physician can successfully, and safely, administer them. In the practice of homeopathic first aid and medical self-help, only the dilutions from tincture through the 200x potencies should ever be used, even by the most skilled lay person.

The homeopathic pharmaceutical manufacturers and associated organizations listed in Appendix One supply convenient kits stocked with remedies for self-help and emergency care use in both the decimal and centesimal systems. The selection of a kit containing remedies in either the decimal or centesimal dilutions is only a matter of individual preference. Homeopathic remedies in the decimal system are recommended for the beginner and intermediate user of homeopathy.

More Is Not Best

We live in a nation that too often thinks more is best. The medical profession also must fight this false thinking of "if one pill is good, two or three are better" all the time. No wonder so many people overdose in America!

The most commonly asked question by the nonhomeopath is: "How can anything that is so diluted possibly work?" This is certainly a good question and deserves an honest answer.

In order for the human body to utilize *any* substance, either for food or for fighting disease, or to combat physical disorder resulting from an injury, it must be broken down by the body into a usable form. For example, even food carefully chewed and swallowed must be further subdivided by the chemicals and enzymes in the digestive tract before it can be absorbed into the system and used. The non-water-soluble Vitamins A, D, and E must first be broken down into micro-diluted form by the digestive process before the body can utilize them as vital nutrients. The same is true for pharmaceutical products.

Homeopathic remedies are already micro-diluted to some extent by the complex process of *trituration*. When introduced into the mouth, they are rapidly dissolved and the mucous membranes of the mouth, which act like sponges for medications, absorb them almost instantaneously into the bloodstream through the capillaries for distribution through the body. *There is no waiting time required for homeopathic remedies to work.* They work immediately. Homeopathy as practiced today began nearly 200 years ago, which permitted enough time for practice and research to have found that potentized, micro-diluted medicines boost the natural vital life force of the body. Homeopathy has found it is not necessary to overwhelm the body with massive doses of many milligrams of medication. Once stimulated by the micro-dose,[33] the system goes to work to overcome the cause of the disease process, just as nature intended.

Homeopathy: Merely a Matter of Mind?

Regardless of what has been said thus far, some people may ask, "With medicines measured in parts per million, or billion, or quadrillion, isn't the ill or injured person merely taking a placebo? Something they only *think* will help them?"[34]

The mind is a marvelous thing. Psychologists and psychiatrists have been attempting to unlock the mysteries of the mind for decades. Often, if a person's belief is strong enough, the mind will bring about what the person thinks or believes, in illness or in health.

Homeopathic remedies, however, are not placebos. They are *system stimulators.* This can be shown through the use of homeopathic remedies in veterinary practice. Yes, there are animal doctors who practice homeopathy and find it works as well as, and sometimes more effectively than, traditional medicine. Any pet owner who has struggled with a favorite cat or dog as it writhed while attempting to get the animal to take medications knows that animals don't think like people and won't assume taking medicine will make them feel better. In truth, many a favorite pet has been saved from destruction when veterinary medicine failed, rebounding to health through homeopathy!

To illustrate, one early evening in 1980, a man whose cat was diagnosed as having cystitis had tried everything the veterinarian had recommended and nothing had worked. He then consulted a homeopath, who explained he wasn't a veterinarian but would look at the cat.

The animal was a 4-year-old neutered tom that had suffered several bouts of "cystitis" every year since his neutering. The conditions had become chronic, the attacks especially acute and growing in frequency. The animal had been treated with every appropriate allopathic drug and catheterized so frequently that his urethra was scarred. Nothing had worked.

In homeopathy there is no such thing as "cystitis"—the common medical term for an inflammation of the bladder. Disease names mean nothing (other than for diagnostic purposes and medical records) in homeopathy. The only important fact is the *total symptom picture* the ill individual shows.

The tom could barely urinate, was obviously in severe pain, and strained repeatedly in its litter box, but passed only a few drops of urine. Often the litter was marked with blood. The most guiding symptom, however, was the cat's inclination to lay splayed out flat against the kitchen floor near a warm oven. This cat was clearly Cantharis. The Keynote symptoms for homeopathic Cantharis in any urinary problem are: scalding urine; urine passes by drops; urine is marked by blood; patient is *better* with warmth, *worse* with cold.

The veterinarian had recommended moist, hot packs on the cat's abdomen which seemed to soothe the cat. If the cat didn't recover, however, a surgical procedure known as *urethrostomy* would have to be performed—the removal of the urethra (amputation of the penis) and a widening of the bladder's neck. Few veterinarians perform this delicate surgery and this one had strongly recommended putting the cat to sleep.

The owner was given a 1-dram vial[35] of Cantharis (of 200x potency), with instructions to give the cat 3 pellets every hour for 2 doses, then stop and wait.

Less than 24 hours later, the man called. The same cat which, the night before, was in pain and sick and listless, was now tearing about the house like a kitten! The man was told to consult his veterinarian about a balanced diet for the cat, a diet low in ash and fiber, and was given another vial of Cantharis to use if the same symptoms ever developed again. They never have.

In another case, an 11-year-old neutered tom was being treated by a veterinarian. This cat also had "cystitis." Every time the cat took its pills, he was fine, but when the medication was stopped, the bladder problem returned. The owner gave this picture of the cat's symptoms: urine passes in drops; great straining in the litter box with little urine passed; no appearance of blood in the urine; cat preferred to lie outdoors on the cool back porch steps.

The veterinarian had suggested that the owner place moist, hot packs on the cat's abdomen to soothe it. Yet every time he attempted this, the cat would hiss, cry out, and fight. A major guiding symptom was established: *worse* from heat; *better* from cold. The remedy of choice in this case of cystitis was not Cantharis but another homeopathic remedy, Apis mellifica. The owner was given a small vial of Apis mel. (of 200x potency) with instructions. Two days later the cat was perfectly healthy. All signs of its bladder trouble were gone.

Homeopathic remedies work quickly and permanently in any disease, *when the guiding symptoms agree.*[36]

Are Homeopathic and Herbal Remedies the Same?

Many homeopathic remedies are derived from plants and herbs. From this some persons may get the idea that homeopathic and herbal remedies are the same. They are not. Herbalogy is both a science and an art. A person seeking herbal treatment for an illness or injury may receive different remedies or different combinations of herbs for the same problem from two different herbal practitioners. The chances of different remedies being suggested under homeopathic treatment are rare, as the treatment is based upon the *total symptom picture* the patient exhibits. Perhaps the following explanation best demonstrates the difference between homeopathy and herbalogy.

We have numerous inquiries from people who think a botanical produces the same action whether it is prepared homeopathically or herbally. In most instances this is a complete misconception.

Actually there are many situations where the homeopathic form of botanical creates the complete opposite reaction from the herbal form, occasionally under certain circumstances the two do treat the same condition, but often there is no connection between symptoms calling for a plant used as an herbal remedy and the same plant used homeopathically.

Where the herbal remedy is administered in the form of a very strong infusion of a plant, it may create the actual symptoms which the homeopathic remedy (very minute amounts of the same plant) is designed to correct. Often, though, the leaves of a plant will be used in the herbal remedy, the root in homeopathy, and the active homeopathic ingredient exists only in the root so there is no relationship between the two remedies. Or homeopathy may use the seed while the herbal remedy is from the stem, and so forth. . . .

In general it is a safe rule that homeopathic remedies from botanical sources should *not* be confused with herbal remedies from the same plant.[37]

There is a danger in intemperate use of herbal remedies. Some years ago a woman complained that every muscle in her body ached. She also said she snapped at people a lot. She believed in "health foods" and raised her own homegrown organic vegetables, took vitamins and minerals, and was "into" herbs. A year earlier she had developed "pleurisy" and had been taking an herbal formula compounded by a local health food store owner. Although she thought she should be feeling better, she really felt worse every day. The label on the bottle of capsules she was taking did not list the quantities of the various herb combinations contained in the preparation, but one of the herbs was white bryony, a European herb also known as English mandrake. The woman had been taking this combination, 3 capsules, 3 times a day, for almost 10 months and was beginning to feel quite awful. Not only did her muscles ache, but she was irritable and suffered extreme dizzy spells every time she got out of bed. When she bent over her head felt as if it were going to crack open, and she had frequent frontal headaches. Her mouth was constantly dry, and she had an incredible thirst. She also felt she needed to lie constantly still, but was "too busy." Her symptom picture was that of an overdose of Bryonia album (Bryonia alb.), the Latin botanical name for white bryony or English mandrake. The homeopath suggested she stop taking the herbal combination. Some weeks later, she was a new woman. The raw herb, in the large dosage she was taking, had actually been *producing* symptoms of severe illness!

This is, of course, not to say that herbal remedies are always dangerous. They are not. The woman mentioned may have had a particular sensitivity to whatever amount of white bryony the capsules contained. Another person may not have been so affected. The health-food store owner, although well-meaning, had not warned this woman of the possible consequences of overdosing with raw herbal remedies (if he even knew the dangers). Herbs, like any other medication, must be used wisely.

When Dr. Samuel Hahnemann first proposed the system of homeopathic medicine, he tested many plant extracts on himself. As the raw substances, taken in large quantity, produced various symptoms of illness, Dr. Hahnemann carefully recorded his observations. Then, taking the same substances, he diluted and potentized them through trituration and found that the now-diluted doses counteracted the symptoms produced by the crude drug. He was then able, as were other physicians who followed him, to match the symptoms with those of known diseases and found that the *most similar* remedies in homeopathic potency counteracted the symptoms of disease. Homeopathy as we know it was born.

Were a patient to come to a homeopathic physician with the symptoms of aching in every muscle, great irritability, vertigo on rising from bed, excruciating pains in the head from bending over, dry mouth and great thirst, and all pains greatly aggravated from the slightest movement, the homeopath would invariably prescribe Bryonia alb. in homeopathic potency as the most similar remedy and produce a cure.

When taking *any* medication, whether allopathic, herbal, or homeopathic, the best advice is to follow the *rule of the golden mean* of the ancient Greeks: *moderation in all things.*

Choice of Remedy Potencies and Repetition of Remedies

As stated earlier in this book, a homeopathic remedy is a *system stimulator.* It should be repeated only until significant improvement of an injury or illness is noticed, then stopped. Clinical practice has demonstrated that the 30x and 30c potencies work well and rapidly in first aid practice.

Normally, the 30x potency is given at 2 to 3 hour intervals for a maximum of nine doses, then stopped. However, other practitioners of homeopathy have found that in especially acute cases, these potencies can be administered every half hour or every hour as necessary, whenever there is a resurgence of pain or discomfort. The author has found the 30x potency to be most useful and repeats it generally in 5-tablet or pellet form for five to six doses, then stops.

In an especially severe illness or injury the 30x potency can be given with complete confidence. Some homeopaths follow several doses of the 30x potency with the 6x potency as required until symptoms abate, especially in severe acute cases. Some practitioners carry all remedies in both the 30x and 6x potencies. This practice may, however, be unnecessarily complicated for most first-aiders. Homeopathic first-aid kits, available from the suppliers listed in Appendix One, are normally available in either the 6x or the 30x potency and in some instances in mixed-potency formats when a specific, intermediate potency, such as the 3x or 12x, has been demonstrated to be most valuable in a certain remedy. For shock, I recommend the first-aider carry both Arnica and Aconite in the higher, 200x potency, which is more rapid-acting than the lower 30x.[38]

The *homeopathic rule* in administering remedies is to give the remedy *best* indicated for the illness or injury on the totality of the guiding symptoms. Repeat the remedy *only as directed* until a noticeable reversal of the condition is seen. At that point, when the person is obviously feeling better, the healing and recovery process is under way and it is time to *stop giving further medication and allow the natural healing process to occur.*

Care of Homeopathic Remedies

Homeopathic remedies are fragile. Some care must be taken in using and in storing them.

One advantage to homeopathic medicines is that they have no expiration date, unlike allopathic drugs. Properly cared for they will not deteriorate and will remain active indefinitely. Some remedies that have been stored for over 75 years have proved to be as active and effective as the day they were first bottled.

The following precautions must be observed to keep your remedies at their peak potency:

1. Keep bottles tightly capped until used and keep the bottle open only as long as necessary.
2. Keep bottles away from direct sunlight and at normal temperatures. Direct sunlight and high heat cause rapid deterioration of homeopathic remedies.
3. Keep bottles away from strong-smelling chemicals such as perfumes, essential oils, camphor or medications containing camphor or menthol, household cleaning agents, and solvents. Once exposed to such materials, homeopathic remedies may neutralize and become inactive.
4. Do not open two remedies at the same time. They may cross-potentize.
5. When administering remedies, be certain *not* to return any spilled or extra tablets or pellets to the bottle. *Throw them away!* They could contaminate the remainder of the contents.
6. Avoid handling remedies as much as possible to avoid contamination. It is best to shake the required number of tablets or pellets from the bottle into the bottle's cap, or into a clean spoon, or onto a clean sheet of paper and then place them into the mouth.
7. When taking homeopathic remedies, do not use mouthwashes or tooth-

paste *for at least 1 hour* before or after. It is probably best not to use mouthwash or toothpaste at all. If you must use a mouthwash, use a weak solution of salt water, or dilute Calendula in water, and substitute salt and baking soda for toothpaste.

8. Strong coffee, tea, and even herb teas may cause homeopathic remedies to neutralize in the body, nullifying or slowing treatment. There is some disagreement on this point. Some authorities believe that the caffeine in coffee and tea, and the medicinal effects of some herb teas, will cause neutralization or otherwise interfere with treatment. *Decaffeinated* coffee or tea may not neutralize the remedy. However, it is best to drink plain water, milk, or fruit or vegetable juices while under homeopathic treatment.

9. It is a well-established fact that certain allopathic drugs seriously interfere with homeopathic remedies. Avoid *cortisone*[39] either orally or topically (as in anti-itch and skin-inflammation ointments containing hydrocortisone) while taking homeopathic remedies. Some anticonvulsive drugs, such as phenobarbital for the treatment of epileptic seizures, may also negate the remedies. *Remember: The first-aider is not a physician. If the patient is taking cortisone or anticonvulsives for a chronic health condition, it may be dangerous to stop taking those medications!* It is better to apply only standard first-aid measures in these cases, and not use homeopathic remedies.

10. Tobacco may nullify the therapeutic effects of homeopathic remedies. It is best not to smoke or chew tobacco at all while under treatment.

One additional advantage to homeopathic remedies is that they are quite inexpensive and easily replaced. With few exceptions of remedies in extremely high or low potencies, all homeopathic remedies are available without a physician's prescription. If you suspect a remedy has been contaminated, throw it away and buy another supply. It is better to be safe than sorry.

Methods of Delivery and Dosages of Homeopathic Remedies

Homeopathic remedies are available in several forms; the most common is a 1- or 1¼-grain tablet in which the medication is suspended in a base of nonmedicinal lactose (milk sugar). Some tablets, most notably specialty combinations, may take the form of a 3-, 5-, or 7-grain tablet the same size as, or slightly larger or smaller than, an ordinary aspirin tablet. Another method of delivery is a round pill called a "pellet," the size of, or slightly larger than, a BB shot, made of sucrose (cane sugar), which has been exposed to a remedy suspended in a bath of ethyl alcohol and water. Yet another form is tiny granules called a "tube dose." The last method is in the form of drops placed directly under or on the tongue. In all cases, the medicine is pleasant-tasting, easy to administer, and directly absorbed into the bloodstream through the minute capillaries that line the mucous membrane of the mouth. Drops are especially appropriate for infants and small children.

Label directions may vary from manufacturer to manufacturer as to how many tablets, pellets, or drops to take. The usual dosages are as follows:

Low Potencies (below 30x): 3 to 5 tablets, or 6 to 8 pellets, every 2 to 3 hours until noticeable improvement is observed. As long as there is steady improvement, no further medication is required.

Medium Potencies (30x): 3 to 5 tablets, or 6 to 8 pellets, every 2 to 4 hours for a maximum of nine dosages. Stop medication after noticeable improvement is observed.

High Potencies (200x): 3 to 5 tablets, or 6 to 8 pellets, *given once or twice only*. In homeopathy, the higher the remedy's potency, the greater is the stimulation of the system. Low potencies may be given more frequently over a longer period (several days, a week, or longer) if necessary to obtain results. The medium potencies—those often employed in medical self-help and emergency care—are administered moderately, usually only for six to nine doses. As their power and rapidity of action are greater than those of the lesser potencies, they require less frequent repetition. The high and highest potencies bear minimum repetition.

Oral Dose: These liquid medications, which seldom exceed the 200x potency and permit longer repetition, are given in doses of 10 drops and are normally given three times daily.

It is best to follow the homeopathic manufacturer's recommendations for dosages and repetition of their remedies. However, this information is provided to give the medical self-helper and first-aider a general guide, and also because many pelleted remedies do not provide these directions on the label.

PART TWO

TREATMENT STRATEGIES

CHAPTER TWO

HOMEOPATHIC FIRST AID IN ACCIDENTS

Topics Covered

Shock
Bruises
Fractures
Sprains
Bone Bruises
Tendon Injuries
Dislocations

Homeopathic treatment, given at the earliest possible moment after an accident resulting in bodily injury, will frequently prevent further suffering, complications, and serious physical disability. Homeopathic first-aid treatments in accidents have proved to be of great value in the rapid recovery from injury. Of course, in all serious injuries from accidents, the person administering first aid, either in its standard form, or utilizing homeopathy as an adjunct treatment toward recovery, will seek skilled medical care as soon as possible. *Remember: The first-aider is not a physician.*

When skilled medical attention is called for, seek it quickly at its nearest source.

One of the "Hurry Cases": Shock

The first-aider must suspect shock in *all* cases of accident and injury. Some individuals react more to shock than others, but shock—the great and silent killer—must be suspected in all cases of injury, even the simplest. Shock is one of the "hurry cases" in first-aid, the others being *cessation of breathing, severe bleeding, and poisoning.*

HOMEOPATHIC TREATMENT
Arnica Montana
Aconite

As a homeopathic prophylactic against shock, the first-aider should administer **Arnica montana,** 200 potency, under the tongue, 5 tablets or pellets, as soon as possible. In cases of severe shock, Arnica can be repeated every 15 minutes until outward symptoms subside. No fluids should ever be given to an unconscious victim. However, Arnica may be given with total confidence, in tablet or pellet form, under the tongue or inside the cheek, even to an unconscious person.

There are two forms of shock: *physiological* and *psychic*. The major symptoms of physiological shock are: pale, ashen-gray, or white color to the skin; profuse perspiration (sweating); pupils of the eyes are fixed (unmoving) and dilated (wide open); the victim of shock may be very lethargic, "shocky," or unconscious.

Arnica is useful in both types of shock. It can prevent shock altogether if given immediately following an injury, and reverse the progress of shock if symptoms have already set in.

Aconite is especially useful in psychic shock, that resulting from great fright or fear. The Keynote symptoms of Aconite are: great fear, anxiety, and worry accompanying every ailment, however minor; fear of death, restlessness, tossing about; shortness of breath and oppressed breathing on the least movement.

Arnica in psychic shock has similar, although somewhat different, Keynote symptoms and the homeopathic first-aider should memorize them: fear of being touched or of the approach of anyone; unconscious; when spoken to answers correctly, *but relapses;* indifference, delirium, nervousness, cannot bear pain, whole body oversensitive; says there is nothing wrong.

Potency and Dosage: Arnica (200x), 5 tablets every 15 minutes until symptoms abate.

A case history will illustrate homeopathic treatment of shock. In 1982, while attending a Boy Scout weekend outing, a 13-year-old Scout cut his finger while carving a stick. The wound was not deep or serious, but it bled profusely. Another Scout nearby proceeded to provide first-aid treatment. The Scout first-aider thought it was necessary to clean the cut because the knife blade was certainly less than clean. He washed the finger under running water then administered the only "antiseptic" he had on hand— 70% isopropyl alcohol—which he poured directly onto the cut. Almost immediately the young Scout turned pale and began to breathe with great difficulty. Beads of sweat formed across his forehead and upper lip, and he fainted, slamming his head into a hard tiled wall. The Scout first-aider, unprepared for such a violent reaction, called for help. The homeopath found that three of the symptoms of physiological shock were present: pale skin, heavy sweating, and unconsciousness. The boy was given 3 tablets of Arnica (200x).

The victim in shock should be kept warm and the feet should be elevated slightly to allow the blood, which has rushed from the brain, to re-enter the head. The boy's feet were propped on top of a cardboard box, and the first-aid Scout supplied his shirt. Within 3 to 4 minutes after receiving Arnica, the boy returned to full consciousness, his normal skin color returned, and his breathing became steady and normal. He was examined for the blow to his head and told to rest for half an hour. There was no further sign of difficulty and he recovered promptly and completely.

The shock reaction had been brought about by seeing a considerable quantity of his own blood, his own fear of his injury (though it was very minor), and the physical shock of having alcohol poured directly into the wound.

The first-aider must suspect shock in all cases of injury, even those that seem minor.

Homeopathy recognizes that every human being is unique and exhibits unique and highly individual reactions to physical and mental stress. In shock, give whichever homeopathic remedy best fits the victim's symptoms.

If you do not have the most-indicated remedy at hand, give either Arnica or Aconite.

Bruises

A bruise, or *contusion*, is an injury caused by the impact of a hard, unyielding object against the soft tissues of the body. In this common type of injury the underlying tissues beneath the surface of the skin are damaged, allowing blood and other body fluids to leak out from the damaged vessels. The result is an extravasion of blood and watery fluid, resulting in the "black and blue" and oftentimes yellow or multihued coloration of the skin. Pain, swelling (moderate or severe), and the discoloration of the skin are all symptoms of a bruise.

HOMEOPATHIC TREATMENT
Arnica Montana
Bellis Perennis
Ledum Palustre (Ledum Pal.)

Depending on the circumstances of the bruising injury and the extent of the tissue damage, skilled medical attention may be necessary, especially if the contused area is large and the tissue damage deep and extensive. However, in *all* cases of bruising, the patient can be greatly benefited by administering **Arnica montana,** 30x potency, for the initial shock that results from any injury. Arnica is a remarkable pain-relieving remedy. Although it has no analgesic action of its own, healing takes place so rapidly with Arnica that pain is naturally and rapidly removed. It has long been known by mountain climbers in Europe, who used to chew the leaves of the Arnica flower whenever they experienced a fall. Arnica is indicated for any bruised, lame, sore, stiff feeling, either from an injury or from simple strain and overexertion.

Another homeopathic remedy that can be well employed in first aid for bruises is the common daisy: **Bellis perennis.** Bellis acts on the muscular tissues and the fibers of the blood vessels in a remarkable manner. After Arnica for the initial shock of any major bruising injury, Bellis should be thought of as *the first* remedy in injury to the deeper tissues. Bellis is best used in the lower 3x and 3c or 6x potencies. When Bellis is employed in first-aid applications, the healing is rapid, pleasant, and totally safe.

Potency and Dosage: 3 to 5 tablets under the tongue every 2 to 3 hours as required is usual for lower potencies.

Ledum palustre (Ledum pal.) is an adjunct remedy in bruises. Made in homeopathic potency from the plant called marsh tea, Ledum pal. has the remarkable ability to remove the lingering discoloration of the skin from a bruise. This may be especially important cosmetically if the bruise is on the face or forehead. Ledum pal. will remove the "black and blue and yellow," but it is Bellis that works to heal the injury itself.

Fractures

Obviously, any fracture requires the early attention of a skilled physician so that the broken bone(s) may be properly set. Sometimes, a fracture may require surgical care to properly realign the bone(s). Suspect a fracture whenever there is swelling in the area of injury; localized pain upon the slightest movement or touch (a sprain will normally distribute pain over a wider area); or any deformity of the injured limb.

> ADVISORY WARNING: Never press in on a suspected fracture as this may cause additional damage and send the victim into deep shock. Seek medical attention promptly in all cases of fracture.

HOMEOPATHIC TREATMENT
Arnica Montana
Symphytum

As a valuable emergency treatment, give the victim *Arnica montana,* 200 or 30x, as a prophylaxis against shock, which will be present in this type of serious injury. Many victims of fracture have died, not from the seriousness of the broken bone itself, but from the resulting shock to the system. Arnica in homeopathic potency not only will *prevent* shock if given immediately, but it will also allay the symptoms of shock following an accident.

The major symptoms of shock are: pale, ashen gray, or white color to the skin; profuse perspiration (sweating); pupils of the eyes are fixed (unmoving) and dilated (wide open); the victim of shock may be very lethargic, "shocky," or unconscious.

Arnica in 200x or 300x potency will also help relieve the resultant pain and make the victim more comfortable.

As an adjunct treatment of fracture following skilled medical care, give **Symphytum** in the 6x potency three times daily for several weeks. Symphytum contains an active healing agent that will assist in the formation of new bone at the site of the injury. Symphytum administered following a fracture can cut healing time by 50 to 75 percent.[40] As in all homeopathic remedies, there is no danger and considerable benefit in this post-fracture treatment.

Sprains

A sprain is a painful injury resulting from trauma to the ligaments—the tough, elastic connective tissues surrounding the joints of the body. The most common sites of sprains are the ankles, wrists, and thumbs.

In a sprain, the ligaments are pulled (stretched), and in severe sprains, they are torn away from the joint. A sprain can be a serious and debilitating injury. The symptoms of a sprain are: *pain* (generally in a sprain, the pain is less localized than in a fracture and covers a larger area); discoloration of the tissues surrounding the site of injury (the discoloration is the result of broken blood vessels beneath the skin surface); tenderness to touch at the site of injury; swelling, moderate to severe. The first-aider will note that the symptoms of a sprain are similar to those of a fracture. In the event of a severe sprain, a fracture should be suspected. Only an x-ray of the injured joint by a skilled physician can determine if the injury is a sprain or a fracture.

In simple sprains, the injured joint should be placed in cold water or an ice pack applied to reduce the swelling and the resulting pain. The injured part should also be elevated to allow for the drainage of body fluids around the site of the injury. As in all cases of physical injuries, **Arnica montana** (30x, 30c, or 200x) should be given to the victim as a prophylaxis against shock and for the relief of pain. Arnica will work rapidly and well in all cases of sprain for the relief of pain.

HOMEOPATHIC TREATMENT
Rhus Toxicodendron (Rhus Tox.)
Bryonia
Calcarea Carbonica (Calc. Carb.)

Homeopathic **Rhus toxicodendron** (a trituration of poison ivy extract), in the 30x potency, may be given every 2 hours for a maximum of five to nine doses. Rhus tox. in its pure, undiluted form causes painful tenderness and stiffness in joints, ligaments, and tendons. Hence, in its homeopathic form, Rhus tox. is almost specific to all injuries to the joints.

Two case histories illustrate the use of homeopathic first aid for the treatment of sprains.

At a summer camp, a 16-year-old boy had jammed his thumb forcefully into the concrete wall of a swimming pool. The thumb was swollen, red, and extremely tender; it was impossible to move without pain. An ice pack was applied to the thumb and hand, and the boy's arm was elevated. Arnica (30x) was given soon after for the pain, and a half-hour later Rhus tox. (30x) was given. Arnica and Rhus tox. were given alternately every other hour for five doses, then stopped. The following day the thumb was still swollen and tender, and all movement was painful and difficult.

Another homeopathic remedy in sprains is ***Bryonia*** (a homeopathic triturated preparation of the wild hops herb). Bryonia is given when *all* movement makes the injury *worse*. When *first* movement is painful, but then becomes better, Rhus tox. is the remedy to use.

In the case of the 16-year-old boy, after 24 hours it was obvious that Rhus tox. was not the most similar remedy. Bryonia (30x) was given. In any case of severe sprain, fracture should be suspected. Without an x-ray, even a physician cannot tell if a joint is sprained or fractured. The boy was taken to a local clinic. X-rays showed the thumb to be severely sprained with probable damage to the joint capsule. The attending physician wrapped the hand in an elastic bandage and told the boy the thumb would be painful and nearly useless for two or three weeks.

Homeopathy, properly applied according to its guiding principles, never fails. One day following his visit to the clinic, and after six doses of Bryonia (30x), the boy returned to the homeopath's office to have his hand examined. He had removed the elastic bandage. All swelling had vanished. There was no more pain or tenderness, and he had nearly complete free movement of the thumb. It had taken homeopathic first aid three days to work. However, according to standard medical advice, the injury should have taken *seven times longer* to heal. Such is often the power and rapidity of homeopathic remedies.

A similar success was seen for an attorney who fell while on a shopping trip. Her wrist was severely sprained. Her husband rushed her to the Emergency Room of a nearby hospital for treatment. The E.R. physician was almost certain the wrist was broken, but x-rays showed only a severe sprain with stretching and tearing of the ligaments. His advice was to soak the hand in ice-water to take the swelling down. She was also to keep it tightly wrapped; was told she would not be able to sleep well for several days because of the pain; and that her wrist would hurt for weeks.

She then called a homeopath to ask if anything could be done homeopathically. The E.R. physician had offered her nothing for pain. The homeopath prescribed Arnica (30x) for the physical trauma of the injury and to help relieve the pain. Movement was difficult because of the intense swelling, but she found that the more she moved her wrist, the less pain she felt. On the Keynote symptoms of the intense redness of her wrist, thumb, and palm, swelling, and *better* from movement, Rhus tox. in the 6x potency (the only potency the homeopath had on hand) was given, which she was to repeat every 2 hours until a noticeable improvement set in. Two days following her fall, she found that the pain was almost gone and the swelling was gone, too. The Arnica had relieved most of the pain, and she had had no problem sleeping. She repeated Rhus tox. (6x) for a few days more. Complete healing of this exceedingly severe sprain under homeopathic treatment took several days, and after 4 days she still had a mild soreness in her thumb, but the injury was hardly as disabling as the E.R. physician had predicted. The fleshy portion below her thumb was intensely black and blue but a few doses of Ledum pal. (30x) soon removed that.

TREATMENT FOR OLD SPRAINS

Often, individuals who have severely sprained, or fractured, joints in the past will experience a continued weakness of the damaged joint. This is quite common in sprains with fractures of the wrists and ankles. These individuals experience continued discomfort and often a permanent, nagging weakness in the joint which is easily reinjured. In such cases, homeopathic *Calcarea carbonica* (homeopathic calcium carbonate), in the 30x or 200x potency, administered *one dose every week*—no oftener—for a month, may greatly assist the weakened joint to complete recovery.

An example of the power of Calc. carb. in an old joint injury is given by a 21-year-old man. The young man was quite heavy, easily fatigued, and slow-moving. These are among the Keynote symptoms of the Calc. carb. patient. Several years before, he had fallen and fractured his ankle. The fracture necessitated surgery to reconstruct the joint. As this young man was an outdoorsman and accustomed to hiking for long distances with a heavy pack on his back, his ankle frequently bothered him; it was continually painful and easily reinjured. Calc. carb. (30x) was prescribed, 5 tablets to be taken once per week until an improvement was noticed. At the end of 2 weeks, the young man fell and twisted his ankle. Normally this would have produced a severe, painful, and debilitating sprain. This time, however, the old injury was not aggravated. As time passed, he noticed that the former tenderness in this ankle had disappeared and his ankle seemed to be returning to the normal condition *before* the fracture. This young man, 8 years later, has had no further discomfort.

The Keynote symptoms of Rhus. tox. in sprains are:

1. Hot, painful swelling of joints
2. Pains tearing in tendons, ligaments
3. Skin red and swollen
4. Pains *better with movement,* change of position, stretching of limbs

The Keynote symptoms of Bryonia in sprains are:

1. Joints stiff and painful
2. Joints red, swollen, and hot
3. Pains *worse on the least movement*

The Keynote symptoms of Calc. carb. in sprains are:

1. A great remedy in old sprains and fractures
2. Patient of Calc. carb. is usually heavy, flabby, easily fatigued
3. Old sprains or fractures are easily reinjured

ADVISORY WARNING: *Do not repeat Calc. carb. too often.* One dose weekly is preferred.

Rhus tox. will normally be the first remedy to think of in a sprain. If the pain is made *worse* from the slightest movement, substitute Bryonia for Rhus tox. If the sprain is severe with much swelling, redness, and pain, suspect a fracture and seek medical attention. If the joint has been fractured, follow the advice for *fracture.*

Bone Bruises and Pulled or Torn Tendons

Frequently an individual will experience a blow to the body that results in a painful bone bruise. This injury is most common in football players, members of hockey and soccer teams, and children and adults who bang their shins into household objects. A *bone bruise* is an injury to the *periosteum,* the sheath covering of the skeletal system. The injury is frequently painful and is manifested by local tenderness, swelling, and discoloration of the skin.

HOMEOPATHIC TREATMENT
Arnica Montana
Ruta Graveolens (Ruta Grav.)
Symphytum

The homeopathic first aid for bone bruise, and for damage to the tendons of the wrists and knees which frequently follows sports injuries, is **Ruta graveolens,** the homeopathic preparation of the common garden herb rue. Ruta is a deep-acting remedy and is specific to this type of injury. Give Ruta (6x to 30x), repeating whenever there is a recurrence of pain. As an adjunct treatment, Ruta ointment may be applied locally. In the event of a deep injury to the surrounding joint, a firm elastic bandage should be applied for support. Inflammation of the synovial lining of the joints, damage to the tendons or the periosteum, and inflammation of the ligaments will respond especially well to Ruta in homeopathic potency. Much pain and disability will be prevented with this treatment.

Should Ruta fail to "take hold" after 24 hours in the case of a periosteal injury, **Symphytum,** the homeopathic preparation of the herb comfrey, can be substituted. Symphytum is a deeper-acting remedy. Symphytum ointment can also be applied locally as an adjunct treatment to Symphytum internally.

The Keynote symptoms of Ruta are:

1. Pain and stiffness in wrists and hands
2. Tendons sore
3. Aching pain in the Achilles tendon
4. Pain in thighs when stretching the limbs
5. Pain in bones of feet and ankles

The Keynote symptoms of Symphytum are:

1. Injuries to sinews, tendons, and the periosteum
2. Acts on joints generally
3. Pricking pain and soreness in periosteum

Dislocations

A dislocation of a major joint is a *serious* injury, requiring the immediate care of a skilled physician who must make a readjustment of the displaced joint. *The first-aider must never attempt to relocate a major joint.* In a dislocation, ligaments (which bind the joints together), tendons (which attach muscle to bone), nerves, and blood vessels may all be involved. This is far too complex for a first-aider to deal with.

HOMEOPATHIC TREATMENT
Arnica Montana
Ruta Graveolens

Treat the dislocation as you would a fracture, immobilizing the joint; and, if appropriate, placing the affected limb in a sling and strapping it with a triangular bandage snugly to the body. Administer **Arnica montana** to control shock and hemorrhage.

The most common dislocations are to the shoulder, although they may occur in any other joint: knees, fingers, thumbs, elbows, jaw, hip, or ankle. The symptoms of a dislocation are swelling (frequently); pain—moderate to severe; and an obvious deformity of the body part.

In a dislocation, a bone end pulls away from the joint, pain is excruciating, and shock is an ever-present possibility. Immobilize the part and, as a homeopathic treatment, give Arnica (200x potency) for the shock and possible trauma to neighboring blood vessels. The Keynote symptoms here will be similar to severe sprain as ligaments and tendons are involved. After relocation of the joint has been accomplished by a physician, **Ruta graveolens** follow well, one dose (3 to 5 tablets) every 3 hours for a maximum of nine doses, or 6x (3 to 5 tablets) repeated for a longer time. Should the area surrounding the relocated joint become greatly swollen, filled with fluid, and *worse* on the least movement, administer **Bryonia** (30x) as above, or Bryonia 6x every 2 hours until symptoms are relieved. Of course, Arnica (30x or 6x) may be given as pain develops.

CHAPTER THREE

SOFT TISSUE INJURIES

Topics Covered

Abrasions
Burns
Open Wounds

Abrasions

An abrasion is caused by scraping the surface of the skin away, as in a fall when the skin slides along a hard, rough surface. A skinned knee or rope "burn" are examples of abrasion. Generally, the damage is not great and is limited to the immediate subsurface of the skin with damage to small veins and tiny capillaries. Although an abrasion may seem minor (and most are) there is considerable danger of infection from anything—dirt, sand, gravel—which may have been ground into the wound.

HOMEOPATHIC TREATMENT
Calendula Officinalis
Pyrogen

By far the best first-aid treatment for an abrasion is to clean the scraped area carefully to remove any embedded foreign materials and to apply a homeopathic preparation of **Calendula.** First, however, if there is considerable pain, **Arnica,** 30x or 200x, should be administered, 5 tablets or pellets under or on the tongue. Arnica works wonders in relieving pain (especially useful if the abrasion happens to a child who has fallen from a backyard swing set or off a bicycle). It will not only relieve the discomfort quite rapidly but will act directly on the broken and damaged blood vessels.

The abrasion should be cleansed with a gauze pad (not cotton, as the loose fibers will cling to the torn, rough skin) dipped into any of the following Calendula products: Calendula succus (the plant juice extract with 18% U.S.H.P. alcohol as a preservative), Calendula nonalcoholic (a preparation of the juice of the Calendula plant in a base of glycerine and water), or Calendula tincture (the tincture of the plant, which contains 41% alcohol). Any of these products is excellent, although I have found the succus and the nonalcoholic preparations most suitable in first-aid use.

Calendula is the homeopathic name of the juice of the African marigold and has truly remarkable healing properties. It is not an antiseptic but rather a bacteriostatic. Calendula does not work directly against bacteria, destroying them, as do allopathic antiseptics such as iodine, mercurochrome, merthiolate, or Betadine. Calendula works to prevent infection by inhibiting bacterial growth. Germs cannot thrive in the presence of Calendula. Calendula also possesses hemostatic or styptic properties. It actually constricts the blood vessels, thereby slowing down or, in many cases, stopping bleeding.

In first aid, Calendula tincture is too powerful to apply undiluted to any open wound, and even the succus form with only 18% alcohol (enough to prevent deterioration of the fresh plant juice) may cause mild discomfort if placed directly on the skin. The first-aider may dilute these two products, adding one teaspoonful to a quarter cup of water. Diluting Calendula does not affect its "antiseptic" properties and allows a typical one-ounce bottle to go quite a long way without replacement.

To treat the abrasion, apply the diluted Calendula to the wound with a gauze pad, removing carefully any embedded foreign material. Any bleeding that is present will slow down or stop altogether, allowing the first-aider to see that all dirt has been removed from the wound. If the wound is contaminated with grease or oil it must be washed with a mild soap first. Green soap or Calendulated soap, or Ivory is much preferred over detergent, deodorant, or antiseptic products. Next, cover the abraded area with a sterile gauze pad and tape it securely to the undamaged skin. Surgical tape is best, but adhesive tape will also work. Apply Calendula directly to the gauze pad, moistening it. If there is a chance that the pad will become soiled (as is likely with children), cover the pad with a gauze bandage. This should be all the first aid necessary. Allow natural healing to set it. *Don't disturb the dressing* "just to look." Every so often in the first 24 hours, it may be a good idea to remoisten the pad with Calendula.

Even in as simple a wound as an abrasion there is the possibility of infection. *Septicemia,* or blood poisoning, is not unheard of, though it is unlikely with Calendula treatment. However, should the abraded area become red and hot, swollen, or painful to the touch, infection is present. Again, homeopathy can deal easily and effectively with this condition.

Pyrogen is a triturated sepsin, derived from natural sources, introduced into homeopathic practice by English homeopathic physicians. It is excellent in treating any wound, whether a cut, scratch, or scrape, that becomes infected. If the wound should show any of the signs of infection, a few doses of Pyrogen in the 30x potency, 5 tablets or pellets under the tongue every 2 to 3 hours, should eliminate it.

Burns: First, Second, and Third Degree

Burns can range from the mildest, *first-degree* burn from touching a hot object such as a skillet on the stove top or a mild sunburn from attempting that first tan of summer, to the most severe or *third-degree* burn.

> ADVISORY WARNING: Extensive burns that cover a portion of the body surface greater than the area of a hand require expert attention. Consult a physician in all cases of extensive first- or second-degree burn, and *always* in third-degree burns. Throughout this manual it has been emphasized that the first-aider is normally not a physician. Above all else, the first-aider must use good common sense and critical judgment in treating any serious injury or illness.

SHOCK IN BURNS

Even in apparently minor burns—the first-degree burn and the second-degree burn that covers little body area—and always in any third-degree burn, shock is to be suspected to some extent. As soon after beginning to treat a burn as possible, the homeopathic first-aider should administer a dose of **Arnica** 200x or, if there is much restlessness and fright, **Aconite** 200x. Either of these remedies, given on the basis of their Keynote symptoms, will serve as a prophylaxis against shock and assist in making the burn victim more comfortable.

HOMEOPATHIC TREATMENT
External Remedies
Hypericum
Calendula Officinalis
Urtica Urens
Cantharis
Causticum

Homeopathy has several remedies that are especially useful in treating burns. The general medical consensus is that *no ointment should ever be applied to a burn,* especially a serious and extensive second-degree or a deep third-degree burn. The reason for this is obvious. Should the burn victim need to be treated by a physician, the doctor will first have to remove the greasy ointment, preventing rapid treatment and causing the victim considerable pain.

THE SYMPTOMS OF DEGREES OF BURNS

First, the first-aider must recognize each of the three degrees of burns.

First-Degree

Redness or discoloration of the skin surface
Mild swelling
Pain

Second-Degree

Redness or a mottled discoloration of the skin surface
Blister formation across the skin surface
Pain—moderate to severe

Third-Degree

Skin appears either white or charred brown, deep-brown, or black
Sometimes the third-degree burn at first resembles a severe second-degree
    burn

First-degree and second-degree burns (or a combination of first- and second-degree burns) are the most painful, with the second-degree, because of its deeper tissue damage, certainly the most painful. Surprisingly, perhaps, the third-degree burn is least painful because it is so deep in its damage of the tissue structures that the nerve endings that transmit the pain message to the brain are destroyed.

There is considerable debate in the medical community, both in allopathic and homeopathic medicine, concerning the best burn treatment. As a discussion of this will only confuse the first-aider, the most standard homeopathic first-aid treatments will be suggested here.

It has already been stated that greasy ointments should not be used in treating burns, except possibly in the mildest first-degree. Homeopathy provides excellent and highly effective alternatives to traditional burn ointments.

Generally it is suggested that when a burn (first- or second-degree) occurs, it should be cooled. Place the burned part in cold water, or apply an ice pack. Cold does, at least temporarily, relieve the painful sensation.

FIRST-AID STEPS IN BURN TREATMENT

Get away from the burning object
Cool the area to normal temperature
Reduce increased blood flow through cooling

Above all, remove the area from heat causing the burn!

Hypericum, made from the plant *hypericum perforatum,* commonly called St. John's wort, is an outstanding remedy for burns. Hypericum is nearly specific in treating any injury where there is damage to the nerves, and in first- and second-degree burns, the nerve endings in the skin are damaged, sending waves of pain signals to the brain. Hypericum is available in two forms for burn treatment: Hypericum tincture (the alcoholic extract of the plant juice), and Hypericum 10% lotion (10% of Hypericum tincture in a bland, nongreasy, water-soluble base of tragocanth). Either form may be used with full confidence in the treatment of first- and second-degree burns.

If Hypericum tincture is used, *dilute* it one teaspoonful to a quarter cup of water, dampen a gauze compress in this solution, and place the pad directly on top of the burned area. As the pad begins to dry, remoisten it with additional Hypericum solution. When using Hypericum 10% lotion, *be certain to shake the bottle well,* then apply a light covering to the burned area. It may be necessary to repeat this treatment several times, as needed.

Another, and very effective, burn treatment for mild first- and second-degree burns is to apply a dilute solution of ***Calendula tincture*** as you would Hypericum, or to apply Calendula gel or 10% Lotion. Calendula is a most soothing burn treatment.

Urtica Urens, a homeopathic preparation of the dwarf stinging nettle, can be used as you would Hypericum, with equal effectiveness. If Urtica were to be dropped undiluted in its tincture form onto the skin, it would produce a stinging sensation, redness, burning, and eventually blisters. Therefore, in its homeopathic form, the usefulness of Urtica in both first- and second-degree burns is obvious. Urtica is also available in either its tincture form (Urtica urens tincture) or as Urtica urens 10% lotion. Again, it is applied as you would either Hypericum or Calendula.

As was stated earlier, the first-aider should suspect shock to some extent in every type of burn. ***Arnica*** 200x, or ***Aconite*** 200x, given on the basis of their Keynote symptoms, should be administered as soon as possible following a burn injury.

The two outstanding homeopathic internal remedies for the *pain* of burns are Cantharis and Causticum.

Cantharis, the homeopathic trituration of the Spanish fly, also known as the blister beetle, is truly outstanding in its ability to eliminate the pain of any burn. Cantharis should be given in the 30x potency, 5 tablets or pellets placed directly under the tongue. It will act quickly to relieve the pain and may be repeated as often as every 15 minutes, or as pain returns.

Causticum, a remedy made from a hydrated mineral caustic, burned lime, and bisulfate of potash, is a powerful pain-relieving remedy in burns, perhaps on an equal with Cantharis. Causticum may be given in the 30x potency, under the tongue, as you would any other homeopathic remedy, repeated as needed for pain.

Another interesting nonhomeopathic remedy for mild burns is recommended by the American homeopathic physician M.B. Panos, M.D.[41] The remedy is the common onion kept in almost every kitchen. According to Dr. Panos, a slice of fresh onion, lightly salted, placed directly over a *mild* burn, removes the pain. In some instances, if you are away from rapid access to your homeopathic first-aid kit, but have an onion and a salt shaker at hand, use it to good advantage!

Two case histories illustrate homeopathic burn treatment.

The summer Boy Scout camp was having one of the hottest summers in memory. A Scoutmaster and his 14-year-old son, a First Class Scout, entered the homeopath's office, and the boy was in obvious and intense pain. He walked stiffly, almost as if he were afraid to move, and he carried his T-shirt in his hand. The boy had a very fair skin and blonde, almost white, hair and blue eyes—just the type to be highly susceptible to a severe sun burn.

All across the boy's chest, on his upper arms, and across the top third of his back his skin was brilliant red, with a large crop of puffy, clear, water-filled blisters. The second-degree sunburn was so painful he could hardly move and he couldn't tolerate anything touching it. The homeopath at the camp poured out one capful of Urtica urens tincture into a glass of lukewarm water. Unfortunately (for the boy), the first thing that had to be done was remove a thick layer of drugstore-purchased burn ointment that the boy's father had applied an hour earlier. The homeopath used green soap and water, working the soap into the grease as carefully as possible until it came off. The boy was in such pain he screamed and cried, tears rolled down his cheeks, and his father had to hold him around the waist to keep him from running out the door. The homeopath in question was treating his very first case and had forgotten about giving Arnica (200x potency) for shock. Even an hour later, Arnica would have greatly aided the boy in relieving his pain.

Once the burn ointment was removed, diluted Urtica urens tincture was dabbed on with a cotton ball. Within 5 minutes of the first application, the boy calmed down noticeably. There was no Cantharis or Causticum in stock to give internally for pain, but the homeopath did have a 30x bottle of Urtica urens in tablet form. Urtica may be used internally, in potentized form, as well as externally for burns. The boy took 5 tablets, dissolving them under his tongue. A few minutes later, he was completely calm. The homeopath explained to the boy's father the seriousness of his burn, and told him to avoid the use of burn ointments. He was given a one-ounce bottle of Urtica urens tincture, with an explanation of its use and a supply of cotton balls; he was told to apply the diluted Urtica every hour back in the campsite. If the blisters broke open, he was to bring his son back immediately because of the danger of infection. It was unlikely that the boy would even be able to sleep that night.

The next day, barely 24 hours later, the man and his son returned. The boy was wearing his T-shirt, whereas the day before he couldn't stand the slightest touch. The blisters were now nearly gone. The father had followed the homeopath's instructions carefully, and that night the boy had slept peacefully. The boy was told to wear a shirt outdoors at all times. Two days later, the last day of camp, there were no blisters anywhere. On top of that, the skin was only the palest pink, and there was no swelling or pain. The boy asked for the name of the remedy and was given the name Urtica urens tincture together with instructions and the name and address of a homeopathic supplier. On the morning of camp check-out, the father told the homeopath, "I've never seen anything like that. When I get back to Red Oak, I'm going to tell my doctor." Undoubtedly the doctor would have never have heard of Urtica urens, and if he knew it was homeopathic, he probably would have sworn it was worse than witch doctoring! But probably the boy and his father would soon learn more about the power of homeopathic first-aid.

A second case history of burn treatment occurred late in 1982. A mother explained that her 2-year-old daughter had scorched the palmar surface of her hand and part of her lower arm on a red-hot waffle iron. Immediately, the mother, a long-time Scouter, had immersed the girl's arm in cold water. That did relieve the pain. As their homeopathic doctor had been out of town, she called a local doctor, who told her to place the arm in cold water and keep it there for at least 30 minutes. The girl had both first-degree and second-degree burns. The doctor told them not to worry. Only if the blisters broke open would the burn be "serious," and if that happened the parents were to bring the girl to his office.

The problem was that, after soaking the child's arm for 30 minutes, the burn was as painful as ever. The child screamed and screamed, was intensely restless, and tears rolled down her face every time her arm was removed from the water.

Their homeopathic doctor was called again, and this time was in. The homeopath had the mother give her 1 tablet of Causticum (30x) for pain while he applied Urtica urens 10% lotion onto the burn. Within 3 minutes the child's screaming stopped (it had been going on for nearly 3 hours). The mother was given the lotion with instructions to apply a light covering every couple of hours, and to give 1 tablet of Causticum (30x) whenever the pain returned. Two days later, the skin that 48 hours earlier had been bright red was now a light pink. All but one small blister had disappeared. The mother found it amazing and said the child had gone right to sleep and slept nearly all afternoon. And she had no sign of any pain.

If standard-trained, allopathic physicians would witness the power of homeopathic remedies in the treatment of burns, they would radically alter their common treatments, which are primitive compared to homeopathy.

> ADVISORY WARNING: Third-degree burns must always be medically treated. The first-aider may provide immediate care to the victim as taught in any first-aid course, administer Arnica (200x) or Aconite (200x) as the Keynote symptoms suggest, and arrange for prompt transportation of the burn victim to the nearest medical care facility.

ADJUNCT BURN TREATMENTS

Many experienced laypersons and health professionals as well are now recommending *Aloe vera* or *Vitamin E* for first- and second-degree burns. I have used both on myself from time to time to see if indeed this treatment worked. It does. Aloe vera[42] is a common household plant with thick, succulent leaves that contain a strong antiburn property. Many homemakers now keep an Aloe vera plant growing in their kitchens, where most household burns occur.

Vitamin E is quite possibly the most valuable nonhomeopathic burn remedy. On Thanksgiving Day some years ago, a woman was basting a turkey when the roasting pan slipped from her hands while she was putting it on top of the stove. She fell backwards, and the boiling grease poured down her stomach, hip, and thigh. Her husband had read extensively about holistic healing methods, and he immediately tore away the grease-spattered dress and undergarments, and applied pure Vitamin E oil from a bottle he had on hand. Then he called his family doctor. The physician told him to pack the burned area with ice and to arrange transportation to the hospital as soon as possible. The man told him he had used Vitamin E on part of the burn and the doctor yelled, "DON'T DO THAT!" The man remembers him shouting over the telephone, "Don't do anything but use ice!"

The woman was treated by the family doctor in the hospital a short time later. The physician, a long-time medical doctor, used standard burn treatment consisting of Silvadene (Flint S.S.D. 1%) ointment. The patient had received an extensive combination of first- and second-degree burns. The pain was severe, and her healing took more than a month. They followed all directives except the physician's orders about using Vitamin E. When the patient returned home, her husband continued to apply the Vitamin E oil to the burn sites. The burned portions to which he had *first* applied the Vitamin E returned to normal quite rapidly. The other portions not first treated with the Vitamin E were painful and very slow to heal under standard medical treatment.

In the treatment of burns, homeopathy works amazingly rapidly and wondrously well in bringing immediate relief and healing. The first-aider should use whichever remedy is at hand, whether it is Hypericum, Urtica urens, or Calendula externally; Cantharis, Causticum, or Urtica urens internally; or Vitamin E or Aloe vera, whichever is most rapidly obtainable.

THINK BURN PREVENTION

Many serious burns can easily be prevented by using common sense. Think before you touch any hot object. Turn the handles of all pots and pans containing boiling water, grease, or warming food away toward the back of the stove. The most common scalding injuries to children result when they reach up to pull at a pot handle dangling over the front edge of the stove.

Sunburn is another frequent and often painful common burn. Regardless of how dark your skin is, whether from natural pigmentation or from a dark suntan, *you will still burn if you expose yourself too long to the sun's direct rays.* Severe and continued sunburn over a period of years has been medically proved to cause premature aging of the skin, severe and irreversible wrinkling and sagging, and various skin cancers, one of which is sometimes fatal. When venturing into the sun, wear a product containing a sunscreen, *para-aminobenzoic acid* (PABA), with a sun protection factor matched to the degree of fairness and sensitivity of your skin. These products vary from a sun protection factor of 4 (offering the lowest level of protection), to a maximum value of 24.[43] Should your skin burn, apply as soon as possible a gel or 10% lotion of Calendula or Urtica urens or Hypericum. These homeopathic products will work rapidly to relieve the pain of the sunburn and to establish rapid and natural healing.

Open Wounds

Open wounds fall into four general types: *abrasions* (which have already been discussed), *incisions, lacerations,* and *punctures.* Following are the main symptoms of each type of open wound.

INCISIONS

An incised wound, or cut, may only involve the immediate surface levels of the skin, producing little damage and only minor or moderate bleeding.

Alternatively, it may also be more severe, involving the deeper tissue structures, larger blood vessels, and producing severe and dangerous bleeding. When an incised wound is especially deep, muscles and connective tissues such as tendons and nerves may be damaged.

This type of open wound is called an incision because the cut itself is relatively clean and straight, such as the kind of cut made by a knife, glass shard, or other sharp object.

LACERATIONS

A laceration produces more traumatic damage to underlying tissues than an incision. The edges of a laceration may be jagged and irregular, the skin appearing as if it had been torn apart. Because of damage to more major vessels, bleeding may be far more rapid and severe than in an incised wound. The immediate dangers in a laceration are from severe and rapid bleeding if an artery is severed and from infection from contamination of the skin's subsurface by foreign material embedded in the wound.

PUNCTURES

A puncture wound is a small wound produced by any pointed object that is forced directly into the skin. A puncture often penetrates into the deepest tissue structures and carries with it contaminated materials from the skin's surface or from the penetrating object itself. The puncture may be caused by a nail, a sliver of wood or metal, a pointed piece of glass, or even a bullet or stabbing implement. Surface bleeding in a puncture wound is normally very minor as the entry point often closes over the wound itself. The greatest danger from any puncture is contamination with bacteria and their toxic byproducts such as in tetanus or botulism.

The Structure of the Skin

The homeopathic first-aider should have a basic knowledge of the anatomy of the skin.

The skin is composed of three layers—epidermis, dermis, and subcutaneous layer. The first or immediate surface layer, the *epidermis,* in turn has four layers, the first layer (*stratum corneum*) being essentially "dead." The second layer of skin is the *corium* or *dermis.* This true skin contains a rich supply of blood vessels: capillaries, small veins, and arteries, as well as nerves, hair follicles, and sweat gland ducts. The third layer is called the *subcutaneous* layer (*tela subcutanea*); it contains larger veins and arteries, sweat glands, fatty tissue, and elastic fibers. The fourth and deepest layer of the epidermis, the *stratum germinativum,* grows at a rapid rate and as it does, the cells move to the surface where, unable to be supplied nourishment by the blood, they die and are continually being sloughed off.

For such a thin tissue that is so often taken for granted, the skin is the body's largest organ and is highly complex in its structure.

Why Homeopathic Treatment Is Superior in Wound Healing

When most people cut themselves or give first-aid treatment to someone who has, the first thing they reach for is any of the numerous and common "antiseptics"—iodine, Betadine, Mercurochrome, or merthiolate—or more often than ever before, various antibiotic ointments that contain one or more topically applied antibacterial agents. The civilized world seems convinced, especially through extensive advertising of these products, that it must destroy every bacterium in order to be safe. But the opposite is true. Medical research has shown that the skin contains some bacteria that are actually "friendly" to the body, assisting the body's natural defenses to fight off "unfriendly" disease-causing bacteria when the skin surface is broken. The common antiseptics and the antibiotic ointments actually destroy these germs as well and inhibit rather than promote healing. Homeopathic remedies, to the contrary, work *with* the body and never against it. Open wounds treated homeopathically seldom become infected and heal faster and more efficiently than under standard treatment.

The first-aider might be interested in how the body works to heal an open wound. In a recent popular scientific magazine, the following article appeared:

> You're slicing through a loaf of bread and suddenly your hand slips. Oops—you've cut yourself. Instantly, your body is called to arms to repair the bleeding wound.
>
> How does it do this?
>
> Within minutes, damaged blood vessels are plugged with a clot fashioned from particles called platelets and from strands of protein called fibrin. Blood that has already escaped into the cut coagulates to form a hard, protective scab at the wound's surface.

Next, with the leaks under control, the body steps up the flow of blood to the site of the injury. There a barrage of white blood cells, which travel to the wound in the bloodstream, kill germs and scavenge cellular debris and foreign material.

Meanwhile, epidermal cells, which form the top layer of skin, reproduce and slide into the cut. Eventually they meet under the scab, restoring the skin's integrity. New blood vessels bud from preexisting ones and penetrate the injured area to bring in oxygen and necessary nutrients.

Now that the immediate emergency is over, the body enters the reconstruction phase. Cells called fibroblasts multiply rapidly to form tissue that fills the wound. Here they synthesize collagen, a tough cablelike fiber that gives the wound tensile strength. In addition, the fibroblasts contract, which in turn pulls the edges of the wound together. Severed nerves sprout fibers to restore some sensation to the healing area, and blood vessels growing from different sides of the cut join together to form a network of vessels.

Eventually the scab sloughs off and the epidermis returns to its original thickness. The area beneath is jammed with fibroblasts and bundles of collagen, which orient themselves along the lines of stress, further reinforcing the strength of the now-healed cut.[44]

It makes more sense to use homeopathic first-aid treatment and assist the body in its healing process than to work against it.

HOMEOPATHIC TREATMENT
Calendula Officinalis
Hypericum Perforatum
Hypercal

The effectiveness of **Calendula** in wound healing has already been discussed. Calendula is the first remedy to think of in treating an incised wound.

The first-aider should let the wound bleed freely for a time (unless, of course, the wound is especially deep and blood spurts from the wound—a sign an artery has been nicked or severed). Barring this complication, in a simple cut, after the wound has bled and in effect cleansed itself of any foreign matter and harmful bacteria, the wound should be flushed with clean water if possible to further assist the cleansing. Apply Calendula non-alcoholic (or succus) directly and undiluted to the wound using a cotton-tipped swab and working *away* from the cut. If the nonalcoholic or succus form is unavailable, a diluted solution of Calendula tincture (one teaspoonful to a quarter cup of water) may be used. Calendula is not a germ-killing agent but actually inhibits the growth of unfriendly bacteria and promotes the accelerated growth of epithelial cells, assisting the wound to heal naturally and more rapidly and safely than under any other treatment. If the wound is small, an appropriate sized plastic strip should then be applied. In a small and simple cut, this is all the first aid that will be necessary.

FIRST AID FOR DEEPER CUTS

If the wound is especially deep, or bleeds profusely, *direct pressure,* using a sterile gauze pad, should be applied directly on top of the wound. Normally direct pressure will staunch the bleeding in a minute or two, and then homeopathic first-aid treatment can be given. Elevating the body part is also beneficial in slowing or stopping rapid bleeding. Should the wound be so deep as to have nicked or severed an artery and *dark-red* blood spurts from the wound, application of direct pressure and elevation must be done imme-diately. In arterial bleeding it may also be necessary to use a *pressure point* where the flat pads of the fingers (never the fingertips!) press against the artery and the bone beneath. All three methods might have to be used in arterial bleeding. Too many people still believe it is necessary to apply a tourniquet to stop severe bleeding. As *all* circulation is stopped in an arm or leg to which a tourniquet is applied, this is a dangerous and serious business. If, and only if, bleeding cannot be stopped using the three foregoing methods, or if a limb has been severed, a tourniquet is applied. *It must be tight, stopping all bleeding.* And, once applied, *the tourniquet must never be loosened or removed.* Doing so can produce immediate severe bleeding, deep shock, or embolism (a blood clot breaks off from the site of injury and travels to the lungs or heart, possibly causing death). *An effective tourniquet must be removed only by skilled medical personnel.*

The homeopathic first-aider should remember Calendula in incised wounds, but **Hypericum** in lacerations. As lacerations are normally deeper and more destructive of the subsurface layers of the skin, they generally affect the nerves. As Hypericum has the Keynote symptom of pains shooting from the site of the injury, it is the first remedy to be thought of in injuries to the nerves. Hypericum's healing effect in lacerations is similar to Calendula's in incised wounds. Of course, if the first-aider does not have the remedy that would normally be used, Hypericum and Calendula may be exchanged one for the other with excellent results. Hypericum should also be diluted before use.

Hypercal is a combination remedy, an equal mixture of 50% Hypericum tincture and 50% Calendula tincture. Unfortunately, it is generally not advertised by homeopathic suppliers but can be purchased on special order from many homeopathic pharmaceutical manufacturers. Alternatively, the first-aider can easily make Hypercal by combining equal amounts of Hypericum tincture and Calendula tincture in a clean bottle for first-aid use. This mixture combines the specific healing properties of both these outstanding homeopathic remedies, and it may be used whenever either Calendula or Hypericum would be called for. Again, because Hypercal is 58% alcohol, it is too strong to be applied directly to any wound without first being diluted with water. One teaspoonful to a quarter cup of water makes an outstanding healing solution.

Incised wounds and lacerations, if deep, may require treatment by a physician, especially if there is any loss of movement that would indicate damage to a tendon.

Occasionally, sutures ("stitches") may be required to close the wound. If the interior of a wound bulges outward and yellowish or whitish tissues can be seen, or if the wound is jagged and badly torn, it will most likely require suturing by a health care professional. Many wounds, however—both incised and lacerated—can frequently be held together by a special bandage called a butterfly. Unlike any other type of bandage, a butterfly closure pulls the edges of the wound together, allowing the wound edges to seal. Butterfly closures are relatively inexpensive and every first-aider should carry several in the first-aid kit. The brand name Steristrips is supplied conveniently packaged and is available from most pharmacies.

In an incised wound or a laceration too large to be covered by a plastic strip, a sterile gauze dressing large enough to cover the injury should be applied and held in place with a gauze bandage or surgical tape. A *dressing* covers the wound; a *bandage* covers a dressing and holds it in place.

A wound should not be disturbed. Constant "peeking" to see if it is healing only slows the healing process by disrupting the cells trying to seal the break. Leave the dressing on, changing it only if it becomes exceptionally dirty. If changing is necessary, first soak the dressing in diluted Calendula, Hypericum, or Hypercal. Attempting to remove an unsoaked dressing may tear the wound open.[45]

The Special Treatment of Puncture Wounds

As most puncture wounds are deep and the penetrating object often drives dirt, dust, bacteria from the skin's surface, and sometimes oil and grease into the deeper tissue structures, the dangers of infection and especially tetanus are far greater than in almost any other injury.

In the basic first-aid treatment of a puncture, the wound should be encouraged to bleed. Bleeding will assist in cleansing the wound of debris embedded in the skin and help flush out other foreign matter and bacteria. Press around the wound, *never over it,* to encourage bleeding.

Homeopathy has a special remedy that is outstanding in the treatment of puncture wounds. **Ledum palustre** (*Ledum pal.*) is the homeopathic preparation of the herb marsh tea. Its use has been well known by homeopaths for decades and is totally unknown in allopathic practice. It is the best treatment for puncture injuries.

Because puncture wounds present a special difficulty, it is best that the first-aider *soak* the site of this injury in a dilute solution of Ledum pal. tincture rather than to merely apply it to the surface of the skin. Soak the injured part, such as a hand or foot, in a 10:1 water and Ledum pal. solution for at least 15 minutes. As nerve pain is frequently present, give Ledum pal. (6x, 12x, or 30x) internally every half hour or every hour or 2 hours as needed for pain. Hypericum in tablet form will also work well here if you do not have Ledum pal. in potency. Ledum pal. has remarkable pain-relieving powers and it also prevents septic conditions.

In any puncture wound (as well as in lacerations) the first-aider must be aware of the possibility of tetanus. Tetanus is a serious disease that may develop from 4 days to 3 weeks after a wound becomes infected by the tetanus bacillus. The tetanus bacillus is anaerobic, requiring no oxygen for it to live or grow, and therefore reproducing best in a deep wound where it is not exposed to air. Until medical researchers developed tetanus toxoid and antitoxin, lockjaw (the old name for tetanus) was nearly always fatal under standard treatment. The homeopaths successfully prevented most cases of tetanus with their wound treatments, using Ledum pal. or Hypericum internally as prophylaxis. However, it is wisest today to be vaccinated against tetanus. I know of no allopath, naturopath, or homeopath who would advocate against such immunization. All cases of deep puncture wounds, and any case of a wound that does not bleed freely, should be treated with tetanus toxoid, with a booster injection if the last immunization was 5 years or more ago, or with antitoxin as a physician indicates. A one-day delay in a booster is all right, giving you time to check your records—thus avoiding an expensive and perhaps unnecessary Emergency Room visit.

HOMEOPATHIC TREATMENT
Ledum Palustre (Ledum Pal.)
Hypericum Perforatum
Hepar Sulphuris Calcareum (Hepar Sulph.)
Pyrogen

The use of **Ledum palustre** internally has already been mentioned in treating puncture wounds. Think first of Ledum pal. in any puncture injury and in any wound that has its Keynote symptom (i.e., the wounded part is cold). **Hypericum** in its potentized form is especially useful when its Keynote symptoms (excessive painfulness and pain shooting upward from site of injury) are present. Ledum pal. also has that latter symptom. Hypericum works best in any wound or injury in which there is nerve pain, such as crushed fingers or toes or a blow to the coccyx ("tailbone"). Hypericum even relieves pain following surgical procedures.

Hepar sulphuris calcareum (Hepar sulph.), a homeopathic mineral remedy, is especially useful in any injury that forms pus or otherwise becomes, or threatens to become, inflamed. Remember that the Keynote symptoms of inflammation are heat, redness, swelling, and pain. Hepar sulph. will handle this situation effectively.

Pyrogen, the homeopathic artificial sepsin, has also been mentioned in connection with abrasions. In first-aid treatment, Pyrogen can deal with inflammation or infection effectively.

Potency and Dosage: 6x–30x every 2 to 4 hours, as required.

ADDITIONAL EFFECTIVE REMEDIES IN WOUNDS

The homeopathic remedies mentioned in the previous section are most commonly found in a well-stocked first-aid kit. In those purchased from homeopathic suppliers, Pyrogen is most frequently omitted.

There are additional remedies which can be thought of in wound treatment.

We don't often hear of ***Gun powder*** in wound treatment anymore, even in most homeopathic literature. However, it is a valuable, but all too often ignored remedy.

Gun powder is a mineral remedy made from potassium nitrate, sulfur, and charcoal. It is a highly effective prophylaxis against any infection, administered as soon after the injury as possible. Dorothy Shepherd, M.D., a British homeopathic physician, devotes an entire chapter in her book, *The Magic of the Minimum Dose,* to the use of Gun powder. It is highly effective in blood poisoning, in septic suppuration, and as a preventive against wound infection. Dr. Shepherd writes:

> . . . the great indication for the use of gunpowder is in *blood-poisoning.* It acts very well in minute doses, in the homoeopathic attenuations. It does not exert a direct germ-killing action; it acts by increasing the normal antiseptic action of the blood, and by raising the immunity. In health, living blood destroys germs; and the reason that in epidemics some persons escape the infection is that their blood is equal to destroying the germs which attack them.[46]

Gun powder is best used in the lower, 3x potency, should the first-aider wish to use the "ounce of prevention" philosophy in wound treatment.

The author frequently uses Gun powder, together with homeopathic external treatment, in wounds that seem to have the greatest possibility of becoming infected. In 4 years of practice, using Gun powder (3x) as an adjunct treatment to homeopathic wound cleansing, I have never had any trouble from infection in a wound so treated.

A case illustration using Gun powder follows. Some wounds are more likely to become infected than others. In the early summer of 1978, in the rugged back country of northern Utah, a group of adult Scout leaders was on a wilderness backpacking expedition. They had camped in a narrow valley in a high pasture used by a local sheep rancher to graze his flock.

Some of the group had gone rock climbing. One of the climbers lost his footing and tumbled and slid 20 feet down and over the rocks, landing hard on the manured ground. He was dazed and shaken, but there was no sign of fracture or concussion from the fall. His shirt, however, was torn and bloody. He had suffered several lacerations that were from 2 to 4 mm deep, and his back and upper right shoulder were considerably abraded, the dirt and manure being well ground into the open wounds.

At the central camp area, the homeopath administered Arnica (200x), 2 doses at 15 minute intervals for shock from the fall and as prophylaxis against bruising from the jarring tumble. The wounds were then cleansed with a solution of Hypericum tincture diluted 1:10 with water that had been boiled and cooled, from a nearby stream. The immediate problem was removing the embedded particles of dirt and manure, which were well worked into the skin's subsurface. A #10-bladed scalpel[47] worked effectively to gently scrape the area and work the small bits of contaminated material from the wounds. The areas were sponged with the dilute Hypericum solution until the wounds were as clean as possible. The jagged wound edges were drawn together by butterfly closures and the exposed skin covered by overlapping 4-inch sterile gauze pads that were bandaged into place. The dressing was saturated with additional Hypericum solution and remoistened periodically as needed.

The danger from infection from this sort of wound is considerable, so the man was given Gun powder (3x) to be dissolved under the tongue every 2 hours. There was little concern from tetanus as his booster was current.

Surprisingly (to him) he experienced almost no pain or stiffness from the fall (a fact attributable to the rapid administration of Arnica), and 2 days later the wounds were healing cleanly with no sign of sepsis.

Echinacea, made from the purple cone flower, is yet another homeopathic remedy exceptionally suitable for wound treatment.[48] It is effective in either its potentized form or in tincture. Echinacea's usefulness lies in the prevention of septicemia (blood poisoning) and in septic conditions generally. It may be applied in a diluted solution of the tincture to any wound where Calendula, Hypericum, or Ledum pal. would be used to good effect. Internally, at any sign of infection, Echinacea in potency will work to combat the inflammation.

Staphysagria is an additional remedy to be mentioned in wound management. In potentized form it is exceedingly valuable in treating the pain from any incised wound, in first aid where there is considerable pain from a clean cut, such as a paper cut, or following surgery when pain emanates from the site of the incision.

Conclusions on Homeopathic Wound Management

For nearly a century in the history of naturopathic medicine, and since at least the decade preceding World War II in the history of homeopathic medicine, people have been warned by nontraditional health care professionals to avoid using antiseptics on open wounds.

The efficiency and often superiority of the homeopathic approach to wound management has already been discussed and demonstrated in this section. Now, in research concluded in 1985 and reported in allopathic medical journals, this belief has been at least indirectly proved.

Separate studies conducted at the University of Florida and at the University of Virginia Medical Center have concluded that the use of over-the-counter and other antiseptics in wound cleansing can actually impede healing. In these studies, medical researchers found that iodine and any antiseptic containing iodine as well as other common and less common antiseptics actually retard healing rather than promote it. Wounds treated by providone-iodine were nearly 60% open following its use after one week; hydrogen peroxide, a common household antiseptic, kept 15% of wounds unhealed after a week's application.

Homeopathic tinctures, properly diluted and applied locally, are the best approach to take in dealing with open wounds—cuts, abrasions, and lacerations. Homeopathic tinctures are not antiseptic but bacteriostatic: they do not permit bacteria to flourish in their presence. They do not, as was discovered in the Florida and Virginia studies, destroy epithelial tissues and the white blood cells which are the body's first-line of defense against infection. Wounds treated homeopathically at the outset rarely become infected, and clinical observations demonstrate that healing is clean and occurs nearly 50% more rapidly than under traditional orthodox approaches.

CHAPTER FOUR

HOMEOPATHIC TREATMENT
OF SPECIFIC CONDITIONS

Topics Covered

Bee Stings
Bites
Boils
Carbuncle
Concussion
Diarrhea
Food Poisoning
Nausea and Vomiting
Earache and Ear Inflammation
Injuries and Inflammations of the Eye
Insect Bites and Stings
Poisonous Plants

Bee Stings

In a simple bee sting, internal remedies are seldom required and are not encouraged. The first-aider should first remove the stinger by scraping (never pulling) it from the skin using a fingernail or knife blade. In effect, when a person is stung by a bee, the insect commits suicide. Its stinger is barbed like a fish hook, and once it punctures the skin it remains and the bee disembowels itself when it flies away, leaving the stinger (which continues to pump poison from its poison sack) as well as its abdominal organs behind. The sting site will be painful, with a soft swelling, and a rosy-red coloration.

HOMEOPATHIC TREATMENT
Ledum Palustre Tincture (Ledum Pal.)
Apis Mellifica (Apis Mel.)
Carbolic Acid

Actually, in a bee sting there are any number of homeopathic remedies that can be considered, with the most useful being Ledum pal. tincture, Apis mel., and Arnica tincture. If none of these are available, the first-aider may freely substitute Urtica urens tincture, Hypericum tincture, or Calendula tincture.

Apply **Ledum palustre tincture,** undiluted, directly onto the sting with a cotton-tipped applicator. Ledum pal. tincture will relieve the pain rapidly. An occasional reapplication whenever the pain returns will normally be all the first aid required. If you do not have Ledum pal. tincture, substitute any of the other external remedies.

If a moderately severe reaction, with much pain, soreness, and swelling, should occur, give **Apis mellifica** (30x or 30c) internally, one to two doses. Apis mel. is the homeopathic trituration of the common honey bee and is effective with the Keynote symptoms of swelling, soreness, sensitivity, stinging pain, *Worse* from heat, touch, or pressure.

Some 1 to 2% of the population, 1 to 2 million people, are hypersensitive to bee stings. The greatest danger from a bee sting is *anaphylactic shock,* a severe and frequently fatal allergic reaction from a foreign protein introduced into the body.

The symptoms of sting-caused anaphylactic shock are as follows: hives covering a large part of the body; itching and burning skin, especially on the face and chest; difficult breathing or gasping for air; collapse, unconsciousness; the skin, especially the lips, may turn blue (*cyanosis*).

ADVISORY WARNING: Anaphylactic shock is a *life-threatening emergency!* Many persons who know they are severely allergic to bee stings or other insect bites carry an Anakit or Epipen (or their equivalent) for immediate use. All such kits contain epinephrine (adrenaline)

1:1,000, which is injected beneath the skin. If any of these kits are at hand, they should be used immediately.

Homeopathic first aid provides for anaphylactic shock effectively in the case of bee sting or other insect bite. The most similar remedy for sting-initiated anaphylactic shock is **Carbolic acid** (200x potency). The homeopathic first-aider should administer it *immediately upon the first symptoms,* 5 tablets or pellets, under the tongue.

The next remedy of choice is Apis mel. (200x potency). Apis is, of course, made from the honey bee, and is technically isopathic (treating the condition with the *same* causative agent) whereas Carbolic acid is homeopathic because it treats a condition with an agent that would produce *similar* symptoms. Obviously, because of the extreme urgency in anaphylactic shock, the first-aider will use whichever remedy is available.

Bites

Bites, whether from an animal, an insect (sting), or a human, are considered puncture wounds and are treated as you would a puncture.

HOMEOPATHIC TREATMENT
Ledum Palustre (Ledum Pal.)
Hypericum Perforatum

The remedy of first choice is, of course, **Ledum pal.,** both externally and internally. **Hypericum** may be substituted and used the same way as Ledum pal. if the latter is unavailable.

The danger from animal bites is, of course, infection and the possibility of rabies—a deadly disease. If possible, the biting animal should be captured and transported to a veterinarian for observation in case it is diseased. If the animal is wild and cannot be safely captured, it may need to be killed (be certain not to damage the head) and a necropsy performed. Almost any animal can carry rabies, although bats, skunks, raccoons, dogs, and cats are the most frequent carriers. The first-aider must not overlook the possibility of infection from a human bite. The mouth is a breeding ground for bacteria, and a human bite wound can easily become severely infected. Treatment with Ledum pal. or Hypericum or Calendula, the first two both externally and internally, will frequently prevent sepsis. Should the bite become inflamed, don't forget the homeopathic internal remedies for infection: **Gun powder, Pyrogen,** and **Hepar sulph.**

A case history of treatment of an insect bite (sting) follows. In 1979, a staff member of a summer Boy Scout camp was stung on the nose and face repeatedly by a horde of angry hornets. He had disturbed their nest unknowingly and suffered the painful consequences. It felt as if a dozen red-hot needles had been jabbed into him, and the pain was excruciating. Tears rolled from his eyes and blinded the man. Clutching his face with both hands, he literally staggered into the dining hall, looking as if he had been shot. A young first-aider nearby knew about homeopathy and hurried the man to the health lodge, where he applied Ledum pal. tincture to the stings. Within 30 seconds the pain began to abate and within 3 minutes it was completely gone. Much angry swelling remained, however. Two doses of Apis mel. (30x), taken a half hour apart, reduced the swelling to near-normal within 2 hours.

Boils

A boil, known by physicians as a *furuncle,* is an acute, tender, inflammatory nodule on the skin caused by staphylococcal bacteria. A boil can occur almost anywhere on the body but most frequently is seen on the neck, face, chest, and buttocks, and normally ranges in size from $1/4$ inch (5 mm) to just over 1 inch (30 mm). A boil can be excruciatingly painful if it occurs on the nose, finger, ear, or scrotum.

Homeopathy provides the most rapid and effective treatment for boils.

HOMEOPATHIC TREATMENT
Hypericum Perforatum Tincture
Tarentula Cubensis

Having treated numbers of boils, the author has seen the most outstanding success with **Hypericum tincture.** The first-aider needs, normally, to do nothing more than paint the boil with *undiluted* Hypericum tincture, cover it with a sterile gauze pad held in place with surgical or adhesive tape, and moisten the dressing with additional Hypericum tincture. The Hypericum tincture rapidly brings the boil to a head; it then suppurates, drains, and vanishes. Several reapplications of Hypericum tincture may be required.

Using homeopathic treatment there is no need to apply hot packs to hasten suppuration or drainage, no need to have the boil lanced, and no need for antibiotic ointments.

Another fine, internal, remedy for boils is *Tarentula cubensis* 30x, a remedy of biologic origin. The Keynote symptoms of this remedy are: purplish skin coloration; burning and stinging pains.

Boils are not uncommon in youngsters, and they seem especially common in young wrestlers, who apparently pick up the staphylococci bacteria from the wrestling mat.

Two case histories are illustrative. An Assistant Scoutmaster at a Boy Scout summer camp brought his son, who was about age 12, to see the homeopath. The boy had a long history of developing boils, sometimes one, sometimes several, every few months. He was in and out of the doctor's office constantly. This recurrent and annoying condition is called *furunculosis* and often occurs in young but otherwise healthy boys and girls. Homeopathy can very effectively deal with furunculosis. The homeopathic physician studies the constitutional nature of the individual and prescribes treatment that removes, often permanently, the predisposition to this disorder. This approach is, however, too complex for the nonmedically trained homeopathic first-aider to handle.

The boy had a newly formed boil the size of a small hen's egg on the posterior thigh, midway between the buttocks and knee. The treatment was simple. Undiluted Hypericum tincture was painted on with a cotton-tipped applicator, the area was covered with a gauze dressing, the gauze was moistened with additional Hypericum tincture, and the boy was told to return the next day. The following day, the boil, which had been nowhere near suppuration, had suppurated and was draining. More Hypericum was swabbed on, and the boil was redressed. The third day, the boil had shrunk to dimesize and had drained completely. Taking the wooden stick of a swab, the homeopathic doctor rolled it from the edge toward the center. A core of dead tissue and pus about 2 inches in length and the diameter of a pencil lead popped out. Again the boil was redressed with Hypericum. On the fourth day, when the boy and his father returned, the boil had completely vanished, leaving normal, smooth skin, with only the slightest hint of redness. The father was amazed and the boy pleased. Usually, under the family physician's treatment, the boils required from 7 to 10 days to heal, and they were usually lanced. Homeopathic treatment cut the healing time by 3 to 5 days, with no pain to the procedure. This man also wanted to learn more about the power, rapidity, and painlessness of homeopathic first aid.

The first case history showed the power of purely external treatment of a boil with Hypericum tincture. The following history demonstrates the power of Tarentula cubensis internally.

One evening, a dentist who had been told often about the power of homeopathy called to ask if the doctor would see his son. The boy was a handsome, athletic 15-year-old, a gymnast and a swimmer. He had developed a marble-size boil in his right groin adjacent to the testicle. Walking was painful and difficult. It was hard to tell who was more embarrassed: a shy teenager with his pants off in front of his father and a stranger, or the homeopath, who had forgotten to restock Hypericum tincture. There was scarcely enough in the bottle for one application. There was also a concern about swabbing it near such delicate tissue for fear it would dribble onto his scrotum and cause a severe burning sensation. But Tarentula cubensis (30x) was also available, and the boy took 5 tablets under his tongue. His father was given a 1-dram vial to take home and instructed to give his son 5 tablets every 4 hours for three to four doses. And his father called a week afterward to report that the boil had completely vanished 3 days later. Such is the power and rapidity of homeopathic treatment.

Carbuncle

A similar disorder to a boil is a *carbuncle*. Although it may be wise for a first-aider not to treat a carbuncle, a case history in its treatment will demonstrate the superiority of homeopathy over standard allopathic treatment.

A carbuncle is a cluster of boils, much larger than a simple boil, with numerous cores. The infection, also caused by staphylococcus, spreads subcutaneously. There is deep and extensive suppuration and often slow healing accompanied by scarring. A quotation from a standard allopathic medical reference text, *The Merck Manual,* will adequately demonstrate the complexity of nonhomeopathic treatment of a carbuncle.

Multiple furuncles and carbuncles require culture and sensitivity studies. Usually a penicillinase-resistant penicillin is required, such as cloxacillin, 250 mg orally q.i.d., or for penicillin-allergic patients, erythromycin in the same dosage. For recurrent boils, antibiotic therapy for 2 to 3 mo[nths] may be advisable. Immunization with staphylococcal vaccines is ineffective. Extensive necrotic destruction may require debridement, but antibiotics have eliminated the need for multilating surgery.[49]

Dorothy Shepherd, M.D., in her book, *The Magic of the Minimum Dose*, reports this history in the homeopathic treatment of a carbuncle.

A boy, aged 10 years, was seen with a large carbuncle on his scrotum; he was almost bent double with the pain and dragging sensation in the scrotal sac and unable to sit down. The swelling was very hard, very tender and red; there was no fluctuation, and no testicles could be made out. His parents had already applied hot fomentations for days with little relief. He was ordered hot dry dressings, a suspensory bandage, and *Tarentula cubensis* four-hourly. The nurse reported two days later that the swelling in the scrotum had disappeared: no sign of any carbuncle was discovered.[50]

From the case histories presented, there can be no doubt that homeopathy offers a superior and pleasant alternative to traditional allopathic treatment for boils and carbuncles. However, most orthodox physicians and, alas, the general public, know nothing of these alternatives, which are so simple to use, so safe to employ, and so successful in their effect.

A successful adjunct treatment of boils and carbuncles is **Echinacea**. The tincture painted on undiluted as one would Hypericum is of unquestionable value and will work as effectively. Echinacea internally, in potency, is especially effective in treating recurring crops of boils that some people seem predisposed to.

Concussion

Nontechnically, a concussion is a bruise on the brain, resulting typically when the head collides with a hard object, as in a fall. The brain, which is encased within the bony skull, is protected by three layers of membranes and between these and the skull itself is cerebrospinal fluid, which acts like a shock absorber. In a severe blow to the head, the brain may slam against the bony skull. Blood vessels may be ruptured, cerebrospinal fluid may escape from cavities within the brain, and the brain may hemorrhage.

A concussion may vary from mild to moderate to severe, relative to the amount of damage the brain receives. In especially severe blows, the brain may become lacerated or the skull fractured. Fluid pressure within the skull may increase, pressing on and compressing blood vessels, limiting oxygen flow to the brain cells in the damaged area.

The symptoms of a concussion are: history of a blow to the head; the victim may complain of dizziness, lightheadedness, or headache; the victim may appear dazed, disoriented, restless, or confused; the victim may vomit or complain of nausea; the victim may show the typical symptoms of shock; the pupils of the eyes may be unequal—one wider than the other—or unreactive to bright-light stimulus.[51]

Standard first-aid manuals say that the first-aider must never administer liquids or foods by mouth to a concussion victim. As in shock, do not give fluids. If unconscious, the victim may choke and aspirate the fluid into the lungs, causing yet another major problem. Because surgery may be required in severe injuries to the skull, as in a compressed fracture, increased fluid pressure, and internal hemorrhage, fluids should never be given. Under anesthesia, the individual may vomit and aspirate the vomitus into the lungs. This is also the reason an unconscious victim is placed on the *side* with the head slightly lower than the feet.

HOMEOPATHIC TREATMENT
Arnica Montana

Arnica montana 200x (or 30x if the 200th potency is unavailable) is the homeopathic remedy of choice in concussion, regardless of how severe. Many concussions are mild, thankfully, and a few doses of Arnica in whatever potency you have will serve well. Even in cases of severe concussion, administering Arnica will never be dangerous, and in fact will do considerable good.

The former fear was that the patient with concussion would fall asleep, and first-aiders were instructed never to allow the victim to sleep—out of fear he or she possibly would never wake up. Sleep isn't dangerous, but the first-aider should check the victim every 15 minutes for lingering or more severe onset of symptoms. Check especially the eyes to make certain the pupils are normal and reactive. Arnica may be given every 15 minutes, every half hour, or every hour as needed.

Diarrhea

If homeopathic remedies fail, they do so for one of three reasons: (1) the prescriber has failed to take into consideration the Keynote symptoms of the remedy and has not properly matched the remedy to the patient's current symptoms; (2) the remedy has been made inert through careless handling and subsequent contamination; or (3) the patient taking the remedy has not done so in a "clean mouth." Remember that coffee, tea, and even some herb teas, mouthwashes, toothpaste, and tobacco may nullify the therapeutic effect of the homeopathic remedy *before* it can be absorbed into the system. *Wait at least 1 hour after using any of these products before giving a homeopathic remedy.*

Boericke's *Materia Medica with Repertory* lists some 114 separate remedies for acute diarrhea. In the following section, only 10 of the most frequently called-for remedies are listed. These should be sufficient to handle most cases of common diarrhea. The prescriber must be careful to select the homeopathic remedy that most closely fits the patient's guiding symptoms.

Sometimes two remedies will show very similar symptoms. The homeopathic first-aider must study the case closely and select the one remedy closest to the patient's symptoms. Give the remedy time to work. If the first remedy fails to work after a reasonable time, or works partially but not completely, the first-aider can then give the next-closest remedy. Single remedies, at least in the 30x potency, should not be administered at the same time.

SINGLE REMEDIES VERSUS COMBINATIONS

Some homeopathic practitioners use combination remedies containing two, three, or more ingredients.

Classic homeopathy, in the mode of Samuel Hahnemann, M.D., and James Tyler Kent, M.D., a famous American homeopath of the early twentieth century, holds that, on careful examination of the Keynote symptoms, there is one and only one remedy that best suits the individual case. At the other end of the spectrum, opposite the classic "purists," are those practitioners who insist that, owing to the complexity of homeopathic prescribing, combination remedies are the simplest form of employing the powers of homeopathic remedies.

Mr. Dana Ullman, Master of Public Health, President of the Foundation for Homeopathic Education and Research, and Director of the Homeopathic Educational Services, calls homeopathic combination remedies "user-friendly homeopathy." Such multiple-ingredient medicines allow a simpler and quicker selection of a homeopathic remedy when dealing with acute cases. The remedies in combination act synergistically, each complimenting the other(s), when the "symptom picture" of a single remedy appears to overlap that of another closely related and complimentary remedy.

The following discussion will assist the reader in understanding and investigating this relatively new approach to homeopathy:

As most followers of homeopathy are well aware, two major approaches to homeopathy are widely accepted. They differ with regard to the form of a remedy given:
   • the modern, combination preparation
   • the classical, single remedy

Hans Heinrich Reckeweg, M.D. [an astute and highly respected West German homeopathic physician; founder of both Biologische Heilmittel Heel (West Germany) and Biological Homeopathic Industries (America)] believed that therapeutic success was more likely through administration of a combination homeopathic preparation than with a single remedy. Dr. Reckeweg felt that combination, or complex, preparations which contained substances from the animal, vegetable, and mineral kingdoms together would have a higher probability of efficacy than a homeopathic dose of a single substance.

As first pointed out by Dr. Samuel Hahnemann, each substance, when prepared homeopathically, will elicit a certain set of symptoms, sometimes called a "symptom picture." This totality of symptoms is characteristic of the given substance and is always recalled when deciding which remedy to administer. The symptom pictures of some remedies are lengthy indeed, covering numerous effects on body, mind, and spirit. When such a remedy is given to a person whose totality of symptoms is included in the remedy's symptom picture, the healing effect can be remarkable. However, just as each substance has a certain, finite realm of effectiveness, it is limited by that range.

Combinations of homeopathic remedies can alleviate the limiting factor of their single components. This is of utmost importance when treating persons with complicated, apparently unrelated symptoms. For example, practitioners nowadays treat many patients who may have deep seated complications from vaccinations or problems resulting from environmental pollution. If such a person develops an acute condition which requires treatment, a single homeopathic remedy will probably not be able to treat both the acute, apparent ailment and the chronic imbalance simultaneously. A complex preparation, though, containing ingredients which focus on both the acute and the chronic symptoms would have a greater likelihood of bringing about an effective stimulation of the body's defense system, leading to health.

Complex homeopathic preparations, due to their broad based composition, are useful in cases without clear, distinctive symptoms. As Dr. Reckeweg stated, the administration of a complex formula sets in motion the evolution of the case to a point where an appropriate single remedy may be prescribed, if desired. This feature seems to many to be preferable to the approach of selecting a single remedy from a nebulous set of symptoms.

Obviously, the act of learning how to repertorize a difficult case [index a set of symptoms of homeopathic remedies known to produce similar "symptom pictures" in healthy subjects] requires a great time commitment. Even to become familiar with a basic number of remedies necessitates more study time than many practitioners are initially willing to invest. Not only might there be difficulty in selecting the appropriate remedy, but the choice of which potency to employ can discourage incipient prescribers. Complex preparations offer therapeutic possibilities to those practitioners not well versed in classical homeopathy yet desirous of treating . . . safely and holistically.[52]

The following discussion on combination remedies appears in an article by Dana Ullman which first appeared in *Homeopathy Today,* a publication of the National Center for Homeopathy.

. . . Recently, one of my customers sought to order a book of which I had never heard by a German physician named Hans Heinrich Reckeweg, called *Homotoxicology.* With some searching, I was able to find it. Before sending it to my customer, I read it myself. The book included the most detailed charts of the physical correlates of Hering's Law of Cure presently available. [as a patient improves, his symptoms will proceed: (1) from within outward; (2) from above downward; (3) from the more important to the less important organs; (4) in reverse order of their appearance] What was particularly surprising to me was that Dr. Reckeweg developed his knowledge from 50 years of experience with combination medicines. I had never heard that the combination medicines work deeply enough to follow Hering's Law . . .

It would perhaps be ideal if consumers could learn the basic principles of homeopathy so that they could know how to pick the one individually-chosen homeopathic medicine to treat various acute, nondangerous conditions. And certainly it would be ideal if everyone had easy access to well-trained and experienced homeopaths to treat the dangerous or chronic health problems. However, few people today know enough about homeopathy to figure out how to use the medicines. Even those consumers who know homeopathy fairly well have difficulty choosing the one individualized medicine. And few people have access to good classical homeopaths, since there are not many such practitioners . . ."[53]

In the author's own practice, while his interest remains closely attuned to single-remedy, classical homeopathy, combination remedies have done yeoman's labor in several common cases in the last several years. One combination remedy, *Gastricumeel (Heel),* containing a synergistic combination of Argentum nitricum, Arsenicum album, Pulsatilla nigrens, Nux vomica, Carbo vegetabilis, and Antimonium crudum, has restored normalcy into the lives of dozens of sufferers from both acute and chronic heartburn, permitting them to again eat the foods they enjoyed without the attendant suffering and without the necessity of continually dosing as they had to with antacids. Six cases of intractable heartburn of 12 and 15 years' duration which had been medically diagnosed and unsuccessfully treated by allopathic means were cleared up, apparently permanently, within 48 hours.

Special combination remedies are supplied by nearly all homeopathic pharmaceutical manufacturers. However, because of the relative simplicity of applying homeopathic remedies in first-aid cases, the first-aider should have little difficulty in finding and applying the one best remedy, with excellent results.

HOMEOPATHIC TREATMENT

Arsenicum Album (Arsenicum Alb.)
Veratum Album (Veratum Alb.)
China
Podophyllum
Colocynthis
Croton Tiglium (Croton Tig.)
Dulcamara

The two most often indicated remedies in the treatment of diarrhea are **Arsenicum album** and **Veratum album** The two remedies are easily distinguished from one another by their peculiar Keynote symptoms.

The Keynote symptoms of Arsenicum alb. are: stools are small in quantity; the patient exhibits restlessness, anguish, and an intolerance to pain; there is considerable thirst, but only for small quantities of fluids, although often; there is great prostration and weakness associated with the diarrhea, although with the small quantity of the stool this would not be expected.

The Keynote symptoms of Veratum alb. are: stools are very loose and profuse in quantity; there is *no* restlessness, anguish, or intolerance to pain; there is great thirst for *large* quantities of cold fluids; great prostration follows the stool; there is profuse and violent retching and vomiting, with vomiting being the most characteristic symptom; stools are forcefully evacuated.

Potency and Dosage for Arsenicum Alb. and Veratum alb.: 6x–30x every 2 to 4 hours, as required.

The Keynote symptom of **China** is: frequent watery stools with gripping abdominal pains.

The Keynote symptoms of **Podophyllum** are: morning diarrhea which is painless; the stool is greenish in color, watery, with a strong, fetid odor; evacuation is *profuse* and gushing.

The Keynote symptoms of **Colocynthis** are: agonizing, cutting pain in the abdomen causing the patient to bend over double; the pain is relieved by pressing firmly on the abdomen; stools are yellowish, or jelly-like and brown.

The Keynote symptoms of **Croton tiglium** are: stools are copious and watery with great urging, always forcefully shot out, with gurgling in the intestines; drinking liquids increases the diarrhea.

The Keynote symptom of **Dulcamara** is: green, watery, slimy stools, often bloody with much whitish mucus, especially in the summer, coming on when weather suddenly becomes cold; *from damp and cold weather.*

Potency and Dosage for China, Podophyllum, Colocynthis, Croton tig., and Dulcamara: 6x–30x every 2 to 4 hours, as required.

SPECIAL KINDS OF DIARRHEA

Antibiotic-Caused Diarrhea

Some persons taking any of a number of antibiotics experience an altered intestinal transit. The antibiotics speed the normal transit time of fecal matter by stimulating the smooth muscle of the intestine. Antibiotic-caused diarrhea can be greatly distressing, as any teacher or businessperson will tell you, who has faced a group of people only to be forced to immediately leave the room.

The homeopathic remedy of choice for this type of diarrhea is *Nitric acid,* in either the 30x or 200x potency. Nitric acid is almost specific to this kind of diarrhea and will promptly relieve it.

Camp Diarrhea

"Camp diarrhea" is frequently the result of eating under less than sanitary conditions outdoors where quantities of grease or oil are allowed to accumulate, often unnoticed, in cooking implements and turn rancid. This special form of diarrhea can also be brought on by drinking impure water or eating foods that have been improperly stored and become contaminated.

The remedy of choice in "camp diarrhea" is *Pyrogen,* a triturated sepsin made from lean beef that has been exposed to direct sunlight and allowed to decompose. From this, a homeopathic remedy is potentized and becomes one of the most powerful of all antiseptic agents. The Keynote symptoms of Pyrogen in "camp diarrhea" are: horribly offensive, brown-black, painless and involuntary stools; stools are large and black, with a decomposed, carrion-like odor, or come in small, black balls; the abdomen is bloated and sore with intolerable cutting, cramping pains; the patient may experience vomiting. The vomitus resembles coffee grounds. Following drinking cold water, the patient vomits as soon as the water warms in the stomach.

Potency and Dosage: 12x–30x every 2 to 4 hours, as required.

Infant Diarrhea

One of the most characteristic remedies for diarrhea in infants is *Nux vomica,* a homeopathic remedy potentized from the poison nut.

The Keynote symptoms of Nux vomica are: diarrhea from eating artificial food such as infant formula; vomiting with much retching after eating; frequent stools with small evacuations.

Potency and Dosage: 6x–30x every 2 to 4 hours, as required.

Food Poisoning

One of the most frequent sources of sudden and violent abdominal pain accompanied by nausea, vomiting, cramping pains, and explosive diarrhea is food poisoning. There are many types of food poisoning. Some forms are the result of ingesting poisonous mushrooms and toadstools (*muscarine* and *phalloidine* poisoning), poisonous plants, either wild or domestic house plants, fish toxins, shellfish poisoning, and chemical contaminants such as insecticide-sprayed fruits and vegetables. Other forms are the result of ingesting bacteria-contaminated foods that have been improperly cooked, handled, or stored. Foods containing high concentrations of protein such as milk, meat, poultry, and eggs that have been improperly refrigerated may bring about intestinal distress.

The so-called "ptomaine" poisoning is the result of *staphylococcal enterotoxin* growing in protein-rich foods left unrefrigerated. Food handlers can also spread "ptomaine" through poor hygiene or when they have a boil somewhere on their skin.

Most common food poisonings are relatively short in duration and self-limiting. The onset of symptoms of acute intestinal distress—nausea, vomiting, and profuse diarrhea—is sudden, but the attack may last from only 3 to 6 hours. Although some potentially fatal forms of food poisoning exist, such as botulism, mushroom, fish, and shellfish poisoning, most forms are merely exceedingly unpleasant but seldom fatal.

HOMEOPATHIC TREATMENT
Arsenicum Album (Arsenicum Alb.)
Kreosotum
Pyrogen

Homeopathy provides a number of valuable remedies for common food poisoning, the so-called "ptomaine."

The most common and telling Keynote symptom of **Arsenicum album** is burning pain. When this symptom is present, together with several of the following symptoms, Arsenicum will be the remedy of choice:

the abdomen is swollen and painful with gnawing and burning pains; nausea, retching, and vomiting occur after eating or drinking; the patient cannot bear the sight or smell of food; stools are small, highly offensive in odor, dark; the patient experiences great debility and prostration *on slightest exertion.*

Kreosotum is a mixture of natural phenols derived from the closed distillation of beechwood. The Keynote symptoms of Kresotum are: nausea; vomiting of food several hours after eating; sensation of coldness in the stomach; bitter taste in the mouth after swallowing water; diarrhea is very offensive, dark brown, and bloody.

Potency and Dosage for Arsenicum album and Kreosotum: 6x–30x every 2 to 4 hours, as required.

Pyrogen is one of the preeminent remedies in most forms of common food poisoning. Together with Arsenicum, Pyrogen most frequently comes to mind in intestinal distress.

The Keynote symptoms of Pyrogen are: intolerable cutting, cramping pains in the abdomen; diarrhea with horribly offensive, brown-black stools that are painless and involuntary; stools are large, black, and with carrion-like odor, or small and passed in black balls; vomiting; water is vomited when it becomes warm in the stomach; the vomitus resembles coffee grounds.

Potency and Dosage: 12x–30x every 2 to 4 hours, as required.

As has been stated, most common food poisonings are short in duration and self-limiting, the troubles ceasing after a few hours, with generally no ill after-effects. However, homeopathic remedies, used according to their Key-note symptoms, are exceedingly effective in cutting the recovery time, often by half.

Two personal case histories of food poisoning provide an illustration of homeopathic treatment. In the summer of 1974, I had occasion to eat an afternoon picnic dinner prepared in a commercial kitchen. The meal consisted of fried chicken, potato salad, and iced melon balls. I noticed that one of the pieces of chicken was less than fully cooked and threw it away after a few bites. I have always been concerned about potato salad served on picnics if it hasn't been under constant refrigeration. But this potato salad was stone-cold and obviously fresh.

About 4 hours after the picnic lunch and back at home, I experienced great chilliness accompanied by a trembling weakness in my arms and legs, and profuse sweating. These symptoms were rapidly followed by severe waves of nausea and violent vomiting. The diarrhea was sudden. I craved cold water, but as soon as I swallowed it, it came back up. Horrible cutting pains slashed across my lower bowel. Within minutes I felt so weak all I could do was literally crawl across the floor, gasping for breath and coming very close to praying for a quick death!

At times it is difficult to think clearly, especially when it is *you* who are experiencing a severe, sudden, and acute illness. Some of the symptoms belonged to Pyrogen: the intolerable cramping abdominal pains and vomiting water as soon as it was drunk. However, on the basis of these two major symptoms alone, Pyrogen would probably have been ineffective.

The Keynote symptoms of Arsenicum proved it to be the *most* called-for remedy: thirst for small quantities of cold water; extreme debility and great weakness overall, and especially in the extremities; sudden and profuse sweating. Arsenicum may be accompanied by diarrhea as well as vomiting. The thirst is a *small* thirst—one swallow at a time, but with frequent desire to drink. These are minor symptoms, but telling ones, in an Arsenicum illness.

I literally dragged myself across the floor to my first-aid kit and found a 2-dram vial of Arsenicum (30x), popped 5 tablets under my tongue, and lay back to "die." Within 15 minutes there was a definite although relatively minor abatement in the symptoms. I took 5 more tablets and waited. Within 1 hour there was a cessation of vomiting and diarrhea, and I could drink the water I craved without having it come back up. I still felt quite weak, but not nearly as weak as I had been. The cramping pains in my lower bowel stopped. Within another half hour most of the debility and prostration had vanished as well. Arsenicum, in homeopathic potency, had worked remarkably well in under 2 hours in what appeared to be a classic case of *staphylococcal enterotoxin* food poisoning.

A very similar poisoning occurred 4 years later. It was midsummer and I was serving as Program Director and Health Officer at a Boy Scout camp in Iowa. Some hours following an evening meal of fried chicken and potato salad, I was struck with nausea, vomiting, weakness in the muscles, and gnawing, burning pains across the abdomen and throughout the lower bowel. The camp director, a retired Air Force colonel, and several other staff members also experienced similar symptoms. On this particular meal, the staff had eaten leftover chicken from the night before as the cooks had run low on the regular dinner menu. None of the Scout campers or leaders were similarly affected. We held quite a "meeting" in the health lodge that evening, but all of us recovered quickly after taking two to three doses of Arsenicum in its 30x potency.

Nausea and Vomiting

Nausea, or nausea accompanied by vomiting, can result from any of a number of different problems, but frequently from eating tainted foods. Homeopathy provides two highly effective remedies for this distressing condition.

HOMEOPATHIC TREATMENT
Ipecacuanha (Ipecac)
Tobacum

Ipecacuanha (Ipecac) comes from the root of the plant of the same name. In its syrup form, available in drugstores, it is a potent emetic, producing vomiting, and is useful as an antidote for many ingested poisons. Because Ipecac produces profuse vomiting and persistent nausea, in its homeopathic potency it reverses the process, hence its great use in homeopathic first aid.

The Keynote symptoms of Ipecac are: continuous nausea with great salivation; persistent, constant vomiting, especially of slimy white mucus; nausea is *unrelieved* by vomiting—this is Ipecac's most important Keynote symptom.

Ipecac is best used in its lower potencies for nausea and vomiting. The 3x and 6x potencies are most effective. In its high potencies, Ipecac is of considerable value in staunching *bright-red* hemorrhages from any part of the body.

Tobacum is made from the tobacco plant. Anyone who has ever used tobacco remembers well the first effects it had: nausea, vomiting, wave after wave of dizziness that was worse from any movement; faintness with a desire for cold, fresh air, and a sick and sinking sensation in the pit of the stomach. Again, what a substance produces as symptoms of illness in an otherwise healthy individual, it will cure in its homeopathic form.

Tobacum's symptoms are similar to those of Ipecac, but distinguished from it by the following Keynote symptoms: nausea and vomiting is *worse* from any motion; *better* with cool, fresh air; considerable dizziness; feeling of faintness with a sick and sinking sensation in the pit of the stomach. If you experience any of these Keynote symptoms, tobacum will promptly relieve the condition.

Potency and Dosage: Tobacum is effective in any of these potencies: 3x–30x every 2 to 4 hours, as required.

NAUSEA AND VOMITING IN MOTION SICKNESS

HOMEOPATHIC TREATMENT
Cocculus

Cocculus, potentized from the Indian cockle plant, is almost specific to all motion sickness. With cocculus, all symptoms are made *worse* by motion—riding in a car, airplane, or a boat or ship.

The Keynote symptoms of Cocculus are: head feels heavy and empty; dizziness and nausea especially when riding or sitting up; nausea from looking at moving objects; Nausea with faintness and vomiting; great aversion to food, drink, or tobacco; metallic taste in the mouth.

AN EFFECTIVE NONHOMEOPATHIC REMEDY

Recent experiences by herbalogists, proved through clinical study, have shown the powdered root of ginger to be highly effective in *preventing* motion sickness. The normal dose is two 650-mg capsules of the powdered root. Ginger appears to have none of the adverse side effects some persons experience from taking Dramamine and other, similar over-the-counter and prescription antivertigo drugs.

CASE HISTORY IN NAUSEA

The author's mother died from metastatic carcinoma (cancer). In the final few months before her death, although she was not undergoing chemotherapy, she began experiencing bouts of constant, unrelenting nausea. Her oncologist (cancer specialist) prescribed Compazine (prochlorperazine), a powerful antinauseant, for severe, persistent nausea and vomiting. Compazine has several possible side effects, the least of which is drowsiness. Jaundice (a yellowing of the skin and "whites" of the eyes) is common, and some sudden deaths have been recorded as prochlorperazine has a suppressant effect on the cough reflex.

While she took Companzine, the drug had little effect on the persistent nausea and profuse vomiting. Ipecac in 3x potency, however, promptly diminished her symptoms. After a few weeks, taking Ipecac only when symptoms appeared, the 3x stopped working. The 6x potency was prescribed and, again, all symptoms of nausea and vomiting ceased. The 6x potency worked well for several weeks before it, too, failed to hold. The 12x potency was given, and this potency held throughout the remainder of her illness, greatly improving the quality of her life until her death a few months later.

Ipecac and Tobacum are of unquestioned value in nausea, or nausea and vomiting, when those remedies' individual, guiding Keynote symptoms are present.

ADVISORY WARNING: Persistent nausea and severe and unrelenting vomiting in children up to the age of 18, following a viral infection such as "flu" or chicken pox, may be a symptom of Reye's syndrome. This disease is of unknown cause, most frequently affecting children between ages 5 and 10. Reye's syndrome has, at present, no known prevention or cure. In the United States it normally occurs in late fall and winter, usually between November and March, and during the period when a child seems to be recovering from the "flu" or chicken pox. Reye's syndrome's usual first symptom is severe, persistent vomiting lasting several hours. This is followed by personality changes: mild amnesia, lethargy, disorientation, agitation, or combativeness. Finally, the child lapses into a coma. Death may follow. If a child exhibits any of these symptoms, Reye's syndrome must be suspected and proved by a blood test. Contact a physician or the emergency service of the nearest medical facility. Let them know you suspect Reye's syndrome, detail the child's recent medical history and current symptoms, and insist on appropriate laboratory tests. *Do not give antinausea drugs of any kind,* allopathic or homeopathic, as these may mask or increase the severity of the disease. Fortunately, the symptoms of Reye's syndrome are becoming more readily recognized by parents and physicians alike. The sooner treatment begins, the better the child's chances of survival. Do not wait! If you suspect the possibility of Reye's syndrome, act immediately. Although there is at present no known cure, the survival rate from Reye's syndrome has increased steadily over the past several years. For further information concerning this disease you may contact the National Reye's Syndrome Foundation in Bryan, Ohio: (419) 636-2679.

Earache and Ear Inflammation

THE STRUCTURE OF THE EAR

Of the five physical senses (taste, touch, smell, sight, and hearing), sight and hearing are the most complex and delicate. The following presentation is not intended to be a complete or exhaustive treatment on the anatomy of the ear, but attempts to give the reader some idea of its complexity.

The ear is composed of three distinct sections: the external ear, the middle ear, and the inner ear. Each section, while separate, interrelates to the other and contains structures essential for normal sound receptivity.

The external ear is composed of the immediately visible *pinna* or *auricle,* a tough, skin-covered cartilage structure. The pinna acts much like a megaphone in reverse, catching and then channeling sound wave vibrations along a narrow canal called the *external auditory meatus,* or ear canal. The canal itself is a relatively short passageway lined with a specialized type of skin or *epithelium,* thinner and more delicate than ordinary skin, and lined with wax-secreting glands that lubricate the *meatus.* The wax, or *cerumen,* secreted from these glands serves to trap and expel foreign particles, even insects, that may enter the ear. At the end of the canal lies the *tympanic membrane* or "eardrum," which receives the directed sound vibrations and separates the external ear from the middle ear.

Internal to the tympanic membrane is the middle ear. An approximately cubical cavity, it contains three bones (the *auditory ossicles*) that conduct sound vibrations from the eardrum: the *malleus, incus,* and *stapes.* Because of their distinctive shapes they are commonly called the hammer, anvil, and stirrup. The incus is situated between the other two and attenuation of noise is accomplished by two small muscles. The *eustachian tube* connects the chamber of the middle ear to the back of the throat, the *nasopharynx,* and is an outside air source. This tube permits an equilibrium of air pressure between the external and internal sides of the eardrum. Additionally, adjacent to the middle ear are the mastoid and the sinuses.

The innermost section of the ear, the inner ear, contains a bony labyrinth and a membranous labyrinth encompassing three semicircular canals, essential to maintain balance and equilibrium, and a bony *cochlea.* Resembling a garden snail's shell, the cochlea divides into bony and membranous chambers containing specialized fluid and the *organ of Corti,* which is lined with fine hairs that respond to sound vibrations and transmit sound-wave impulses along the eighth cranial nerve to the brain.

The ear is such a complex and delicate mechanism that the first-aider and medical self-helper must be aware of the limitations of non-medically supervised treatment.

ADVISORY WARNING: Although homeopathic remedies are exceptionally effective in treating conditions of the outer and middle ear, should the best-indicated remedy fail to significantly reduce, then eliminate, the condition within 48 hours, consult a physician.

EARACHE

Simple earache may be caused by exposure to cold, damp chill, and drafts, or it may be the result of a viral cold extending from the sinuses or eustachian tube into the ear. An earache may also be caused by a diseased tooth, in which case a dentist must be consulted to eliminate the cause of the infection.

HOMEOPATHIC TREATMENT
Chamomilla
Ferrum Phosphoricum (Ferr. Phos.)
Mullein Oil
Plantago Majus Tincture

Ferrum phosphoricum is a homeopathic "tissue salt"—a trituration of the mineral iron phosphate.

Ferr. Phos. is the pre-eminent biochemic first-aid. It is the *oxygen-carrier.* It enters into the composition of haemoglobin, the red colouring matter of the blood. It takes up oxygen from the air inhaled by the lungs and carries it in the blood stream to all parts of the body thus furnishing the vital force that sustains life. It gives strength and toughness to the circular walls of the blood vessels, especially the arteries. Freely circulating, oxygen-rich blood is essential to health and life and for this reason Ferr. Phos. should always be considered, as a supplementary remedy, no matter what other treatment may be indicated by the symptoms.

Congestion, inflammatory pain, high temperature, quickened pulse, all call for more oxygen, and it is Ferr. Phos. that is the medium through which oxygen is taken up by the blood stream and carried to the affected area. This tissue-salt can be given with advantage in the early stage of most acute disorders, and it should be administered at frequent intervals until the inflammatory symptoms subside.[54]

Ferr. phos., given in 5-tablet doses every 15 to 30 minutes at the very beginning of any inflammatory condition, will work to good effect. It is one of the first remedies to consider in simple earache and is best employed in the lower 3x to 6x potencies.

For simple earache, *Mullein oil* is recommended. Mullein oil is not really an oil at all but a dark-brown fluid extract of *Verbascum thapsus.* It has pronounced effect on the ear, in simple earache. Mullein oil is supplied by homeopathic pharmacies in 1/2 oz. and 1 oz. dropper bottles. Best results are obtained when 3 to 4 drops of the *warmed* oil are instilled into the affected ear. The oil may be warmed by placing the bottle in a pan of hot water for a few minutes, or warming the oil in a clean, heated spoon. A small ball of cotton, large enough not to slip down into the ear canal, is then inserted to keep the oil from dribbling out. Repeat this treatment twice daily.

Plantago majus is the tincture extract of the plantain plant, usually considered by gardeners and yardkeepers as a noxious weed. Not only do the young, tender, unsprayed leaves make a fine addition to the summer salad, but also, in its homeopathic tincture, Plantago majus is an excellent and effective remedy in simple earache, especially when the ear pain is associated with a toothache. Of course, the underlying cause of the toothache will have to be assessed by a dentist. Here Plantago majus tincture pulls double duty, as homeopathic remedies so often do. One or 2 drops of the tincture on the painful tooth will stop the pain temporarily, if the pain is associated with a cavity.

The Keynote symptoms of Plantago majus are: stitching pain in ear(s); noise is painful; pain goes from one ear to the other through the head; pain plays between teeth and ears; earache is often associated with toothache.

In administering Plantago majus tincture, follow the same guidelines for Mullein oil.

Chamomilla comes from the German chamomile flower and is especially useful in earaches in young children. Considered predominantly a children's remedy, Chamomilla also has proved effective in adults.

The Keynote symptoms of Chamomilla are: ringing in ears; earache with localized soreness; swelling and heat in ear driving patient frantic; ears feel stopped up. Employ Chamomilla in any available potency: 3x, 6x, 12x, or 30x, with the lower potencies repeated more frequently until symptoms subside.

EAR INFLAMMATIONS

Ear inflammations, for the purpose of first aid and medical self-help, may be classified as inflammations of the *external auditory meatus* (*otitis externa*) or the middle ear (*otitis media*). Sometimes there is excessive accumulation of wax in the ear canal, or foreign objects may become trapped in the canal. Employing the indicated homeopathic remedies and associated techniques, the first aider or self-helper may expect excellent and rapid results. However, should the indicated remedy fail after 36 to 48 hours, or if the irritation or pain persists or becomes worse, do not hesitate to consult a licensed health-care professional.

HOMEOPATHIC TREATMENT

Aconite
Belladonna
Chamomilla
Ferrum Phosphoricum (Ferr. Phos.)
Pulsatilla

The Keynote symptoms of ***Aconite*** are: ear(s) very sensitive to noises; sounds (music) are unbearable; external ear (pinna) hot, red, painful, swollen; earache with sensation of a drop of water in (left) ear.

The Keynote symptoms of ***Belladonna*** are: tearing pain in external ear; humming noises occur in the ear; patient is sensitive to loud noises; pain causes delirium; parotid gland is swollen; eardrum bulges and is bright red with injected blood vessels.[55]

The Keynote symptoms of ***Chamomilla*** are: ear pains are violent, with stitching pain; pain is *worse* from warmth; patient is fretful and restless; ear(s) feel stopped up; swelling and heat drive the patient frantic.

Chamomilla is *almost* always the specific remedy in earache in infants and small children.

The Keynote symptoms of **Ferrum phosphoricum** are: ear is sensitive to sound; pain is throbbing, or with intermittent sharp, stitching pain.

Ferr. phos., a homeopathic tissue salt of considerable value in any inflammatory condition, should be thought of as a concurrent and complementary remedy given with any of the remedies listed, whether the Keynote symptoms for it exist or not.

Pulsatilla, a remedy compounded from the wind flower, exerts a great curative effect over external ear inflammations and should always be considered when its Keynote symptoms agree. The Keynote symptoms of Pulsatilla are: ear is hot, red, and swollen; severe darting, tearing, or throbbing pains are present, which are generally *worse* at night.

AUXILIARY REMEDIES FOR EXTERNAL EAR CONDITIONS

Echinacea tincture, an extract of the purple cone flower, is an important remedy to consider in localized inflammation of the external ear canal. A dilute solution of Echinacea tincture, 9 parts of purified or distilled water to 1 part tincture, can be instilled into the ear canal, or applied by a cotton-tipped applicator *lightly* inserted into the external canal, *but no farther than your unaided eye can see.* The diluted Echinacea tincture is especially useful in the treatment of a boil in the external canal or of local irritation caused by insect bite or stings of the immediate external opening or the pinna.

Otologists (specialists in the treatment of ear diseases and hearing disorders) and E.N.T. (ear, nose, and throat) specialists do not recommend inserting *any* objects into the ear. The lining of the ear canal is thin and easily damaged and, when damaged, is prone to infection. Inserting pointed objects, such as toothpicks, pen caps, pencils, and so forth into the ear may only lead to trouble.

SWIMMER'S EAR

Generally, external ear inflammations are caused by a boil (furuncle) in the canal, or by several varieties of bacteria, or rarely by a fungal infection. Frequently during the summer months swimmers will suffer from an external otitis called "swimmer's ear." This annoying condition often results when water becomes trapped by debris or accumulated wax and is allowed to pool in the ear. The epithelial lining of the ear becomes macerated, and bacteria may invade the tissues and spread, resulting in acute infection.

Swimmer's ear is generally associated with itching and pain along the ear canal, possible hearing loss if the canal becomes inflamed and swollen, and later oozing of a foul-smelling, purulent discharge from the opening.

Simple Home Remedy for Prevention of Swimmer's Ear
Although a number of over-the-counter remedies exist for the prevention of swimmer's ear, a simple home remedy often works effectively. After swimming, instill 3 to 4 drops of a dilute solution of distilled white vinegar (5% acidity), 1 part vinegar to 3 parts purified or distilled water, into the ear and allow to drain by tilting the head to the side. This treatment alters the pH of the ear canal, preventing or inhibiting the growth of harmful bacteria. In fact, physicians often employ a 0.5% acetic acid solution (the same acidity as in 5% distilled white vinegar) three times a day for 7 days to cure otitis externa.

HOMEOPATHIC TREATMENT
Aconite
Belladonna
Chamomilla
Pulsatilla
Echinacea Tincture
Mullein Oil

Swimmer's ear yields brilliantly and rapidly to homeopathic treatment. Because the symptoms of swimmer's ear often overlap the first three remedies, a useful combination remedy called *"ABC"*—the homeopathic combination of Aconite, Belladonna, and Chamomilla—in the 6x or 30x potency, is especially valuable. Some homeopathic pharmaceutical houses or local homeopathic pharmacies will specially compound this remedy upon request, and ABC is available in the 6x potency from one or two American homeopathic manufacturers. The author has used ABC in the 30x potency for swimmer's ear any number of times, with 100% effectiveness within 24 to 36 hours.

A case history is illustrative. One of the staff members at a Boy Scout summer camp, a 16-year-old boy on the aquatics staff and an active competitor on his school's swim team, was constantly developing otitis externa. His symptoms were itching along the ear canal and stitching pain, often tearing in nature and unbearable. The homeopath gave him Belladonna (30x), 5 tablets to be taken 4 times a day for 2 days, and a local application of Echinacea tincture. The treatment worked rapidly and, within less than one full day, all symptoms of the inflammation had disappeared. Since then, every time the symptoms of swimmer's ear occur, his father administers Belladonna and Echinacea tincture, and the symptoms vanish in 24 hours.

For years the author has used either the foregoing treatment or **Pulsatilla** alone when its Keynote symptoms indicated it was the most effective remedy, or ABC-30, all with the same results. The inflammation was reduced a few hours later and vanished completely, usually within 24 to 36 hours.

It always amuses me when, after some 12 years of work with homeopathy, I am told, usually by a traditionally trained physician with an M.D. degree, "That 'medicine' doesn't work." It used to make me angry. Now I only look at these people with a smile of bemused tolerance and attempt to re-educate them. It's a slow process. Homeopathy *does* work, time after time, if the symptoms of the disease are matched closely to the remedy's Keynote symptoms. Following is a case history from the experience of a well-known British homeopath, Dorothy Shepherd, M.D.

In one way children are difficult to treat, as you have to depend entirely on your powers of observation; you cannot ask any questions as regards the nature, the seat, and the character and directions of the pain. On the other hand, their objective signs and symptoms are clearer, not disguised or hidden by crude drugs and large doses of medicines taken in the past.

This baby was eight months old and just passing through its difficult period of dentition [cutting teeth]: breast fed, with a good careful mother, a happy, contented mortal, always cooing and laughing. Suddenly it all changed, the face became scarlet and felt very hot to the touch; the temperature was 102 degrees, and he was delirious during the night, constantly shrieking with piercing shrieks, the throat was intensely red, and the left eardrum was bulging. Did I incise the eardrum? I should have, according to recognized and orthodox teaching. I depended on the homoeopathic scalpel, which in this case was *Belladonna*. The district nurse was sent in to watch the case, and if necessary, send [the baby] to hospital; but again the simple remedy conquered the foul disease; the temperature went down to 99 degrees the next morning and never went up again, and the child recovered as quickly as it was stricken down.[56]

At times the best-indicated remedy will work well, only to fail to "hold."

This usually occurs when the remedy is not, as the homeopaths say, "deep" enough. Then, a complementary and deeper-acting remedy will be needed.

An example of this occurred a few years ago with a friend's 4-year-old daughter. The mother was somewhat acquainted with homeopathy. She had been taking Arnica for the muscle soreness and stiffness she often felt following gardening or an aerobics class she attended. The Arnica worked well and she also learned about several other useful remedies. One evening she called to say her daughter had turned fretful, was running a fever of over 102 degrees, and was complaining of a sore throat and earache.

The child's throat was bright red and shiny, and her right ear was intensely painful. Nearby noises, even the sound of the television, hurt her ear. Swallowing was painful. Belladonna (30x) was indicated on the basis of the Keynote symptoms (bright-red, shiny throat, *worse* swallowing liquids, *worse* right side, hearing acute and noise painful). In about 24 hours the throat cleared well—no more pain and the child drank milk and water—and the earache vanished, too. But the child relapsed, and her symptoms changed. Her throat was now painful on the left, still dry but not shiny. She was able to drink, but cold milk disagreed with her, although hot tea soothed her throat. The earache reappeared in the left ear, whereas it had been on the right before. The problem called for another remedy, and in accordance with Boericke's *Materia Medica with Repertory,* her symptoms were clearly **Lycopodium.** Lycopodium is made from the ground seed spores of club moss. A highly regarded homeopathic remedy in higher potencies, it has no value in traditional medicine. The Keynote symptoms of Lycopodium were here (dryness of the throat, *better with warm* drinks), and the most telling symptom also was present (disease characteristically moves from right to left). The child received Lycopodium (30x), four doses, after which the symptoms disappeared and never returned.

Her mother, by the way, was a Lycopodium patient. Every physical complaint she experienced *always* was either limited to the right side of her body, or moved from right to left—the eczema she had suffered from for years, the frequent right-sided temporal headaches, and the sore throats that always began on the right and either stayed on the right or moved on to the left. Lycopodium cleared up the eczema she had suffered with for 20 years, and it proved to be the only remedy she has ever needed for her peculiar right-sided headaches and sore throats. To the traditionally trained physician, "sidedness" means little or nothing. Going to a doctor's office saying, "All my illnesses are *always* right-sided, or left-sided, or move from left to right, or right to left," would probably be met with an arched eyebrow and a quizzical look. It wouldn't mean much. To a homeopath these symptoms, called *modalities,* are highly important.

INFLAMMATION OF THE MIDDLE EAR

A number of disorders and infections afflict the middle ear, ranging from aerotitis resulting from unequal air pressure on the eardrum, as in descending in an airplane or the pressure exerted in scuba diving, to various bacterial, viral, and mycoplasmal infections. The only subject which will be discussed in this section is *acute otitis media*—a bacterial or viral infection of the middle ear. All other problems should be seen by a licensed health-care professional.

> ADVISORY WARNING: In any ear problem, if the indicated homeopathic remedy best fitting the patient's symptoms fails to work, or if the problem persists beyond 36 to 48 hours, stop treatment and consult a physician.

Keynote Symptoms of Otitis Media
Normally acute middle ear inflammation occurs in infants and young children between 3 months and 3 years of age, the result of microscopic organisms traveling from the nasopharnyx into the middle ear through the eustachian tube. Symptoms include a sudden, severe earache, a possible loss of hearing acuteness, nausea, vomiting, diarrhea, and fever. *Serious complications may result from untreated otitis media.* A generally effective means of determining whether the inflammation involves the middle ear or the external ear is to pull gently on the *pinna* and to press on the *tragus* (the small cartilaginous projection nearest the face). Resultant pain or discomfort from this simple test tends to indicate an *external ear inflammation.* If the first-aider or medical self-helper has an otoscope or orotoscope available, examination can determine if the eardrum is swollen (bulging outward) and bright red, with engorged blood vessels.

External treatments such as with Mullein oil, Plantago majus tincture, or Echinacea tincture are of no use in the middle ear infections.

HOMEOPATHIC TREATMENT
Aconite
Belladonna

Aconite should be thought of whenever there is a sudden and violent onset of pain *with fever.* Accompanying the pain and fever there may be considerable restlessness, both physical and mental. These two symptoms—*physical and mental restlessness*—are the most characteristic of aconite. Aconite is generally the first remedy to consider in any sudden inflammatory condition. Aconite is a quick and brief-acting remedy and is useful only in the very early stages of acute inflammatory conditions.

Belladonna most often exhibits the Keynote symptoms of middle ear infection. The eardrum is congested with blood vessels and is bright red, and the eardrum itself bulges outward from the pressure behind it. There will be considerable tearing pain in the affected ear, with throbbing or beating pains deep within the ear. Through experience, belladonna has proved itself almost specific in middle ear inflammations, frequently bringing about a complete and rapid cure.

A valuable combination remedy in middle ear infection is *ABC*—the homeopathic combination of Aconite, Belladonna, and Chamomilla. Generally available from homeopathic suppliers in the 6x potency, ABC will act quickly in most acute middle ear conditions. In using the lower potency of ABC or any single remedy, increase the recommended dosage on the label to every 2 hours. In the higher 30x potency, administer the remedy every 2 to 4 hours for a maximum dosage of nine applications.

Another homeopathic remedy is often employed in the treatment of acute middle ear infection, *Hepar sulph.,* and a number of pre-prepared combination remedy specialties contain it. It is advisable for the first-aider or medical self-helper *not to use Hepar sulph.* in treating a middle ear condition. Hepar sulph. tends to increase suppuration and may act so strongly as to rupture the eardrum! A ruptured eardrum is a medical emergency and may lead to complications. The first-aider will recall the first principle for first aid from the Introduction: *to do no harm.* The use of Hepar sulph. in ear inflammations is best left to the skilled homeopathic practitioner.

EXTERNAL EAR OBSTRUCTIONS

Mechanical obstructions of the outer ear are not uncommon, especially in small children who have a bad habit of inserting any object that fits into their ears. These objects range from dried peas and beans to beads from a broken necklace. Obstructions in the ears of adults most frequently result from an accumulation of wax in the canal.

There is considerable debate over whether a first-aider or medical self-helper should attempt to remove *any* object from the ear canal. The reader will recall the warning from ear and ear, nose, and throat specialists never to insert any object into the ear. Most of us do, however, even though we've been warned.

A guiding rule for the self-helper or first-aider here might be that, if the object is clearly visible to the unaided eye, it might be removed safely, without danger. Perhaps the best way is to flush the ear with water using a syringe. Do not, however, use water on a dried bean or pea as it will swell and may block the ear canal completely. If the object does not flush out easily, take the person to a health care professional. *Do not attempt to probe into the ear canal with tweezers or forceps.* This may only push the object further into the ear canal, injure the eardrum, or in some way further complicate its removal.

Many adults suffer from an accumulation of ear wax, which may reduce hearing acuity. Although there are a number of commercial, over-the-counter preparations that claim to "soften" wax, they are best left on the shelf. Many of these products may macerate the delicate tissue lining the ear canal and produce an appropriate environment for a bacterial or fungal infection. An appropriate homeopathic treatment is to use **Calendula,** a dilute solution of one teaspoonful to a quarter cup of purified or distilled water. Warm the diluted Calendula solution to body temperature, or just above (*not hot*), and instill this solution into the ear by syringe. The warm Calendula solution will soften the wax and allow its easy and safe removal. Unlike harsh chemicals, Calendula will not injure the specialized epithelial tissues lining the ear canal and will create a bacateriostatic environment that will inhibit the growth of harmful bacteria.

Another note of caution: although cotton-tipped swabs are advertised as a safe way to clean the ear, they should never be used in the ear canal! Read the small print on the box. Attempting to remove excess wax with a cotton swab may only impact it further into the canal, fracturing one or more of the three delicate bones, and result in hearing loss or infection. Cotton swabs are safe to use to clean the external *pinna* only.

Injuries and Inflammations of the Eye

"BLACK EYE"

The so-called black eye results when the small vessels in the delicate tissues surrounding the eye, or the lid itself, are ruptured. This usually results from a blow, as from a thrown ball or a fist, impacting the area. A black eye is nothing more than a bruise. Of course, should the eye itself be injured, the victim should be examined by a health care professional.

HOMEOPATHIC TREATMENT
Arnica Montana
Ledum Palustre (Ledum Pal.)

Ledum palustre, the homeopathic remedy made from the plant marsh tea, is almost specific to any bruising injury where there is a discoloration. ***Arnica*** relieves pain, repairs damaged vessels, and cures a bruised feeling. Ledum pal. attends to the discoloration itself. In Arnica pain is *worse* from damp cold; in Ledum pal. it is *better.* Remember Arnica in pain relief and the repair of damaged tissues and Ledum pal. to assist in the resorption of the blood and the return of the discolored portion to normal in a relatively short time.

   Potency and Dosage: 6x–30x every 2 to 4 hours, the 30x potency for a maximum of nine doses.

EYE STRAIN

Although optometrists and ophthalmologists may not agree, the overuse of the eyes from reading, studying, or performing close work for a long time, or working in dim light, often produces "eye strain." The eyes ache, may feel hot, and may be bloodshot. There may be a feeling of pressure in the eyeballs or around the eye, often accompanied by headache.

HOMEOPATHIC TREATMENT
Arnica Montana
Ruta Graveolens

Arnica deals effectively with the bruised, sore feeling in the eyes following close work and the tired, weary feeling from sightseeing or viewing slides or films. If these are the symptoms experienced, a few doses of Arnica will greatly relieve the problem.

   Another fine remedy for eye strain is ***Ruta graveolens*** triturated from the common garden rue. Ruta's symptoms are somewhat similar to those of Arnica, and Ruta is most often thought of first in eye strain.

   The Keynote symptoms of Ruta are: eye strain followed by headache; eyes red, hot, and painful from sewing or reading; disturbances in visual accommodation—eyes fail to focus well, vision is blurred; pressure deep in the eyeball(s) or over the eyebrow.

A bruised feeling in the eye would tend to indicate Arnica as the most appropriate remedy, whereas blurred vision and redness would best indicate Ruta.

Potency and Dosage: 6x–30x every 2 to 4 hours, as required.

SUBCONJUNCTIVAL HEMORRHAGE

Briefly presented in the Introduction together with a case history, a subconjunctival hemorrhage is a leakage of blood from the small vessels in the "white" (sclera) of the eye. Occasionally occurring spontaneously without cause, most frequently the hemorrhage occurs following a hard cough or sneeze. Although the sclera will appear greatly inflamed and almost completely red, the condition is self-limiting, usually lasting from 5 to 14 days. A rebleed is not uncommon on the fifth day. The condition is not dangerous because the hemorrhage occurs beneath the conjunctiva and *not* in the eye itself.

HOMEOPATHIC TREATMENT
Arnica Montana
Hamamelis
Ledum Palustre (Ledum Pal.)

Arnica is often thought of as the first remedy in subconjunctival hemorrhage. The eye appears bloody and greatly inflamed. The Keynote symptom for Arnica in this condition is great bloody redness with a bruised soreness in the eyeball. A few doses of the remedy in the 30x potency, or in the lower 6x, will frequently bring about a reabsorption of the blood and alleviate any pain.

Hamamelis, made from the herb witch hazel, is often the most immediate remedy in this condition. Hamamelis works to rapidly and safely reabsorb the effused blood. It has nearly identical eye symptoms to Arnica and follows favorably if Arnica is given first but fails to work, or to hold.

The third remedy to be considered is *Ledum palustre.* There is an extravasion of blood beneath the conjunctiva, sometimes accompanied by an aching sensation.

Potency and Dosage: For first aid, the preferred potency for each of these remedies is 30x, but 6x will work effectively although it may require more frequent repetition.[57]

STYE

A stye is an acute, local, pus-forming infection of the gland(s) of the margin of the eye lid. Sometimes a stye occurs beneath the lid itself. Thus, there are both external and internal sties. Usually the result of staphylococcal bacteria, the stye normally develops with localized pain and tenderness of the lid margin and later forms a small round pustule. In essence, a stye is a small boil.

A number of homeopathic remedies can be considered, with value, in the treatment of this annoying condition, but three are often found most useful.

HOMEOPATHIC TREATMENT
Sulphuris Calcareum (Hepar Sulph.)
Pulsatilla
Sulfur

Sulphuris calcareum (Hepar sulph.) a mineral remedy (calcium sulfide), is especially useful in treating pus-forming papules that tend toward suppuration. In Hepar sulph. there will be redness and inflammation of the lid(s) with considerable sensitivity to touch and even to cool air and drafts.

Pulsatilla, made from the wind flower, is generally considered the most valuable remedy in sties. W.A. Dewey, M.D., considers Pulsatilla "a remedy for styes [without] equal . . . caus[ing] them to abort before pus has formed."[58]

Sulfur is yet another useful remedy in persons whose constitutions tend toward recurring sties. Sulfur is of great value in conditions that relapse as sties often do, especially where there is localized heat and burning with itching, made worse from heat. In Sulfur, burning is a Keynote symptom to the remedy.

CONJUNCTIVITIS

This greatly annoying eye condition is most often caused by either bacteria or virus and sometimes by allergy. The causal agent is relatively easy to determine, although in homeopathy the totality of guiding symptoms is of more importance than the causative factor. Bacterial conjunctivitis produces a purulent discharge from the eye, often accompanied by a moderate swelling of the lid. The eye does not itch. Viral conjunctivitis produces a clear discharge accompanied by minimal lid swelling and no itching. Allergic conjunctivitis may produce a clear, mucoid, or stringy discharge. Lid swelling may be moderate to severe and accompanied by intense itching. Aside from these causes, conjunctival irritation may follow exposure to polluted air, wind, dust particles, bright light, and reflected light.

HOMEOPATHIC TREATMENT
Aconite
Arnica Montana
Arsenicum Album (Arsenicum Alb.)
Belladonna
Euphrasia
Pulsatilla
Sulfur

Each of the listed remedies is specific to acute conjunctivitis regardless of the cause, but the selection of the appropriate remedy must be made on its specific Keynote symptoms.

The Keynote symptoms of *Aconite* are: eyes are red and inflamed; eyes feel dry, hot, and gritty, as if sand were trapped under the eyelids; lids are swollen, hard, and red; there is a great aversion to light of all kinds, and to glare and reflection; profuse watering occurs after exposure to cold, dry wind.

Arnica is especially useful in eye irritations of a mechanical cause where there is inflammation (redness, heat, and swelling) accompanied by a bruised, sore feeling.

The Keynote symptoms of *Arsenicum album* are: burning in eyes with acid-like tearing or watering; lids are red, granulated, or ulcerated, scabby, and scaly; lids are swollen—especially there is puffiness around the eyes; watering is *burning and hot;* external inflammation is extremely painful; intense aversion to light of all sources.

Belladonna is a preeminent eye remedy, recognized by the intensity and violence of its Keynote symptoms: eyes feel swollen as if they were bulging outward; conjunctiva is red, dry, and burning; eyelids are swollen; there are shooting or throbbing pain(s) in the eye(s); patient has an aversion to light.

Euphrasia is triturated from the herb appropriately named eyebright and is considered one of the preeminent eye remedies. It shows special value in eye irritations of an allergic origin. Euphrasia may be well employed in its triturated form or used locally as an eyebath. To use Euphrasia locally, dilute

2 drops of the tincture in an eye cup of sterile, purified, or distilled water and flush the eye(s) with it several times a day. This latter treatment is especially useful in seasonal hayfever allergy with itching, watering, and burning of the eyes.

The Keynote symptoms of *Euphrasia* are: acrid, thick discharge from the eyes; acid tearing or watering; eyelids burn and swell; frequent inclination to blink; eyes water constantly; intense aversion to light, especially artificial indoor lighting; small, clear blisters on the cornea.

The Keynote symptoms of *Pulsatilla* are: thick, profuse, yellow, nonacrid discharge; eyes itch and burn; profuse tearing or watering; general condition of the eye(s) is *worse* from warmth; lid(s) are inflamed; eyes matted shut by sticky mucus.

Sulfur is an especially valuable remedy in any chronic inflammation of the eye lids when there is *burning* or ulceration, or both, of the margins. It follows Arnica or Aconite in acute eye disorders, especially if soreness continues. In chronic eye inflammations, Sulfur follows Arsenicum alb. well when irritation continues but no acute inflammatory condition is present. The Keynote symptoms of Sulfur are: *burning* or ulceration, or both, of the eyelid margins; sensation of heat and *burning* in the eye(s); eyes burn and itch constantly.

Potency and Dosage for All Remedies Above: 6x–30x, 3 to 5 tablets every 3 to 4 hours, as required.

FOREIGN OBJECTS IN THE EYE

Often dust, dirt, or sand particles will enter the eye, or sometimes small insects. This irritation sets up an itching, burning sensation accompanied by intense watering as the eye attempts to flush the irritating object free.

If an object enters the eye, flush the eye with cool water to attempt to rinse it out. If this fails and the object is trapped underneath the lid, roll the lid back against the support of a cotton-tipped applicator or swab and use a *damp—never dry*—swab to remove the object. After the object is removed, if irritation continues, the homeopathic first-aider may flush the eye in an eye bath containing 2 drops of *Calendula succus* or *tincture,* or *Hypericum tincture,* or *Euphrasia tincture. The first-aider must never attempt to remove an object that has become embedded in the surface of the eye.* If an object, such as a piece of glass, gravel, or other object, becomes embedded, the eye should be covered with something that will not exert pressure against the object and cause further injury. As odd as it may sound, the best procedure is to place a paper cup over the eye and bandage the cup in place. Aconite is the remedy *par excellence* for the pain of eye injuries and also acts as a sedative if the victim shows extreme fear or anxiety. Two doses of the 30x, or one of the 200x potency, should be given. *Ignatia* (200x) substitutes well in place of Aconite and will alleviate the emotional upset, which is often out of proportion to the seriousness of the injury. It will not relieve pain, however. The first-aider, of course, should never forget Arnica (200x) or Aconite (200x) if signs of shock appear and as a preventive against shock in any injury of this nature. Arnica is a great pain-reliever in mechanical injuries, Hypericum in crushing injuries and when there is pain where nerves are obviously involved.

ACUTE INFLAMMATION OF THE EYELID

The final inflammatory condition to be presented in this section deals with a condition termed *blepharitis,* which simply refers to an acute inflammation of the margin of the eyelid. There is redness and thickening of the margin, frequently accompanied by the formation of scales or crusts along the margins and sometimes shallow ulcerations. The condition may be caused by a bacterial infection or by allergy.

Blepharitis is often an indolent disorder that does not yield well to traditional allopathic treatment. Homeopathy, on the other hand, often effects a rapid and pleasant healing of this condition.

HOMEOPATHIC TREATMENT
Graphites
Mercurius
Pulsatilla

Graphites is the homeopathic name of the element carbon, also called black lead. The Keynote symptoms of Graphites in acute marginal inflammations include: eyelids *red and swollen; dryness of the lids;* eczema (scales and crusts) along the lid margins.

Potency and Dosage: 3x, 3 to 5 tablets every 3 to 4 hours, as required.

Mercurius is triturated from the element mercury and exhibits great power over eye inflammations of this type. Its Keynote symptoms include:

red, thick, and swollen lids; profuse, acrid, and burning discharge from the eye.

Pulsatilla, the wind flower, shows a special affinity to the eyes. It exhibits the Keynote symptoms of: itching, inflammation, and burning; margins of the lids are red and mattered; thick, profuse, yellow and *nonacrid* discharge.

Pulsatilla is especially suited to anyone whose disposition is ever-changing, at one moment gentle and mild-tempered, the next instant sad and weepy. The Pulsatilla patient is changeable and contradictory, always better from cold and open air, worse from heat and indoor atmospheres. These symptoms are called *homeopathic modalities;* they are important considerations in prescribing Pulsatilla and should be considered together with acute symptoms. Such symptoms mean nothing to the traditional allopath but everything to the trained homeopath.

CONCURRENT REMEDIES IN EYE INFLAMMATIONS

A remedy that should not be forgotten at the very beginning of any acute inflammatory condition is the tissue salt *Ferrum phosphoricum (Ferr. phos.).* Although too frequently overlooked in favor of other remedies, Ferr. phos. (iron phosphate) is especially valuable in conditions accompanied by burning, redness, and general inflammation. In Ferr. phos. there is no purulent secretion. Best administered in the lower 3x or 6x potencies, Ferr. phos. has continually proved its value as an adjunct or concurrent remedy in nearly every inflammatory condition of the eye.

The instances in which the author has been called upon to treat blepharitis have yielded easily to the appropriate homeopathic treatment. Most frequently the remedy has proved to be Graphites, in the lower 3x to 6x potency. Ferr. phos. is also given concurrently, and the two remedies together have worked effectively.

Once such case involved a university professor in his early thirties who complained of itching, red eyes. The margins were red and slightly swollen, with a dry crust along the border. He had seen a physician's assistant, who diagnosed acute marginal blepharitis and prescribed an antibiotic ophthalmic ointment (bacitracin). Apparently this worked well in the acute stage, but the problem became chronic and continued to recur. Based on the Keynote symptoms, Graphites (3x) proved the remedy of choice and eliminated the condition in 3 days with no recurrence. A.B. Norton, M.D., appears to be correct when he states that "[Graphites] comes nearer being a specific in blepharitis than any other [remedy]."[59]

WOUNDS OF THE EYE

A "wounded eye" in this section refers only to a cut or laceration of the eyelid, not of the eyeball itself. Any injury to the eyeball requires medical attention. If the eyelid has been cut and is bleeding, the most appropriate homeopathic remedy is to compress the closed lid with a 50/50 solution of *Calendula,* succus or tincture, and water. Calendula is hemostatic; it slows down, diminishes, or stops bleeding, and its "antiseptic" (actually bacteriostatic) properties work to prevent infection. Use cold water, as cold also works to constrict blood vessels. If there is pain, give *Arnica* in 6x, 30x, or 200x potency, but *never* apply Arnica tincture to an open wound, as it will cause a severe skin irritation.

Insect Bites and Stings

The homeopathic treatment of bee and hornet stings has already been presented, the remedies of choice being *Ledum pal.* tincture applied undiluted directly to the sting and *Apis mel.* in potency administered internally. However, there are other types of biting and stinging insects, and homeopathy is armed to deal effectively with these.

MOSQUITO BITES

Most frequently, a mosquito bite does nothing more than raise a small welt, which itches for a short while, then disappears. The itching is produced by the insect's injecting an anticoagulant into the skin prior to removing blood. Male mosquitoes are harmless; only the female insects bite. Sometimes, however, in persons especially sensitive to mosquitoes, the bite can become quite large and appear very much like a hive, red at the center and raised on a hard, white weal. These inflamed areas can be as large as a quarter. Small children appear to be most greatly affected, although a good number of adults also suffer considerable distress from these bites.

HOMEOPATHIC TREATMENT
Ledum Palustre Tincture (Ledum Pal.)
Staphysagria

The homeopathic remedy of choice is *Ledum palustre tincture,* which is nearly a specific antidote for the bites and stings of most insects. A drop or two painted on with a cotton swab, using the undiluted tincture, very frequently relieves the itch in seconds and tends to greatly reduce the swelling. Ledum pal. may also be given internally in potency from the 3x to the 200x, adjusting the repetition of the dose accordingly. The modalities of *Ledum pal.* are *better from cold, worse from heat.*

Although I have never had occasion to use it, **Staphysagria** has developed a considerable reputation in persons hypersensitive to mosquito bites. Staphysagria comes from the delphinium or stavesacre plant. It has as well the reputation of *preventing* mosquitoes from biting.[60]

Those individuals who have shown special sensitivity may wish to attempt desensitization by using a combination remedy. Hri-Dolisos HRI-20 Insect Allergy Drops may afford considerable relief if taken prior to the summer months and in maintenance doses throughout the insect season. HRI-20 contains six insect poisons in the 6x trituration (*Formica rufa* [ant], *Vespa crabo* [wasp], *Apis mellifica* [bee], *Pulex irritans* [flea], *Aranea diadema* [Papal-cross spider], and *Blatta americana* [American cockroach]).

Naturopathic Preventive Measures
Obviously if a person reacts unfavorably to mosquito bites, an "ounce of prevention is worth a pound of cure." Repellant products are now available that contain D.E.E.T., a highly effective chemical repellant, which lasts for hours. For those preferring an absolutely natural approach, *oil of citronella* is also effective, and many experienced outdoorsmen swear by *thiamine hydrochloride* (Vitamin B_1). A water-soluble member of the Vitamin B Complex group, Thiamine is perfectly safe to take. What the body does not need is passed off harmlessly in the urine. Thiamine appears to produce an odor to the skin which is offensive to mosquitoes but unnoticeable to humans, or gnats. The normal dose is 100 mg/day.

CHIGGER BITES

Chiggers are minute parasitic insects that burrow beneath the skin and lay their eggs in the host body. They are so small as to be nearly impossible to see with the naked eye. For something so small, they produce an incredible itch. The homeopathic remedy that has proved to be most effective against chiggers is Ledum pal. Paint the undiluted tincture onto the skin and be amazed at how rapidly the irritation vanishes. One patient who first used Ledum pal. several years ago was so impressed by it that neither he nor his family will leave home without it.

GNAT BITES

Gnats, small flying insects, rarely produce more than a minor localized irritation. However, in some hypersensitive individuals, a gnat bite can produce a greatly inflamed local swelling. The eyelids seem most frequently affected. *Cantharis* at 200x (Spanish beetle) taken internally produces rapid remission of symptoms.

A woman acquaintance had been highly susceptible to gnat bites for years. The bites produced a severe burning, stinging irritation. The skin was hot and greatly swollen. She enjoyed camping during the summer along the Missouri River except for the constant gnat bites she suffered. Traditional medical treatment had proved effective but slow. She was advised that, the next time she was bitten, she take Cantharis (200x), repeating the dose once in 15 minutes, if necessary. Cantharis brought about a remarkable remission of symptoms, usually within 2 to 4 hours.

It is useful here to reproduce a case history experienced by M.L. Tyler, M.D., on the remarkable effectiveness of Cantharis:

Last Tuesday, 10 P.M., a fine sharp stab just above right wrist, and a flimsy little demon flew gaily off. Almost immediately thereafter a hard wheal appeared, pricking and extending. At night, awakened by a stab in finger of left hand, and then a second finger wounded. All Wednesday—*those bites!* By Thursday, absolutely obsessed, to the exclusion of thought or interest in anything else, by the incessant urgent necessity of handling and nursing the torment, and struggling against the impulse to scratch and tear. Wrist; round wrist; up arm; farther and farther round wrist; high and higher up arm; round fingers; over back of hand: everywhere, burning, itching, swelling; spreading more and more widely. On Thursday afternoon, things were at their worst, when, . . . a friend-in-need produced a few globules medicated with *Canth*[*aris*] 30[c], which were obediently sucked; and a second dose, to be taken later on, was provided. The rapidity of the relief was unbelievable: the suffering was soon negligible, then forgotten. Able to concentrate again!—able to experience the thrill of the Wembley Tattoo. And on this [Friday] morning, arm and fingers are again normal—except for a few scratch-marks. But why record all this? Because such airy demons are not the last of their kind, and because someone else, some day, may be glad to prove the merits of *Cantharis*, in potency, for *gnat bites*.[61]

FIRE ANT BITES

In recent years the south and southwestern portions of the United States have experienced an invasion of an especially venomous insect from South and Central America—the fire ant. Building large mounds in pastures, fields, and meadows, these ants attack livestock and humans, producing localized redness, and intense itching, stinging, and burning.

HOMEOPATHIC TREATMENT
Formica Rufa (*Myrmexine*)
Ledum Palustre Tincture (*Ledum Pal.*)
Urtica Urens Tincture
Xerophyllum

If you live in localities where fire ants are present, **Formica rufa,** in potency, taken over a period of time may assist in establishing desensitization. **Ledum palustre** is a near-specific remedy in most stings of insects, both locally and in potency internally. **Urtica urens,** made from the stinging nettle, produces on the skin itching blotches and red rash accompanied by burning heat, formication, and violent itching. **Xerophyllum,** the Tamalpais lily, also called basket grass flower, produces (and therefore in its homeopathic potency, relieves) intense itching, stinging, and burning pains of the skin and red rash with the formation of small blisters. The modalities of Xerophyllum are *worse from cold water* and *better from hot water applications.*

Poisonous Plants

POISON IVY, POISON OAK, POISON SUMAC

Among the most troublesome complaints experienced during the summer months, especially in the temperate climates, are the skin irritations caused by poison ivy (*Rhus toxicodendron*), poison oak (*Rhus diversoloba*), and poison sumac (*Rhus venenata*). The Rhus family of plants contain an oily resin called *urushiol* and, on contact with the skin, often cause an allergic contact dermatitis. In her book, *Homeopathic Drug Pictures,* the British homeopathic physician M.L. Tyler, M.D., vividly describes the effects of

Rhus poisoning on a homeopathic "prover" (a healthy person who volunteers to test effects of homeopathic remedies):

[Eruption] with numerous vesicles that burst, and secreted for eight days a slimy liquid. After 24 hours itching and burning commenced, lasting from half-an-hour to two hours. After 36 hours, swelling of the parts, with violent itching and burning, increased on touching or moving; the parts affected as if pierced by hot needles. White transparent vesicles appeared on the highly red and inflamed skin. Covered from head to foot with a fine red vesicular rash, itching and burning terribly, especially in the joints; worse at night causing constant scratching, with little or no relief, and which felt very hard when pressed with the finger: skin burning hot. The face became red, enormously swollen and oedematous, then also the hands and the skin of the whole body became covered with a scarlet-like exanthema, with intolerable itching; . . . on the fourth day, the back of the hands and legs became covered with blisters which burst and slowly desquamated. Violent vesicular [rash] on the face and hands, attended with a high state of fever.[62]

Although a case of Rhus poisoning such as Dr. Tyler describes would occur perhaps only in the most hypersensitive of people, it has been estimated that nearly 70% of the population, or 177 million persons, in the United States are sensitive to urushiol, the active ingredient in these plants.

NATURAL IMMUNITY

Persons sometimes claim to be immune from the effects of poison ivy. One man bragged that he had fallen in it, even rolled in patches of the plant, all without any reaction whatsoever. That same man, a year later, merely strolled past a large crop of poison ivy along a wilderness trail. He did not even come into direct contact with the plants, yet within a few hours was covered with an intensely itching, bumpy red rash. A person can go for months, or even years, without being affected by Rhus poisoning, only to later develop a galloping case of it.

Case after case of supposed immunity to these plants could be cited, which in the long run proved foolhardy and invalid. Natural immunity to urushiol is rare, and no one should take needless chances as exposure. One

15-year-old boy, so convinced of his "immunity," actually rubbed his face and hands with poison ivy. A short time later, his face had swelled into a nearly shapeless mass and his eyes had puffed nearly completely shut.

All persons venturing outdoors should be able to recognize the poisonous plants—ivy, oak, and sumac—that grow natively in their particular geographic area. Of these three plants, poison ivy is the most widespread. Native only to North America, poison ivy grows wild in all areas of the United States except the southwest. It is easily recognized by its shape: the plant always has three shiny leaves growing from a single stem. The stem may be a light red or pinkish color. In the late fall, during seed time, poison ivy develops crops of white berries and the leaves often become bumpy and oily. No other plant has the same configuration of three leaves growing from a single stem. An old folk rhyme goes: "Leaves of three, let them be," and that seems sound advice.

Poison ivy may appear as a small plant growing low to the ground, or as a vine creeping up a tree trunk or entwining around a fence post, or as a bush. All portions of the plant contain the oily resin which causes the intense, red, blotchy, itching rash. Tests have shown that the urushiol clings to clothing and, despite months of disuse and numerous washings in strong detergents, the resin remains embedded in the cloth, still sufficiently concentrated to produce a local dermatitis.

HOMEOPATHIC DESENSITIZATION

Emphasis must be made that, to date, no method of desensitization to poison ivy, poison oak, or poison sumac is 100% effective—either homeopathic or allopathic. Traditional (allopathic) medicine has recently made available "poison ivy shots," in which minute amounts of the causative irritant are injected over a period of weeks or months. These desensitization injections appear to work fairly effectively in those persons especially sensitive to poison ivy.

Homeopathy goes one important step farther in assisting those especially sensitive persons. Homeopathy offers remedies *given by mouth*—not hypodermic injection—which have proved nearly 90% effective in clinical use. The most common desensitizing remedy is ***Rhus toxicodendron (Rhus tox.)***. In either the 30x or the higher 200x potency, given orally once or twice a week 4 to 6 weeks prior to exposure, Rhus tox. has proved highly effective in either preventing or greatly lessening the allergic reaction to all three of the Rhus family plants.

Rhus tox. frequently demonstrates a peculiar pattern in the remission of a Rhus poisoning rash. Desensitivity is often shown in the first year, but the patient will develop a minor rash on a certain body part. The following year desensitivity is still in effect, but a rash, smaller than that of the year before, appears in exactly the same location. In following years, frequently no rash will appear at all.

A case history demonstrates the effectiveness and this odd feature of Rhus tox. in establishing immunity to poison ivy and the other members of the Rhus family.

One man, a middle-aged farmer, loved the outdoors but was unable to enjoy camping, hiking, or even his normal farming activities during the summer months. Every summer he developed a serious case of poison ivy. He broke out in an intensely itching, knobby, red rash that spread rapidly over his body. Once his reaction was so severe he sought treatment from his family physician. He was given oral cortisone, a powerful steroid, highly effective in the management of poison ivy-caused dermatitis. His hypersensitive reaction to the drug sent him to the Intensive Care Unit of the hospital for three days. When he was later told about oral homeopathic immunization, he was quite willing to try anything, especially when he learned that homeopathic treatment could not produce any life-threatening side effects. He was given Rhus tox. (200x potency), which he took 6 weeks before exposure. That summer he did develop a poison ivy rash, but its severity was nowhere near what he would normally have expected. Only a small patch of red rash appeared on his forearms. It did not spread, nor was it at all debilitating. The patient mentioned he still had poison ivy, but he was told about the peculiar rash pattern that sometimes accompanies Rhus tox., especially in highly sensitive persons. He was told to take the remedy again the following season. Again he developed a rash, much smaller this time, and in exactly the same location. But other than that small patch, he remained free of poison ivy. The third year he developed no rash whatsoever and, in five years, has had no recurrence of poison ivy rash.

Rhus tox. is not the only desensitizing remedy for Rhus poisoning in the homeopathic *Materia Medica*. In fact, Boericke's *Materia Medica* lists 28 separate remedies. "Homeopathy has never recognized the 'one cause, one cure' approach. Even where the cause is irrefutable (you walk into a patch of poison oak, you break out), homeopathy offers a number of remedies to help relieve the misery for different individuals."[63] Homeopathy is the only major system of medicine to recognize the intense individuality of people. We are not clones of one another. Because each of us *is* special, separate, and highly individual, a remedy that may serve one person (your next-door neighbor, for example) may not serve you as well. Complete desensitization to Rhus poisoning, as far as it is possible, may be from **Croton tiglium** (croton-seed oil) in one person, **Anacardium** (marking nut) in another, and **Xerophyllum** (Tamalpais lily) in yet another. The well-trained homeopathic physician will be able to determine the constitutional type of the individual patient and, using modalities peculiar to that patient, determine which of a number of remedies is most effective. This process is too complex for the nonphysician. Therefore, for the first-aider and medical self-helper, a number of homeopathic pharmaceutical companies have developed specialty, compound remedies containing two, three, or more combinations of the most generally effective remedies. Standard Homeopathic Company in Los Angeles manufactures *Hyland's Poison Oak Tablets* containing a combination of Rhus toxicodendron, Croton tiglium, and Xerophyllum. HRI-Dolisos, a French-based firm now manufacturing in Las Vegas, produces **HRI-11** *Poison Ivy Drops,* a combination of Rhus toxicodendron, Croton tiglium, Allium cepa, and Myosotis pulv. which has also proved of high clinical effectiveness. These combination remedies are not only preventive (immunological) in their nature, but can as well be used curatively if acute Rhus poisoning develops.

If you are sensitive to poison ivy, poison oak, or poison sumac, it is, of course, best to consult a homeopathic physician and seek his or her recommendation. However, if there is no homeopath near you, you may try Rhus tox. in the 200x potency as directed here, or use any of the proprietary "house" combination products available from homeopathic pharmacies. The chances are excellent that one will work well for you.

Internal Remedies for Rhus Poisoning
If you are not especially sensitive to Rhus poisoning and have not attempted desensitization but develop the annoying itchy, red rash, there are a number of highly effective remedies available in the homeopathic *Materia Medica.*

HOMEOPATHIC TREATMENT
Rhus Toxicodendron (Rhus Tox.)
Anacardium

Listed here are only two of the 28 possible remedies for poison ivy, poison oak, and poison sumac, because of the 28, these two remedies have proved greatly effective for the majority of sufferers.

The Keynote symptoms for **Rhus tox.** are: skin is red with eruptions of small blisters containing a transparent liquid, and these blisters, which are the size of a pinhead, rest on the base of abnormally reddened skin; intense itching and burning *not relieved by scratching;* the eruption resembles "leopard skin"; In especially severe cases the eyelids and face may be swollen, puffy, and red. The modalities in Rhus tox. are: itching is *relieved by hot applications,* either moist hot cloths or baths, and *made worse by cold*

Anacardium is closely related to Rhus tox. in dermatitis and most closely resembles it in skin irritations. Its Keynote symptoms are: *intense* itching; blister-like eruption on the skin which is reddened at the base of the eruption; in especially severe cases there may be considerable swelling of the eyelids and face. The modalities for Anacardium are: itching is *not relieved by hot applications* and is *greatly aggravated by heat.*

In treating an acute case of dermatitis caused by Rhus poisoning, select the remedy closest to the symptoms, paying special attention to the modalities of the remedies. In Rhus tox., hot water applications relieve the intense itching; cold makes them worse. In Anacardium the itching is greatly increased by heat. Either remedy works effectively in nearly any potency. For normal first aid and self-help applications, the 30x potency is the first to consider, repeated a maximum of nine times, then stopped. Lower potencies (3x and 6x) may require more frequent repetition.

The first-aider should not be alarmed if, on giving either Rhus tox. or Anacardium, the patient experiences a sudden, increased aggravation of the symptoms. This is not uncommon in especially sensitive individuals. This is called a "healing reaction" and lasts but a short time. Healing establishes itself quickly afterwards. In my experience these brief intensifications of symptoms have been uncommon.

External Remedies for Rhus Poisoning
Before beginning this section on effective homeopathic remedies used externally in treating Rhus poisoning, some ineffective, or at least less-than-effective, allopathic ones are discussed.

Zinc oxide, the old family standby for minor skin irritation, is sometimes called upon to treat poison ivy, but it is not very effective. Calamine lotion and similar products under various brand names tend to relieve the itching briefly, but they color the skin pink and very soon crack and peel and flake off. Many products now on the market and available without prescription contain 0.5% hydrocortisone. Cortisone is a powerful steroid. But these ointments, creams, or sprays *have absolutely no effect* on Rhus-caused dermatitis in its acute inflammatory stage. Such products may assist in relieving some of the annoying itch, but they are effective only when the irritation is less acute.

Traditional medicine employs tap-water soaks during the acute inflammatory stages and often oral corticosteroids are employed. Oral cortisone is not recommended, however, in treatment of adolescents as it may interfere with the teenager's normal maturation for as long as a year.

All things being considered, homeopathy offers the safest, most rapid, and most effective treatment for poison ivy, poison oak, and poison sumac.

HOMEOPATHIC TREATMENT
Grindelia Tincture
Plantago Majus Tincture
Erechthites Tincture

Often in the treatment of Rhus-caused dermatitis, the first-aider is well advised to take a "double-barreled" approach, using both internal and external measures. Each of the three tinctures listed has proved to be of considerable value in arresting the intense itching and reducing the overall irritation of Rhus poisoning. Either the undiluted tincture may be used, or a 5:1 solution of water to tincture. Thoroughly wet a cloth or gauze pad and allow this to remain in contact with the affected area. Remoisten when necessary.

Grindelia comes from rosin-wood (Grindelia robusta and Grindelia squarrosa), both varieties being nearly identical in their actions. Grindelia is also one of the 28 remedies listed in Boericke's *Materia Medica* for internal use in its potentized form for Rhus poisoning. *Erechthites,* or fireweed, produces in its raw form, in homeopathic provers, symptoms identical to those of acute Rhus poisoning. Boericke lists no modalities to differentiate the skin symptom pictures of either remedy.

Plantago majus is the botanical name for the common plantain, a so-called "noxious weed" that grows in yards, parks, and many wilderness areas. Some people use the tender young, pale-green leaves of the plantain as a salad vegetable, and American Indians used a poultice of the crushed leaves as an effective treatment for hives (urticaria) and any itching, burning skin irritations. Plantago majus has been used in homeopathy for over 100 years and has developed a strong reputation in earache, toothache, urinary incontinence, and middle ear inflammations. It is sometimes effective as a cure for the tobacco habit, as Plantago tends to cause an aversion to tobacco in some persons.

Used on the red, itching rash of poison ivy, poison oak, or poison sumac, Plantago has been found to be exceedingly effective in quickly stopping itching and reducing the local inflammation. In fact, Plantago is so effective against Rhus poisoning that traditionally trained allopathic physicians are now beginning to advocate its use. In a letter to the prestigious *New England Journal of Medicine,* Serge Duckett, M.D., advises poison ivy sufferers to crush the leaves of plantain and rub them directly against the skin, noting that it puts a prompt end to the itching.[64]

Some Naturopathic Remedies

Two effective nonhomeopathic home remedies that have developed a considerable reputation in treating Rhus dermatitis are *sea salt* and *Aloe vera.* James H. Stephenson, M.D., noted the effectiveness of bathing in ocean salt water on acute poison ivy.[65] Norman Goldstein, M.D., of the University of Hawaii, highly recommends squeezing the juice of the Aloe vera plant onto the rash of poison ivy. It relieves the local irritation almost immediately.[66]

Sea salt may be purchased inexpensively from any health food store. Aloe vera is also readily available relatively cheaply from health food outlets in a gel or spray liquid form. The author has used Aloe vera on any number of skin irritations from insect stings to first-degree and mild second-degree burns.

A case history is illustrative. A 15-year-old boy had an especially severe case of contact dermatitis after having slept overnight on a bed of cedar boughs as part of the requirements for a Boy Scout merit badge. The rash spread rapidly over his entire body, leaving only his face, the palms of his hands, and the soles of his feet clear. It was not unlike poison ivy with its intensely burning, itching, red, blistered rash. The first-aider on duty, an Emergency Medical Technician, had first used zinc oxide, and later Calamine lotion—both to no effect. The boy remained extremely uncomfortable. When the homeopath applied Aloe vera, 99.6% gel, he remarked that almost instantly the burning and itching stopped. Additional Aloe vera was left with the EMT with directions for its use. As the boy had a history of allergies, the EMT and the homeopath both felt he needed more detailed treatment and he was sent to a local clinic. The Aloe vera, however, had made him comfortable for the first time in several hours. Because Aloe vera is hypoallergenic, there is no danger in its use.

ADVISORY WARNING: Some individuals react with special severity to Rhus poisoning. Whenever the face swells and becomes severely contorted, or the eyelids swell shut, or there is any evidence of difficulty in breathing, that person must obviously seek advanced medical treatment. Urushiol may be inhaled if poison ivy, poison oak, or poison sumac is burned. In sensitive individuals, this may cause edema of the esophagus and lungs, constricting the normal flow of air. *This is a medical emergency* and must be handled by qualified medical personnel.

CHAPTER FIVE

HEAT-CAUSED ILLNESSES

Topics Covered

Heat Cramp
Heat Exhaustion
Heatstroke

Heat Cramp

Heat cramp, also variously known as stroker's cramp, fireman's cramp, and miner's cramp, results from the loss of sodium chloride—salt—owing to profuse sweating from heavy work in temperatures exceeding 100 degrees F, especially in persons unaccustomed to working in oppressive heat.

It is better to prevent heat cramp, using sensible precautions, than to treat it after it develops. If you are going to perform heavy muscular work under conditions of high temperatures and humidity, dress accordingly in noninsulating, lightweight clothing, and maintain an adequate intake of fluids, preferably pure water.

There is a good deal of misunderstanding concerning the use of salt as a preventive of heat stress, even among well-trained first-aiders and physicians untrained in sports medicine. Most people do not lose much salt in sweat. Therefore, they *do not require* such strong measures as salt tablets or adding large quantities of salt to their drinks or to food. Recently, a commercial drink product has been marketed under several brand names, which contains the mineral salts (sodium chloride, potassium) and glucose commonly lost during heavy outdoor exertion. It is used by athletes and others who work out-of-doors to maintain the essential electrolyte balance in the body by replacing the mineral salts and glucose lost during heavy exertion. However, many athletic trainers, nutritionists, and sports medicine specialists feel it is too strong, and, if used at all, should be diluted half and half by water. Commercial salt tablets, available in any drugstore, also work to replace lost salt. These, however, are not recommended because they are highly concentrated and few people take them with sufficient fluids. Salt tablets may erode the lining of the stomach. As a result, many persons experience stomach distress from taking salt tablets.[67]

Well over a century ago, British military personnel serving in the warm climates of the world made an important discovery. Many of the British soldiers suffered abdominal distress and cramping after drinking ice-cold fluids on hot days. They found that drinking warm liquids on hot days ended the problem. Many people suffer undue distress during hot weather from drinking iced tea or cold soda pop too quickly. Usually these products contain large amounts of sugar, which increases thirst. In spite of the fact that they are cold, they do not replace the electrolytes lost in hot weather.

The Keynote symptoms of heat cramp are: the onset of the cramp is sudden; the victim may lie flat with the legs flexed (owing to abdominal cramping) or roll about crying out from extreme pain of muscular spasms; most commonly the arms and legs are affected, but the abdomen and muscles are also affected with knots and spasms; body temperature is normal (98.6 degrees F), but the skin is pale and damp.

Heat cramps may last for hours if left untreated and are extremely debilitating. Standard first-aid measures should be followed, including removing the victim to a cool place. Lay the victim down and give a half-glass of water in which a half-teaspoonful of salt has been dissolved. Give this salt and water solution every 15 minutes for up to 1 hour. The muscle spasms and knots may be relieved by exerting firm pressure and muscle massage.

Magnesium Phosphorica (Mag. Phos.)

Perhaps one of the most useful and powerful homeopathic antispasmodics is the trituration of the mineral magnesium phosphate. ***Magnesium phosphorica*** in the 6x potency will frequently relieve muscle spasms and cramps in a few minutes. It is unusual in that it works best dissolved in *hot water,* 15 to 20 tablets, and given in half-glass doses, combined with ordinary table salt, every 15 minutes.

The author has used Mag. phos. frequently with rapid and highly satisfying results. Mag. phos. works in muscle cramps affecting any part of the body.

Heat Exhaustion

Heat exhaustion results when the body, in an attempt to lose excess heat, pools the blood in the capillaries of the skin. This excessive blood pooling deprives the vital organs—the lungs, heart, and brain—of oxygen. The smaller veins constrict as the body attempts to compensate for the reduced blood supply. The symptoms of heat exhaustion are: the victim's skin is cool and moist (clammy), pale or white; the body temperature is normal or only slightly elevated; the victim may faint, but normally recovers consciousness rapidly when the feet are elevated higher than the head; the victim may complain of nausea, dizziness, bodily weakness, or cramps.

Veratrum Album (Veratrum Alb.)

As an adjunct to standard first-aid treatment (given later) for heat exhaustion, the victim can be greatly benefited by giving ***Veratrum album*** in homeopathic potency. Veratrum alb. corresponds to the classic symptoms of heat exhaustion: the skin is cool, pale or bluish, clammy, and there may be vomiting accompanied by cramping in the extremities. In acute cases give one dose every 15 minutes.

STANDARD FIRST AID FOR HEAT EXHAUSTION

Standard first-aid measures call for removing the victim to a cool, shaded place. Loosen all tight or restrictive clothing, which will assist the body in regulating its temperature. Raise the victim's feet higher than the head and give cool (*not cold*) water to which one-half teaspoon of ordinary table salt has been added. Give this salt water mixture in sips as the victim may vomit from ingesting fluids too rapidly. Cool the body by applying cold cloths or by fanning to stimulate air circulation. *In acute cases, the victim may require advanced medical assistance.*

Heatstroke

Heatstroke is *a life-threatening emergency.*

In heatstroke, the body's temperature-regulating mechanism becomes severely disabled and the body is unable to maintain a normal temperature (98.6 degrees F). The victim's temperature may soar to 106 degrees F or higher. At temperatures this high the major organs begin to suffer severe, often irreversible damage. Kidney failure and heart failure are not uncommon. Temperatures of 108 degrees F and higher will result in irreversible brain damage. In cases of severe heatstroke, deep, profound shock and circulatory collapse may result.

Symptoms of heatstroke are: onset may be sudden and acute, or occur gradually, preceded by bodily weakness, headache, dizziness, and nausea; prior to the full manifestation, the victim may experience diminished perspiration, or perspiration may stop altogether—this is an important symptom; the skin is red, hot, and dry (the opposite of heat exhaustion); the pulse is bounding, 160 beats per minute (bpm) or higher, and the victim may experience increased, rapid respiration of 20 to 30 inhalations per minute; the victim may be listless, anxious, or *unconscious;* the pupils of the eyes may at first be contracted (smaller), but later dilate (become wider).

EMERGENCY FIRST-AID TREATMENT

1. Strip the victim naked. In this extreme medical emergency, modesty is superseded by *the need to save a life.*
2. Sponge the body with cool water or apply cold packs, and, if possible, place the victim in a bathtub of cold water, but *do not add ice.*
3. *Never give alcohol or any kind of stimulant.*
4. *Call for advanced medical assistance as soon as possible.*

The victim's temperature may be monitored, best done through the rectum. The body temperature must not be allowed to drop below 101 degrees

F. Vigorous muscle massage is indicated to help stimulate circulation and assist the body in regulating the elevated temperature. *Hypothermia* (greatly lowered body temperature) is a possible later result. If the temperature drops below 101 degrees F, the victim may need to be covered to maintain body heat.

ADVISORY WARNING: Heatstroke is a serious, life-threatening, medical emergency. Call for advanced medical support at the earliest opportunity!

HOMEOPATHIC TREATMENT
Belladonna
Glonoine
Aconite
Gelsemium

Homeopathy provides several extremely useful remedies that assist in combating the symptoms of heatstroke. The two remedies most frequently called for are **Belladonna** and **Glonoine.**

Belladonna has the following Keynote symptoms: victim's face is flushed bright-red or bluish-red, skin is hot and shining; the victim is conscious, experiencing great dizziness, extreme throbbing in the head, and pain, especially in the forehead; the victim exhibits heavy, labored breathing.

Belladonna, if symptoms agree, may be given immediately, 5 tablets or pellets in the 200x or 30x potencies, repeated every 15 minutes until symptoms begin to subside.

Glonoine is a homeopathic preparation of nitroglycerine. Its Keynote symptoms include: mental confusion with dizziness; the victim's head is heavy with violent throbbing and bursting pains.

Glonoine is best given, if symptoms agree, in the same dosage and potency as Belladonna, and repeated every 15 minutes until symptoms subside.

Aconite corresponds to the following Keynote symptoms: victim experiences a full feeling in the head; skin is hot and the victim complains of bursting head pains with *outward pressure,* made *worse* from sitting upright; there is great anxiety and fear of death.

Gelsemium, made from the yellow jasmine flower, has the following Keynote symptoms: face is hot and flushed; victim is giddy, as if intoxicated, *on attempting to move;* victim complains of a band-like feeling around the head, with the pain located in the occipital (rear portion) of the head.

Homeopathic remedies, applied according to their Keynote symptoms, as an immediate first-aid measure, together with standard first-aid treatment, will greatly assist the victim of heatstroke toward recovery. The remedies can do no harm and only good.

Homeopathy is especially well suited to dealing with the late, after-effects of heatstroke.

Many persons, having experienced heatstroke, complain of annoying and debilitating symptoms that recur especially in hot weather. Homeopathy can greatly assist these persons to return to a more normal lifestyle during the warm months of the year.

HOMEOPATHIC TREATMENT
Natrum Muriaticum (Nat. Mur.)
Natrum Carbonicum (Nat. Carb.)

Natrum muriaticum is the homeopathic trituration of sodium chloride. Nat. mur. has proved exceedingly effective in dealing with the persistent and chronic after-effects of heatstroke, when the Keynote symptoms agree. The Keynote symptoms for Nat. mur. are: throbbing, blinding headache; "aches as if 1000 hammers were knocking on the brain."

Potency and Dosage: Give 3 doses of Nat. mur. daily in the 6x, 12x, or 30x potency for 2 to 3 days and await results.

Natrum carbonicum is the homeopathic trituration of the mineral sodium carbonate. In the chronic after-effects of heatstroke, Nat. carb. has proved of considerable benefit. The Keynote symptoms for Nat. carb. are: great debility caused by summer heat; head aches *worse* from sun and the return of hot weather.

A case history is illustrative. Several years ago, a young English woman mentioned that her 13-year-old son had suffered a severe sunstroke while on a camping trip near London 2 years before. The boy had been hospitalized, and ever since the illness her son had been nearly a prisoner of the air-conditioned indoors during the summer months. The boy suffered severe headaches every time he spent a few hours in the summer sun. The problem obviously greatly restricted his activities with his friends.

Having come from England, the woman was acquainted with homeopathy, although her physician at home had been an allopath. A simple mineral salt, sodium carbonate, in homeopathic potency, which was totally safe, was suggested to her in the hope that it might help her son eliminate the problem altogether.

The boy did not have the typical Nat. mur. headache (severe throbbing "like 1000 little hammers"), so Nat. mur. would have been an inappropriate remedy. The local health food store carried Nat. carb. as a tissue salt[68] and the mother purchased a bottle in the 6x potency. The results of this homeopathic remedy on her son were immediate. Taking a maintenance dose of 5 tablets each day throughout the summer and whenever the weather turned warm, the boy was able to enjoy the outdoors as a normal adolescent. This woman reports that over the years her son has had no more heat-caused headaches.

THINK PREVENTION OF HEAT-CAUSED ILLNESSES

Common-sense precautions used during hot weather will prevent a great deal of later suffering. If your skin is particularly sensitive, wear a sunscreen before venturing outdoors. Remember that a number of synthetic detergent soaps can photosensitize the skin to the sun's ultraviolet rays, as can certain perfumes and cosmetic products. Wear a loose-fitting head covering when outdoors in the direct sunlight for any period of time, and wear clothing that is most suitable for the weather. Drink fluids (especially water) to maintain normal body fluid levels and maintain adequate sodium intake, especially if you are working for a long period during high heat.

CHAPTER SIX

RESPIRATORY AILMENTS

Topics Covered

Prevention of Flu and Colds
Treatment of Flu and Colds

In the common respiratory diseases caused by viruses, homeopathy has continued to outshine allopathic medicine. In 1918, just at the conclusion of World War I, a great pandemic—an influenza ("flu") epidemic of enormous proportions—swept across war-torn Europe as well as the United States. Thousands of deaths were reported both here and abroad. Traditional medicine of the time found itself faced with disaster and nearly helpless.

In the early part of the 20th century, influenza vaccines did not exist. Nor was there a host of appropriate antibiotics to treat secondary bacterial infections or pneumonia, which often developed in the most serious cases, especially among infants and the elderly. Homeopathy was, however, prepared to treat the disease, just as it had been decades before and in the decades which have followed. Traditional medicine could only palliate, attempt to make the victims more comfortable, and prescribe bed rest and fluids. It was hoped that the victims' own resistance was sufficient to sustain them. Too often it was not.

Exact figures for the mortality rates of victims treated by standard methods versus those treated by homeopathy are not available, but homeopathic physicians of the time, in medical reports closely scrutinized and verified by traditional medical authorities, demonstrated a nearly 100% recovery rate, usually within 48 hours, and without fatal, or even serious, complications.[69]

Why was such astounding success available to homeopathy and not to traditional medicine?

Since shortly after its refinement by Dr. Samuel Hahnemann and those pioneering physicians who followed him, homeopathy has been able to treat the *whole person* based solely upon the unique symptoms she or he shows while in ill health. Homeopathy has never been forced to scramble to find the cause of a disease, fumble for a diagnosis, or "shoot in the dark" searching for a drug or series of drugs that will effectively treat an illness. In the von Economo's influenza epidemic that swept Europe and America in 1918–1920, the peculiar symptom pattern clearly showed **Arsenicum** as the most effective remedy, based upon the totality of the symptom picture victims showed.

Dorothy Shepherd, M.D., a homeopathic physician in London at the time of the great pandemic, personally treated over 150 cases ranging from the mildly to the most seriously ill. "There was not a single death in the whole of this series and no subsequent complications."[70] Homeopathic physicians in Europe and in the United States were united in their treatment of the 1918 "flu"—it was Arsenicum flu. One rarely finds such a totality of agreement for diagnosis, or methods of treatment, even today among the traditional medical community.

Although modern medical research in the coming years will undoubtedly produce many more successful antiviral drugs, it is no secret that traditional medicine can do little to treat viral diseases such as flu. Medicine can only palliate the symptoms by prescribing aspirin and acetaminophen for the aches, pains, and fever, bed rest, and an adequate intake of fluids. It can recommend using a humidifier to reduce congestion and a syrup for the hacking cough, but little else.

Vaccination, although it does not guarantee absolute protection against the flu, has proved to be from 60 to 90 percent effective. However, even the manufacturers and physicians admit that owing to unpredictable mutations of flu-strain viruses from year to year, a vaccine may afford no protection against the newest strains.

According to a Du Pont Pharmaceuticals report, in 1980 in the United States alone, 85 million work days and 61 million school days were lost because of the flu, and between 1968 and 1981, over 200,000 cases of influenza proved fatal![71] Those are not encouraging statistics.

Now let us turn our attention to the homeopathic treatment and *cure* of influenza.

Homeopathic medicine is armed against the flu with remedies that have, through their employment for nearly 200 years, proved of high clinical value.

Prevention of Flu and Colds

Although no method of immunization can be guaranteed to afford complete protection against the flu, either allopathic or homeopathic, homeopathy can go a long way toward achieving considerable protection for every family member. In addition, this protection is achieved through *oral vaccination* and not through the discomfort of hypodermic injections.

HOMEOPATHIC PREVENTIVE TREATMENT
Influenzinum/Bacillinum
Oscillococcinum
HRI-2 Influenza/Cold Drops

I was first introduced to homeopathic immunization against the flu while a teenager touring England in the early 1960s. I had developed a severe cold as I so often did as a youngster and went to a private physician in London for help. I didn't realize then that the man behind the desk was a homeopathic medical doctor, nor would it have made any impression on me if I had. I was unaware at the time that the tiny pellets he prescribed were homeopathic remedies. All I remember is that the following day my most severe symptoms had vanished. However, during our interview the physician asked if I frequently developed colds or caught the flu. Yes I did. Often the colds lingered for a week or more, and my typical winter flu laid me up for many days with fever, muscle and body aches, headaches, and a lingering desire to lie in bed and be left completely alone.

I later learned that the London homeopath's remedy was a combination of **Influenzinum** and **Bacillinum** compounded for him by a local chemist (the English version of a pharmacist, although American pharmacists are seldom called upon these days to compound drugs). Influenzinum is a homeopathic trituration of all the various influenza viruses that have caused flu since the great epidemic of 1918–1920. Bacillinum is a maceration of tuberculous lung and, in its *safe* homeopathic potentized state, affords both preventive and curative power over acute and chronic nontubercular diseases, catarrhal conditions, oppressed breathing due to congestion, suffocating coughs, and other pulmonary conditions.

The doctor advised that I take Influenzinum/Bacillinum (30x) prior to the normal flu season, usually from late fall to the beginning of spring, one dose weekly. I do not recall ever being troubled with the flu since I first began taking this combination remedy in 1964—over 20 years ago. And colds? Although my friends and relatives cough and sneeze and snort and I am constantly exposed to people with the severest cold symptoms, I have not had a cold.

Influenzinum alone, or in combination with Bacillinum, *cannot guarantee absolute immunity from colds or flu.* However, it can afford considerable protection. Bacillinum should never be used in potencies below the 30x and Influenzinum below the 15x.

Another valuable remedy has just come onto the American homeopathic market. *Oscillococcinum* is one of the few patented remedies in the homeopathic *Materia Medica.* First developed in France by Joseph Roy, M.D., Oscillococcinum has proved itself repeatedly as both extremely reliable and effective taken at the very beginning of flu-like symptoms. Manufactured by Laboratoires Boiron of Lyons, France, it is distributed in the United States by Boiron-Borneman of Norwood, Pennsylvania. Oscillococcinum contains a high concentration of RNA and DNA and has been proven to be nearly 95 percent effective in aborting the flu if taken immediately upon the first symptoms.

Another valuable remedy that can be used both preventively and curatively is the compound remedy *HRI-2 Influenza/Cold Drops* recently introduced in America by Health Research Institute-Dolisos, a French and American firm. This compound contains eight homeopathic remedies that have proved exceedingly effective clinically in both viral colds and flu: Influenzinum, Ferr. phos., Aconite, Eucalyptus glob., Byronia alb., Gelsemium, Eupatorium perf., and Arnica montana. Although this combination is truly a "shotgun" approach, which would not be approved by homeopathic purists, there can be no question as to the effectiveness of the remedies it contains.

It is important to forewarn the reader that Influenzinum may produce an "artificial cold" or flu condition in some users. The symptoms are far from severe and may last only a few hours. To the homeopath this condition indicates a "healing reaction," which is actually a sign that the body is throwing off accumulated toxic matter better removed from the body than left in. Under homeopathic treatment, a cold or the flu can certainly be caught, but the symptoms do not last long, they are not nearly as severe, and the convalescence is considerably shortened.

Treatment of Flu and Colds

HOMEOPATHIC TREATMENT
Aconite
Arsenicum Album (Arsenicum Alb.)
Belladonna
Bryonia
Eupatorium Perfoliatum (Eupatorium Perf.)
Gelsemium
Mercurius Solubus (Mercurius Sol.)
Nux Vomica
Pulsatilla
Rhus Toxicodendron (Rhus Tox.)

Aconite has not established a reputation in flu, but it is of considerable value in treating colds *in their earliest stages*. Like the tissue salt Ferr. phos., which it complements, Aconite is one of homeopathy's first remedies in inflammations. Taken at the very first sign of cold symptoms, Aconite may well abort the cold. Any acute, sudden, and violent attack with fever calls for this remedy. The Aconite cold often comes on after exposure to dry, cold weather. There is chilliness followed by fever and nasal congestion. There may be a throbbing frontal headache and sneezing accompanied by a hard, dry cough. The modalities of Aconite are: all symptoms are *better* in the open air.

Arsenicum album is a major flu remedy of considerable value. It corresponds well to the typical gastric flu when the patient *cannot tolerate the sight or smell of food*. Nausea, retching, and vomiting follow eating or drinking. There is an accompanying anxiety in the pit of the stomach—

uneasiness. The patient may experience periodic chills with prostration, weakness, and restlessness. The prominent and unmistakable Keynote symptom of Arsenicum alb. is in the eyes. They water and burn, and the tearing is acid in nature. The lids are red and swollen. The nasal passages are congested, stopped up with a modality of *worse* in open air; *better* indoors. The early stages of an Arsenicum alb. cold or flu may begin in the upper chest, especially with darting pains radiating through the upper right lung. The bronchi feel congested, respiration is wheezing. The modality here is: fear of suffocation from lying down; must sit upright; respiratory symptoms are *worse* lying down. Arsenicum appears to cover more typical influenza symptoms than any other remedy and is the first to consider when symptoms agree.

Belladonna is a major "chill remedy" with its symptoms developing suddenly, often after getting the head wet. Fever will follow with the face and eyes flushed and red. Symptoms of redness and heat predominate in Belladonna, as do the mental symptoms of excitability and restlessness, including during sleep. The head is hot and throbbing with a feeling of fullness especially in the forehead but also at the back of the head and at the temples. The modalities of Belladonna are: *worse* in the afternoon and on lying down; *better* sitting partially upright.

Belladonna alternates well with Aconite, which is complementary in the early stages of illness, brought on by becoming wet or chilled.

Bryonia corresponds especially well in those cases of colds or flu in which there is much aching, as in the muscles, the back, the neck (with painful stiffness), and the extremities. The head shows the Keynote symptoms of a bursting, splitting headache with great outward pressure, often expressed as if a hammer were beating inside. The headache is worse from motion and sitting up. The Bryonia throat feels dry, scraped, and constricted and is often accompanied by a hard, dry, hacking cough. The cough is often so hard as to make the patient believe the chest could explode, and the congestion and constriction of the respiratory passage make the person take long, deep breaths in an effort to fully inflate the lungs. In the Bryonia cold or flu, the symptoms normally begin in the head and then travel down into the chest, producing the typical symptoms of "chest cold." In chest symptoms, the right side is affected most often, and symptoms are often relieved by pressing or lying on the right side.

The modalities of Bryonia are: *worse* from warmth, movement, hot weather, exercise, and touch; patient cannot sit upright and feels sick or faint if he or she does; all symptoms are *better* from cold, rest, and pressure.

Bryonia alternates well with Gelsemium, which is complementary.

Eupatorium perfoliatum, also known as thoroughwort and boneset, is a preeminent remedy in febrile diseases, such as influenza, in which there is great soreness in the muscles and aching throughout the body. Eupatorium perf. acts remarkably and promptly in relieving these Keynote symptoms. The head figures critically in this type of influenza. There is much throbbing pain and pressure across the entire head. Pain is most noticeable along the top and back of the head, often accompanying soreness in the eyeballs. The tongue may have a yellow coating, and the patient is thirsty. A bitter taste lingers in the mouth. In Eupatorium perf. there is vomiting preceded by thirst, and stools are frequent and watery. A major Keynote symptom is great chilling, often in the early morning, *preceded by thirst with great soreness and aching of bones.*

Gelsemium is a truly remarkable remedy and is often used prior to the flu season or immediately after exposure to someone who has the flu as a prophylactic. Many homeopathically oriented lay people take doses of Gelsemium at the first outbreak of flu and report they achieve total protection. Gelsemium is especially useful taken at the very beginning of influenza or severe cold symptoms when the person typically comments, "I think I feel the flu coming on." There is a dullness and heaviness about the body, sometimes with dizziness and drowsiness and general prostration and weakness. The person feels tired and is not mentally alert. The general listlessness prompts him or her to seek quiet and to be left alone. In a full outbreak of flu, the Gelsemium patient will feel chilly, desire to be kept warm, and express a generalized dullness and apathy toward everything.

Mercurius solubus is a remedy that shows all symptoms worse at night and in damp, cold, wet weather, but all symptoms are also made *worse* by warmth, either the heat of a room or the warmth of the bed. Nasal symptoms predominate in Mercurius sol. There is much sneezing, often with a yellow-green discharge from the nose, which is acid in nature. There is a strong sense of soreness and rawness of the nasal passages with considerable discharge that burns or smarts. There is often a metallic taste in the mouth accompanied by increased salivation; the tongue is thickly coated and has a moist, yellow appearance, and is easily indented by the teeth.

Nux vomica works against a cold or flu in which chills predominate. There is chilliness on being uncovered and the patient feels he or she must be covered. However, a peculiar symptom emerges here: *the patient does not allow himself to be covered.* A major Keynote symptom in Nux vomica is great irritability and hypersensitivity. The patient cannot tolerate noise, odors, or light, is sullen, finds fault easily in everything, and does not desire to be touched. The nose is congested and stuffed up, especially at night, whereas in the daytime the nose runs freely with an acid discharge *yet accompanied by a stuffed-up feeling.* Nausea and vomiting may also predominate, the nausea coming on especially in the morning and after eating, and there are belching and retching with sour and bitter tastes. The stomach is extremely sensitive to any kind of pressure or the slightest touch.

Pulsatilla has proved to be an effective remedy in the late stages of a cold. The mucous membranes are affected with thick, yellowish discharges that do not burn or excoriate. The nasal passages alternate between being stuffed up in the evening and running fluently in the morning. The eyes may be inflamed, itch, and burn with profuse tearing. A major modality in Pulsatilla is that the patient *always feels better outside in the open air.*

Rhus toxicodendron is a remedy not often considered in flu, yet it can play a major role in its treatment. Rhus tox. has the symptoms of severe aching, pains, and stiffness, especially in the joints, with the Keynote symptoms being worse on *first* movement, but *better* after continued movement. In Rhus tox., when the patient limbers up, walks, moves about, or stretches, the pains are greatly relieved. Like Belladonna, Rhus tox. is associated with great restlessness with a continued desire to change position. As with Gelsemium, the patient is also listless, but this is not as marked as in Gelsemium. Rhus tox. eyes are red and swollen and painful from pressure. There is sneezing and the throat is often sore. The glands may be enlarged and inflamed and, on swallowing, a sticking pain predominates. Stomach symptoms include no desire for food but a considerable and unquenchable desire for liquids, especially milk. The throat and mouth are always dry.

There are many other remedies that correspond to colds and influenza, but those listed here are the most frequently called upon.

An adjunct combination remedy exists that has demonstrated considerable value in flu and severe colds, **"AGE."** AGE (Arsenicum iodatum, Gelsemium, and Eupatorium perf.) covers a majority of typical cold and flu symptoms. Arsenicum iod., not to be confused with Arsenicum alb. (Arsenicum trioxide), is especially useful in acute respiratory conditions in which there is a hacking, racking cough, always dry, with little expectoration, and when nasal symptoms produce a thin, watery, highly irritating discharge. Some homeopathic pharmacies carry AGE as a house specialty. It appears of special value in the 6x and 30x potencies. AGE-30 can be specially compounded by Ehrhart & Karl, Inc., Chicago. AGE-30 complements the Influenzinum/Bacillinum combination when the latter fails to establish complete immunization. Dosage is generally recommended at four doses, 3 hours apart for one day, then three to four doses every 4 hours the following day, then stop.

COMMON-SENSE SUPPORTIVE TREATMENTS

Of course, common sense dictates that in the treatment of severe colds and certainly flu the patient get plenty of rest and drink quantities of liquids—water or fruit juices—to prevent dehydration and to assist the body to rid itself of accumulated toxins. These measures should be followed also under homeopathic treatment. Complications of the flu, especially in the very young and the elderly, are not uncommon, such as secondary bacterial infections and pneumonia. They are rare under the appropriate homeopathic treatment. However, should the patient, upon recovering from the flu, suffer a relapse or show acute respiratory symptoms, the first-aider or medical self-helper should always consult a qualified, licensed health-care professional.

ADVISORY WARNING: The importance of suspecting and diagnosing Reye's syndrome cannot be overstressed. Should a child under the age of 18 who is recovering from the "flu" experience severe, persistent vomiting and noticeable personality changes—forgetfulness, weakness, disorientation, or anger—suspect Reye's syndrome and consult your family physician or nearest medical center *immediately.* Reye's syndrome can be fatal!

CHAPTER SEVEN

SKIN DISEASES

Topics Covered

Eczema
Wet, "Weeping" Skin Lesions
Warts
Hives (Urticaria, Nettle Rash)
Cold Sores ("Fever Blisters")

Often, the most prominent and common medical problems seen in physicians' offices are diseases of the skin.[72] The various types of dermatoses—eczema, urticaria, dermal lesions, impetigo, psoriasis, rashes, and itches of various sorts—send patients flocking to general practitioners, family specialists, and dermatologists with great frequency. There's an old joke among physicians. *Question:* "What is the best specialty in medicine?" *Answer:* "Dermatology. The hours are regular, patients seldom die, and usually they never get better." Admittedly, that's a bad joke, but all too often not very far from the truth.

Homeopathy has been opposed from its beginning to treating skin disorders solely externally with salves, creams, and ointments. The homeopathic and naturopathic professions united in dismay when, in the 1950s, traditional medicine employed x-rays as a common treatment for cystic acne. Thirty years later, many of those patients so treated still bear the pits and scars and red discoloration of the acne they had as teens. Professional and popular literature have reported cases in which some patients so treated required cosmetic and reconstructive surgery to repair radiation-damaged skin.

Allopathic medicine turned from radiation to antibiotic therapy, using tetracycline as a standard treatment for acne. And tetracycline works—as long as the acne-sufferer continues to take it internally in massive doses, or uses a lotion formula. But its disadvantages are notable. Internally, it sterilizes the bowel of beneficial bacteria required for the proper absorption of vital nutrients, and it can produce as a side effect behavioral mood changes. As Drs. Dodd and Chi have observed, it can also cause inflammation of the genitals.[73] One very recent therapy using an analogue of Vitamin A has been connected with birth defects in children.

The major problem with traditional allopathic medicine is, as was stated earlier, a lack of a truly unified theory to support its system of health care delivery; homeopathy, on the other hand, has never lacked that vital element. In treating diseases of the skin, traditional medicine relies on powerful drugs which all too often produce adverse reactions; these drugs may indeed cure or lessen external symptoms, but frequently they only palliate. Some diseases, such as psoriasis and chronic eczema, traditional medicine pronounces "incurable." Yet homeopathy, using its potentized microdoses, frequently can treat effectively these and many other diseases and disorders that fail to respond well, if at all, to standard methods: asthma, essential hypertension (high blood pressure), colitis (irritable bowel), rheumatoid arthritis and osteoarthritis, and Meniere's syndrome, to name a few.

This book is not intended to enable the medical self-helper to treat chronic disease. However, this section will present some of the most common, acute skin conditions and relate their effective symptomatic treatment.

Eczema

Homeopaths recognize two types of eczema: constitutional and acquired. The less common of the two types, constitutional eczema, is that which is normally acquired in infancy and continues on well into adulthood. This is the so-called "chronic eczema." Acquired eczema, by far the more common form, is considered by homeopaths a condition of delayed allergy. Constitutional eczema requires the careful efforts of a well-qualified homeopathic physician, who must closely scrutinize the individual *as a unique biological entity* and determine that patient's constitutional "type" prior to initiating treatment. Acquired eczema can be treated successfully by the lay person, following the Keynote symptoms of the acute disease.

ECZEMA OF THE SCALP

Scalp eczema is common both to infants and adults.

HOMEOPATHIC TREATMENT
Calcarea Carbonica (Calc. Carb.)
Natrum Muriaticum (Nat. Mur.)
Sulfur

In infants, the chalkish-white to light-yellow crusting skin often yields effectively to **Calcarea carbonica** (calcium carbonate). The modalities of Calc. carb. are: patient is usually *worse* from cold—air, water, wet weather—and *better* with dry warmth.

In a similar scalp condition, when the flaking dry crusts appear near the hairline rather than in the hair itself, consider homeopathic sodium chloride, **Natrum muriaticum** This remedy is also often effective in clearing up oily and greasy eruptions on hairy body parts and in treating dry, crusting eruptions occurring in the *bends* of joints and behind the ears. The modalities of Nat. mur. are: patient is *worse* from warmth and heat; *better* from open air, cold water, and cool weather.

Often complementary to the foregoing two remedies and sometimes required to complete the curative action of them is **Sulfur** in homeopathic potency. Sulfur in its crude form produces—and, therefore, in its triturated and potentized form, cures—dry, scaly, flaking skin eruptions, especially if they itch, burn, and are *worse* from scratching or bathing. The modalities of Sulfur are: *worse* from moist warmth, washing or bathing; *better* from dry warmth.

Potency and Dosage: 12x–30x.

OTHER FLAKING SKIN ERUPTIONS

The major similarity among the homeopathic remedies is the appearance of the skin, and it is therefore important to carefully observe the skin's texture to differentiate among the remedies.

HOMEOPATHIC TREATMENT
Arsenicum Iodatum (Arsenicum Iod.)
Natrum Sulphuricum (Nat. Sulph.)
Petroleum

Arsenicum Iodatum is useful in treating rough, dry, scaly skin when the flakes (plaques) are relatively *small*. Itching accompanies the scaly eruption, and as the plaques flake off they leave a raw-appearing and *watery* skin surface beneath.

Natrum sulphuricum, a homeopathic tissue salt, often effectively treats ailments in which the skin is rough, dry, and scaly with *medium* to *large* flaking plaques usually yellowish-white in color. As these plaques slough off, the skin is red and shiny and *dry*.

Some people experience the appearance of a dry, scaly, although at times moist skin eruption in the winter months or during cold weather. This condition disappears during the summer and during warm weather. This "periodicity," as homeopaths call an on-and-off again condition, marks **Petroleum.** If you meet a skin condition characterized by these symptoms and showing the modalities of *worse* in winter and from dampness and cold, and *better* in summer and from dry warmth, Petroleum is the most likely remedy.

Wet, "Weeping" Skin Lesions

Graphites, a carbon-based remedy, is especially effective in treating conditions in which the skin breaks open and exudes a thick, honey-like discharge. The Keynote symptom of the remedy is the thick, syrupy ooze from the broken skin. This weeping secretion dries to form a thick yellow to light-brown crust. Graphites eruptions often appear on the palms of the hands, between the toes, around the genitals and mouth, and sometimes around the nipples.

The modalities for Graphites are: *worse* with warmth and, in women, during and following menstruation; *better* with local cold applications.

Potency and Dosage: Graphites seems to work best in its lower potencies, 3x or 6x, and it may also be used locally as an ointment. Ointments (called *cerates* in homeopathy) are fine and have their uses, but it is best to treat skin conditions with internal potencies, using cerates as adjunctive treatments as needed.

A case history is illustrative. A young man in his middle twenties asked the homeopath about an annoying skin irritation for which he had consulted two physicians, first his family doctor and second a dermatologist. The condition was totally localized around the fleshy portion of his left thumb and extended some distance onto the palm. The skin first formed crops of tiny blisters barely the size of a pinhead, and the skin itched intensely. The blisters ran together, broke open, and oozed a thick yellow discharge. Following this oozing, the surface crusted over. Both physicians had prescribed a hydrocortisone ointment, which had only limited effectiveness. The condition would disappear for a time, only to reappear, sometimes worse than before. All the Keynote symptoms of Graphites were present and, after taking Graphites in 3x potency, 5 tablets 4 times daily for 2 weeks, the young man experienced a total remission of symptoms and regained perfectly clear skin without further treatment.

Warts

Warts are truly amazing, and perhaps no one has so well—almost poetically—described them than Lewis Thomas, M.D.:

> Warts are wonderful structures. They can appear overnight on any part of the skin, like mushrooms on a damp lawn, full grown and splendid in the complexity of their architecture. Viewed in stained sections under a microscope, they are the most specialized of cellular arrangements. . . . They sit there like turreted mounds of dense, impenetrable horn, impregnable, designed for defense against the world outside. . . . As it turns out, the exuberant cells of a wart are the elaborate reproductive apparatus of a virus.[74]

Poetic thoughts aside, warts appear in numerous forms and some people appear more susceptible to them than others. As is usually true in homeopathy, there is no one remedy that is specific to all types of warts. Therefore, the self-helper must pay close attention to the description of each listed remedy.

HOMEOPATHIC TREATMENT
Thuja Occidentalis

One of the first remedies to think of in nearly any kind of wart is **Thuja occidentalis,** made from the arbor vitae evergreen. Of special value in treating warts around the anus and genitals, Thuja does have a beneficial effect on warts in other locations. A few doses of Thuja in the 30x potency are often sufficient to remove many warts. It can also be applied locally in undiluted tincture, painted on the wart and allowed to dry. Using the tincture may be of value in children who, psychologically, like to see that something is being done externally to treat their warts.

TREATING WARTS BY TYPE AND LOCATIONS

Warts on Hands and Feet

Plantar and palmar warts are merely terms of location. Plantar warts appear on the soles of the feet, whereas palmar warts grow on the inner surfaces of the hands. Anyone who has had one or several plantar warts knows how painful they can be. Plantar warts tend to grow inward; they are shaped like an ice-cream cone, and the sharp base of the cone presses on deep tissue structures, causing severe pain and making it difficult for the victim to walk. Some plantar warts, however, are quite painless. Plantar and palmar warts may appear individually, or severally as well-spaced individual warts, or in small crops close together (mosaic warts).

HOMEOPATHIC TREATMENT
Antimonium Crudum (Antimonium Crud.)
Nitric Acid

Treatment of these and most other types of warts may be benefited by **Thuja** as an adjunct remedy. Thuja is effective in most potency ranges, but preference may be to the midrange 30x potency. Thuja should not be used too often; one standard dose per week is usually sufficient. Together with Thuja, employ one of the following remedies according to its description.

Antimonium crudum is very useful in treating either plantar or palmer warts, single or mosaic, when the wart is hard and cornified. Antimonium crud. will treat warts on any body part so long as they meet this description.

If you spill *Nitric acid* on the skin, the surface turns yellow to yellow-orange. A wart that has this color, especially if it produces a sharp, pricking pain (as in plantar warts) or bleeds easily, has Nitric acid as the homeopathic remedy of choice. Nitric acid alternates well with Antimonium crud. and a weekly dose of Thuja.

Warts Under and Around the Fingernails

HOMEOPATHIC TREATMENT
Causticum
Graphites

Warts appearing under the nails bear the medical term of *subungual verrucas*. In warts of this nature **Causticum,** alternating with a weekly dose of Thuja, is the remedy of choice. A Causticum wart may be smooth but most often is large, is jagged, bleeds easily, and may even be located on the tip of the nose!

Graphites treats another kind of wart, the *periungual qualified verrucas*—those growing beside the nail. This kind of wart is hard, horny, very jagged in appearance, white surfaced, and very rough. It may bleed easily. *Graphites* (3x to 6x), in alternation with Antimonium crud. and a weekly dose of Thuja, will often remove this wart.

One last word on warts. Homeopathic treatment is usually very effective and always painless. Eight in ten cases of warts can be cleared using the indicated homeopathic remedies. Do not expect the remedies to work overnight. Experience has shown that in the eight of ten cases in which homeopathy eradicated warts, treatment required from 2 weeks to 30 days. Sometimes, even using homeopathy, direct intervention is required by a physician—local application of 40% salicylic acid, cantharides, or electrical desiccation. Do not, however, pare away a wart yourself; it will simply grow back, or spread, and you may damage yourself in the process.

Hives (Urticaria, Nettle Rash)

Hives, called *urticaria* by physicians and sometimes *nettle rash* by the public, may result from drug-induced allergy, from insect stings, or from eating certain foods (fruits, nuts, eggs, shellfish). They may sometimes follow streptococcal and certain viral infections. Hives may be *acute* or *chronic*. Acute urticaria is a self-limiting condition in which the intensely itching red wheals appear rapidly and last from one day to a week. Chronic urticaria, a condition that lasts for weeks, may be symptomatic of an underlying allergy or a chronic infection.

ADVISORY WARNING: *Chronic urticaria should be treated only on the advice of a physician, preferably a homeopath.*

SYMPTOMS

Usually hives develop rapidly, forming large, inflamed red blotches on the skin anywhere on the body. They may be round or irregularly shaped, generally red and puffy, sometimes pale white in the center surrounded by a red border. They itch intensely and may spread at an alarming rate.

HOMEOPATHIC TREATMENT
Apis Mellifica (Apis Mel.)
Belladonna
Urtica Urens

Consider **Apis mellifica,** the homeopathic trituration of the honey bee, when the following Keynote symptoms are present: rapid onset of symptoms; skin swells, is puffy, color is a rosy-red hue; violent stinging, itching, and burning. The modalities of Apis mel. are: *worse* with heat, touch, pressure; *better* with cold applications.

Potency and Dosage: 6x to 30x every 3 to 4 hours.

Belladonna treats hives that show the following Keynote symptoms: blotches are yellowish-red; hot and burning; condition may be accompanied by a violent headache; much mental restlessness. The modalities of Belladonna are: rubbing *relieves* the itching.

Potency and Dosage: 6x to 30x every 3 to 4 hours.

Urtica urens, made from the stinging nettle plant, is often highly effective in treating acute urticaria. If the allergic reaction is brought on from eating shellfish, it is the *first* remedy to consider, as it will act as an antidote to the ill-effects. The Keynote symptoms of Urtica urens are: itching skin blotches accompanied by burning heat and violent itching. The *modalities* of Urtica urens are: *worse* from local cold applications and touch.

Potency and Dosage: 6x to 30x every 3 to 4 hours.

Cold Sores ("Fever Blisters")

Cold sores and fever blisters are the outward symptoms of the herpes simplex virus, which nearly everyone carries dormant in the body. They frequently appear around the mouth and lips following a viral infection (hence the name "cold" sore), during times of stress, and even following exposure to the sun. Although they pose no danger, they are annoying and unsightly.

HOMEOPATHIC TREATMENT
Natrum Muriaticum (Nat. Mur.)
Rhus Toxicodendron (Rhus Tox.)
Lycopodium

There are few remedies in the homeopathic *Materia Medica* that are specific to any particular disease. However, in fever blisters, **Natrum muriaticum** comes close to being *the* remedy in nearly every case.

The Nat. mur. fever blister begins anywhere on the lips or around the mouth and nose. A major Keynote of this remedy is *the blisters appear like pearls around the mouth*. Experience has shown that, taken at the first sign, Nat. mur. prevents fever blisters from growing larger or spreading, and will most frequently dry them up in 24 hours.

Potency and Dosage: Use the 30x potency, repeating at 2-hour intervals during a 24-hour period.

Nat. mur. does not stand alone, however, in relieving fever blisters. When cold sores follow a cold or the flu, accompanied by fever, when the patient has been restless, and especially when the tongue is dry, dark-coated and red-tipped, consider **Rhus toxicodendron** (the homeopathic trituration of poison ivy). The blisters of Rhus tox. appear red, are water-filled and swollen, and itch intensely.

One final remedy needs to be considered: **Lycopodium.** This remedy, like Nat. mur., works best in higher potencies (30x and higher). Lycopodium is a *right-sided* remedy; afflictions begin on the right side and remain here, or shift from right to left. Skin lesions may ulcerate, itch violently, and bleed easily when rubbed. Lycopodium should be considered in fever blisters whenever they appear on the *right* side of the lips or mouth and when the patient suffers predominantly from right-sided complaints during illness.

Symptoms guide the prescriber in the use of these three remedies. Positive benefit can be derived from using the *most similar* remedy.

CHAPTER EIGHT

SORE THROAT AND TONSILLITIS

Sore throats are estimated to cost American business over 100 million lost workdays annually. Therefore, sore throats are more common than influenza in causing illness in the United States.

Most people lump sore throats and tonsillitis together, but it is informative to differentiate between the two. Physicians call the "sore throat" *pharyngitis,* an inflammation of the throat producing pain on swallowing. Pharyngitis is most often caused by a virus, although sometimes a streptococcus and less commonly by staphylococcus bacteria. Tonsillitis, on the other hand, is an inflammation of the tonsils themselves, producing severe pain on swallowing, the pain often shooting into the ears, accompanied by fever, lethargy, and sometimes headache and vomiting; vomiting is especially common in children. Tonsillitis is caused most frequently by streptococcal bacteria and less commonly by a virus.

The orthodox medical community is still undecided on whether the simple "sore throat" should be treated by antibiotics. Most often, rest, aspirin, and salt water or hydrogen peroxide gargles are suggested. Remember that antibiotics have absolutely no effect on viruses. However, if the physician obtains a throat culture and discovers a bacterial infection, antibiotics will be prescribed.

One of the greatest demonstrations of the power and rapid action of homeopathy can be seen in the treatment of both pharyngitis and tonsillitis using the remedy *that most closely matches* the patient's symptoms. If the prescriber has remembered and followed the proper administration of homeopathic remedies, he or she can expect marked improvement or complete cure of both conditions regardless of cause in as little as 24 to 36 hours. Homeopathy has a large arsenal of remedies for pharyngitis and tonsillitis, but the following remedies will cover nearly any set of symptoms.

HOMEOPATHIC TREATMENT
Aconite
Apis Mellifica (Apis Mel.)
Belladonna
Hepar Sulphuris Calcareum (Hepar Sulph.)
Lachesis
Lycopodium
Phytolacca

Aconite, made in homeopathic potency from the monkshood plant, is most effective at the *very beginning* of throat pain and ineffective once the sore throat is well established. The Keynote symptoms are: throat is red, dry, with a constricted feeling; patient complains of pain and difficulty on swallowing or speaking; throat is redder than normal, but not deep-hued or glossy, and the patient may complain of burning and pricking sensations. The modalities are: *dislikes drinking either hot or cold liquids.*

Apis mellifica, the homeopathic trituration of the honey bee, is a major remedy in sore throats of any kind when Keynote symptoms agree: throat is swollen noticeably both inside and out, accompanied by stinging pain and a sensation of constriction; throat or tonsils appear fiery red and puffy and the *uvula* (the tiny punching bag-shaped organ at the back of the throat) is often swollen and fiery red; sometimes the Apis patient complains of a feeling as if a fishbone were stuck in the throat. The modalities of Apis mel. are: *worse* from heat in any form, swallowing hot liquids, pressure, and touch; *better* from cold liquids.

Belladonna, made from the deadly nightshade plant, is effective with these Keynote symptoms: throats that are dry, angry red, and shiny as if glazed; throat feels constricted, accompanied by great difficulty in swallowing; the Belladonna throat often feels as if it contained a lump. The modalities of Belladonna are: *worse* on right side; from swallowing liquids; and from touch and pressure.

Hepar sulph. is a mineral substance compounded by Dr. Samuel Hahnemann ("Hahnemann's calcium sulfide"). Keynote symptoms are: throat feels as if a plug or a splinter were stuck in it; stitching pains run from the throat to the ear when swallowing; patient may attempt to hawk up a clinging mucus from the throat; is constantly clearing the throat, which produces pain; in the Hepar throat, the tonsils may appear ulcerated or abscessed. The modalities of Hepar sulph. are: *worse* from cold, touch, lying on the affected side; *better* from warmth and after eating.

Lachesis is a powerful homeopathic remedy triturated from the venom of the Surucucu snake and is totally harmless in its homeopathic microdilutions but extremely effective in its curative powers whenever symptoms agree. The Keynote symptoms are: lachesis throat is exceptionally dry, intensely swollen both inside and out, and painful from the slightest touch or pressure; lining of the throat often shows a dusky, purplish-red membrane; pain from the Lachesis throat runs into the ear, and the pressure from a collar or tie must be relieved; patient complains of a severe sore throat; tonsils may be enlarged and dark-hued or purplish; patient constantly attempts to clear the throat, but the mucus clings and cannot be forced up or down. The modalities are: *worse* on left side, and on swallowing liquids; pain greatly aggravated by hot drinks; *better* after warm local applications to the neck.

Lycopodium, a remedy made from the club moss plant, is totally unknown to the orthodox medical profession. Its only use at one time was in microscopic measurement owing to the mathematical evenness of the spores. In its homeopathic triturated form, however, Lycopodium is one of the most powerful allies in treating illnesses with which its symptoms agree.

The characteristic Keynote symptom of Lycopodium is its "sidedness" and periodicity. Symptoms of illness *always* begin on the right side and either remain right-sided or move from right to left. Aggravation of symptoms begin from 4:00 P.M. to 8:00 P.M. Of course, "sidedness" and periodicity mean absolutely nothing to the allopathic physician. The Keynote symptoms are: the Lycopodium sore throat is *dry with thirst;* throat is inflamed, accompanied by stitching pains on swallowing; food or drink often regurgitates through the nose as if liquids were being forced upward through the nasal passage.

The modalities of Lycopodium are: *worse* from cold drinks; condition begins on the right and remains on the right or moves to the left; warm local applications to the throat; *better* from warm drinks.

Phytolacca is made from the poke-root herb and holds an excellent reputation in sore throat and tonsillitis. The Phytolacca Keynote symptoms are: throat is dark red to bluish red in color; soft palate (the fleshy portion behind the roof of the mouth) may be very sore, and the tonsils are swollen, dark red or bluish; there is considerable pain at the root of the tongue; pain shoots into the ears on swallowing; in advanced cases, the throat and tonsils are ulcerated, with grayish-white spots, and a thick, yellow mucus clings to the throat and tonsils; the throat feels hot and burning, making it difficult to swallow any liquids; in tonsillitis the *right* organ is most frequently affected. The modalities are: *worse* on swallowing hot liquids.

All of the remedies listed here are found in the well-stocked homeopathic first-aid or home-remedy kit. Studying the Keynote symptoms and modalities of each remedy will enable the first-aider and medical self-helper to prescribe the *most similar* remedy to the disease, regardless of its cause.

In each remedy, any potency will work well. Lower potencies (3x, 6x) bear frequent repetition, although the most rapid resolution of the condition will come from the 30x potency—the potency most often used in first aid and medical self-care. Under homeopathic treatment, pharyngitis and tonsillitis will most often resolve in 24 to 36 hours. Certainly marked improvement will follow soon after the most similar remedy is given according to homeopathic principles.

ADVISORY WARNING: As in all cases of illness, should the condition not improve, or become worse, consult a licensed health care practitioner.

The first-aider or self-helper may find it most convenient to carry a combination "sore throat" remedy when weight or bulk is an important consideration. Each homeopathic pharmaceutical supplier listed in Appendix One sells specialty combinations containing several of the remedies listed here. They are usually supplied in the lower 3x or 6x potency and will work but require more frequent repetition of the standard dose.

CHAPTER NINE

HAYFEVER

Topics Covered

Symptomatic Treatment
Desensitization through Homeopathy

Hayfever, sometimes called pollinosis, rosefever, or perennial allergic rhinitis, is an acute seasonal allergy generally caused by inhaled, wind-borne pollens from flowers, plants, trees, and even mold spores.

Hayfever symptoms vary from person to person, from mild to moderate to severe. Anyone who suffers from this allergy knows well the disadvantages of over-the-counter as well as prescribed drugs so often used in its treatment. Antihistamines often have a sedating effect on the central nervous system, making the user drowsy. Concentration can become difficult. Tasks requiring the utmost awareness—driving and operating power tools and machinery—become dangerous to self and others.

Credit must be given, however, to orthodox allopathic medicine. Only recently has allopathic research produced a class of drugs for the symptomatic treatment of seasonal allergies that do not easily penetrate the blood-brain barrier and therefore do not produce, in most people, the sedating effects of traditional antihistamines.

Perhaps it is only homeopathy that offers the hayfever sufferer any real hope for long-term and permanent results, however. Unlike nearly all allopathic drugs, homeopathic remedies have none of the side effects of antihistamines. They do not interact with alcohol (which intensifies antihistamines' sedative effects) or with most other medications, nor do they cause sleepiness. Best of all, homeopathic remedies, carefully selected according to the total pattern of symptoms, can produce a permanent remission of hayfever symptoms.

This section is divided into two treatment modes: the temporary *symptomatic* treatment of acute allergic conditions, and the permanent *desensitization* approach.

Symptomatic Treatment

The symptomatic treatment of hayfever palliates—lessens or removes—outward allergic symptoms: the sneezing, sniffling, running nose, and red, itching, burning, and watering eyes. Symptomatic treatment does not cure the underlying allergic sensitivity to whatever is causing those symptoms, but it does offer immediate relief.

The beginner to homeopathy may prefer to select one of the many proprietary combination remedies for hayfever symptoms manufactured by homeopathic chemists, which are readily available in many health food stores or from any of the homeopathic suppliers listed in Appendix One at the back of this book. Such combination remedies generally prove quite effective; they are combinations of naturally occurring ingredients working together to produce the desired effect—stimulating and strengthening the body's own defense system.

Most seasonal hayfever sufferers find that one of these combination remedies serves their needs well. They may have to experiment, however, to find the one (with the proper combination of remedies) best suited to their particular symptoms. Many hayfever sufferers who have used these products have been able to stop taking over-the-counter or physician-prescribed antihistamines altogether and are well pleased with the results.

Homeopathy, through its *Materia Medica,* offers many single remedies to treat hayfever symptoms, and the following list should not be considered exhaustive. These single remedies, however, are most often considered in the treatment of seasonal hayfever allergy.

HOMEOPATHIC TREATMENT
Arsenicum Album (Arsenicum Alb.)
Ambrosia
Allium Cepa
Euphrasia Officinalis (Euphrasia Off.)
Naphthalin
Pulsatilla

Always remember when selecting a single remedy to *match the symptoms of the remedy with the overall symptoms experienced.* Employ the homeopathic "three-legged stool." This is a device for selecting the most similar remedy as old as homeopathy itself. You cannot balance on a two-legged stool, but put three legs under it and it is solid. In homeopathic prescribing, find *three* Keynote (or major) symptoms under a single remedy that most match the most prominent symptoms and, nine times out of ten, you will have found the correct remedy for that particular symptom pattern.

Arsenicum album is the remedy made from the compound arsenic trioxide. Arsenicum is frequently found to be very useful in treating hayfever symptoms and, in its homeopathic form, is perfectly safe. It should not be used below the 6x potency. Arsenicum's Keynote symptoms are: thin, watery discharge from the nose; discharge *burns* the upper lip; nose is stuffed up; much sneezing, but sneezing brings *no* relief; all symptoms are *worse* in the open air and *better* indoors.

Ambrosia is not the "nectar of the gods" of Greek mythology to hayfever sufferers. It is the Latin botanical name for the common ragweed, which so often brings on hayfever symptoms to millions as it pollinates in the fall. Ambrosia's Keynote symptoms are: much watering from the eyes with *intolerable itching* of the eyelids; nose and head feel stuffed up sneezing with watery discharge from the nose.

Allium cepa, a remedy that is frequently called upon when the hayfever sufferer does not sneeze, is made from the common red onion. Anyone who has sliced an onion well knows this pungent vegetable's effects! As already noted, in homeopathy, the symptoms a substance can produce it can also cure. Allium is one of homeopathy's most effective and most often called on remedies for hayfever *when the Keynote symptoms agree:* acid, burning discharge from the nose; nose becomes red and sore; eyes are red and water profusely, but the discharge is bland and nonirritating; eyelids are sore and burn.

Naphthalin is a coal tar compound and is often found in combination with other remedies. Alone, Naphthalin's Keynote symptoms are: much sneezing; eyes are inflamed, painful, and burn; eyelids are often swollen; head feels hot.

Euphrasia officinalis is a wonderful remedy in hayfever in which eye symptoms predominate. In fact, the common name of this herb is eyebright. *Euphrasia's* Keynote symptoms include: acrid, thick discharge from the eyes; acid tearing and watering; eyelids burn and swell; frequent inclination to blink; eyes water constantly; intense aversion to light, especially artificial indoor lighting; small, clear blisters form on the cornea.

Euphrasia is best used in the lower 3x or 6x potencies internally and its diluted tincture employed locally as eyedrops or in an eyebath. To use Euphrasia locally, dilute 2 drops of the tincture in a quarter cup of sterile, purified, or distilled water and flush the eye(s) several times a day. The latter treatment is especially useful in seasonal hayfever allergy when the eyes itch, water, or burn.

Pulsatilla, the homeopathic preparation of the wind flower herb, shows great benefit in treating seasonal allergies. The Keynote symptoms of Pulsatilla are: thick, profuse, yellow, non-acrid discharge from the eyes; eyes itch and burn; profuse tearing and watering; the general condition of the eye(s) is *worse* from warmth; lid(s) are inflamed; eyes are matted shut by a sticky mucus.

Potency and Dosage: 3x, 6x, or 30x every 2 to 3 hours, as needed.

Desensitization through Homeopathy

The most significant advantage homeopathic treatment can offer the majority of hayfever sufferers over its allopathic counterpart is painless and permanent desensitization.

Annually, thousands of hayfever and allergy sufferers flock to allopathic allergists' offices to undergo first a series of skin patch testing to determine the specific substance(s) to which they are allergic, and second to submit to a lengthy series of weekly or twice-weekly injections. This method, called *isotherapy,* employs minute amounts of the allergens to which the person is allergic—house dust, pet hair, molds, pollens, even food substances—to establish desensitization. Not only is the procedure lengthy, lasting a year or longer, but it is also uncomfortable and very expensive.

Although they may not realize (or admit) it, allergists using isotherapy are employing a form of homeopathy. Although true homeopathy, in the treatment of allergies, may employ not the specific substance to which a person is sensitive but a substance which, in crude form, would produce a very similar symptom picture, homeopathy also employs isotherapy.

On the basis of a complete health history and a thorough analysis of the patient's guiding symptoms, a homeopathic physician, or a naturopathic physician employing the homeopathic method, can locate and prescribe *the* single isotherapeutic substance in homeopathic potency that most fits the overall allergic symptoms.

As is true of allopathic practice, homeopathic desensitization requires great care in effective prescribing, and usually a 2- to 3-year course of treatment is required for long-term remission of symptoms. But the results are very often well worth the time required, and the advantages are numerous: no need for hypodermic injections, no continued office visits, and no inordinate expense for homeopathically prepared remedies.

Allergy management is tricky at best. The lay person should not expect to desensitize himself or herself. However, using classic homeopathy, once the most similar single remedy is found that covers the totality of symptoms, the lay prescriber can take that remedy at least 6 weeks prior to the usual onset of seasonal symptoms and in effect produce a significant seasonal desensitization.

The effectiveness of the homeopathic approach to allergy management has been well documented over decades of clinical practice. Its safety and positive results are well known in homeopathy, naturopathy, and holistic health care.

CHAPTER TEN

HOMEOPATHIC TREATMENT OF COMMON DENTAL PROBLEMS

Topics Covered

Preoperative Treatment
Anxiety
Anxiety Reactions in Children
Homeopathy in General Dental Conditions

Homeopathy offers excellent results in the treatment and prevention of many dental conditions and has been used successfully for many years by lay practitioners. In recent years more and more dentists have come to study postgraduate homeopathic medicine and then employ the time-tested remedies in their practices.

The homeopathic first-aider will find the following treatments completely safe, highly effective, and—perhaps of equal importance—painless.

Preoperative Treatment

In a psychological study conducted several years ago, groups of people were asked to identify the health care professional they least like to visit. The overwhelming response was the dentist.

No matter how carefully the modern dentist, today very much a medical specialist, designs his or her office, patient anxiety is high.

The hypodermic syringe used to inject Novocaine is large enough to cause apprehension, and the instruments required to extract an impacted wisdom tooth resemble the tools designed to change an automobile tire.

Today's dentists are doing all they can to eliminate this anxiety. Intravenous sedation, producing the so-called "twilight sleep," is becoming more and more common. It is also one of the leading controversies in dentistry. Intravenous sedation has been associated with serious reactions; it can send a patient into anaphylactic shock or cause the heart to stop. The use of certain sedative or analgesic drugs on children has produced devastating results—permanent neurological injury (brain damage, paralysis) has been recorded. Using homeopathy, however, there is no need to fear dental procedures. Homeopathic preoperative treatment for both adults and children is designed to relieve stressful anxiety and to work safely and without the possibility of side effects. For these reasons, more and more dentists are gaining knowledge of homeopathic remedies in their practices.

Anxiety

Homeopathy recognizes two categories of stress-anxiety: weak and strong. In weak anxiety, the patient shows a general *loss of power* prior to dental treatment. The opposite is true in strong anxiety, in which the patient is nervous, highly agitated, and anxious. Using the following remedies according to their indications will greatly relieve these two types of predental stress.

WEAK ANXIETY

HOMEOPATHIC TREATMENT
Gelsemium

Gelsemium taken several hours before a dental visit frequently brings about a relaxation of tension and anxiety. Give one dose in the morning and again at night *before* visiting the dentist and another dose 1 hour before entering the office. The Keynote symptoms of Gelsemium are fear, tiredness, general weakness, and an overall loss of power. The remedy is especially indicated for those persons who, in anticipation of seeing the dentist, experience "the nervous shakes" and diarrhea. Preferred potencies range from the 12x to 30x.

STRONG ANXIETY

HOMEOPATHIC TREATMENT
Argentum Nitricum (Argentum Nit.)
Aconite
Arsenicum Album (Arsenicum Alb.)
Calcarea Carbonica (Calc. Carb.)
Ignatia

Argentum nitricum is a very useful remedy for stress-anxiety in adults, but shows the opposite symptom picture of Gelsemium. In Argentum nit. the patient is full of power (compare with Gelsemium's loss of power), very anxious, nervous and highly agitated. Give one dose in the morning and again the night *before* visiting the dentist, and another dose 1 hour before entering the office. Preferred potencies are 12x and 30x.

Aconite, another powerful antianxiety remedy, is similar to Argentum nit., yet different. The Keynote symptoms are physical and mental restlessness, great fear and anxiety, fear of impending doom, and fear of death. Give in the 30x or 200x potencies, one dose in the morning and evening the day *before* the dental appointment and another one hour prior.

Arsenicum album, given in high potency when stressful symptoms agree, frequently brings about excellent results in negating stress. In strong anxiety, its Keynote symptoms are great exhaustion and irritable weakness, and great anguish and restlessness, especially with a nighttime aggravation. Dentists may use the remedy in the highest potency, but the nondentist should restrict the remedy's potency to the 30x or 200x.

Calcarea carbonica, another remedy for strong anxiety, is appropriate for patients who are *apprehensive;* their overall symptoms are usually *worse* as evening falls. A Keynote symptom is palpatation of the heart induced by stress and fear. Calc. carb. should be taken in the 30x potency following the indications for Argentum, Aconite, and Arsenicum alb.

Ignatia, potentized from the St. Ignatius' bean, is paramount in treating highly excitable persons. The patient is easily excited and filled with contradictions: alert, rigid, trembling, erratic in behavior, subject to swift mood changes from silent, uncommunicative brooding to tearful sobbing. Preferred potencies are 30x or 200x taken one dose morning and evening 24 hours prior to the dental visit and another dose 1 hour before any dental procedure.

Anxiety Reactions in Children

Anxiety reactions in children may be very similar to those experienced by adults and are often the result of parents' expressing their own fears and influencing their sons and daughters. Sometimes the stress-anxiety is brought about when an older sister or brother scares the younger child with highly exaggerated stories about how awful it was to visit the dentist.

HOMEOPATHIC TREATMENT
Chamomilla
Coffea Cruda

The remedy called on most often in children's anxiety is **Chamomilla.** Chamomilla demonstrates a *strong anxiety;* a weak, passive response contraindicates this remedy. All the child's anxiety responses are strong: whining, restlessness, wanting things and then refusing them. The child must be constantly cajoled; he or she is peevish, impatient, intolerant, extremely sensitive, spiteful, snappish, and constantly complaining. All children's complaints showing Chamomilla are full of anger and strength. Quarrelsomeness and an intolerance to pain of any kind are Keynote symptoms. This remedy is without equal for children who exhibit these symptoms, but it is also well indicated in adults whose symptoms match. To use Chamomilla as an anxiety preventive, give one dose of 30x or 200x the morning and evening *before* the dental visit and another one dose one hour before the office call.

Coffea cruda is indicated for the nervous child who is overactive and frequently has difficulty sleeping. The Keynote symptom is that the very thought of pain upsets the child. Coffea cruda is *not* indicated for adults who are habitual coffee drinkers, who are quite probably immune to its homeopathic action. It will work well in children and also in adults who are not coffee drinkers, symptoms agreeing.

Homeopathy in General Dental Conditions

Homeopathy is, of course, excellent in preventing other physical problems that a dental visit can cause: postoperative infection, swelling, bruising of delicate tissues, and bleeding all respond well to homeopathic preventive treatment. Many modern dentists are discovering that giving homeopathic remedies prior to dental surgery prevents or greatly relieves common complications. Examine the following preventive techniques.

BRUISING AND SWELLING

Arnica montana acts favorably on blood vessels and the soft tissues of the body to prevent excessive bruising and swelling from the procedures of dental surgery as well as to combat pus-forming infections. It also assists in alleviating gum soreness due to dental probing, scaling of plaque and tartar, and tooth extraction.

Potency and Dosage: As a preventive measure, take one dose of Arnica in 12x or 30x potencies 2 to 3 times daily for 2 to 3 days prior to the dental operation and one additional dose 1 hour before any surgical or teeth cleaning procedure.

ADVISORY WARNING: Arnica tincture must never be used on any open wound as it produces a serious reaction in the tissues. In its triturated (nontincture) form, however, Arnica is perfectly safe.

PREVENTING INFECTION

HOMEOPATHIC TREATMENT
Pyrogen
Hepar Sulphuris Calcareum (Hepar Sulph.)

Arnica montana has already been mentioned for its value in preventing pus-forming infections from dental surgery. Other remedies are considered of great value in preventing postoperative infections.

Remember that the human mouth is a breeding ground for bacteria of various types, and any surgical procedure of the mouth—on the gums or in tooth extraction—may lead to infection. As an outstanding preventive, the following remedies are recommended.

Pyrogen is a highly desirable remedy to take *following* any dental surgery. It works exceptionally well to prevent infection.

Potency and Dosage: The recommended dose is one dose, twice daily, for 3 to 5 days following oral surgery. The preferred potency is 12x or 30x.

Following the recommendations given here, Pyrogen has been used successfully by dentists trained in homeopathy.

In the arsenal of homeopathy, perhaps no other remedy is as useful against suppurative infections (pus-forming) as **Hepar sulph.** This combination mineral remedy will prevent as well as treat any pus-forming condition. However, an extreme paradox exists. Used in potencies *below* 30x, Hepar sulph. tends to produce pus formation rather than prevent it. Therefore, *never* use Hepar sulph. in potencies below 30x.

PREVENTING DENTAL BLEEDING

A common problem following tooth extraction is hemorrhage from the socket. This is often the result of a nicked blood vessel that has not closed through clot formation. In most cases, postoperative bleeding can be prevented, or greatly lessened, by giving *Phosphorus,* 12x or 30x, one dose the night *before* and another dose the morning of the tooth extraction. Should the socket bleed following surgery, one or two doses of Phosphorus should stop the flow.

> ADVISORY WARNING: Any serious bleeding from the mouth following dental surgery may require packing or suturing by a dentist or an emergency room physician. Do not hesitate to see a dentist or physician should serious bleeding occur, which does not stop within 15 minutes of taking a dose of Phosphorus.

TREATING DENTAL BLEEDING

Homeopathy recognizes three highly effective remedies in dental hemorrhage.

HOMEOPATHIC TREATMENT
Ferrum Phosphoricum (Ferr. Phos.)
Ipecac
Phosphorus

Any of these remedies in homeopathic potency is highly effective in stopping bleeding from any dental surgery. **Phosphorus** has already been mentioned. Phosphorus shares in common with **Ipecac** any *bright-red* bleeding, often profuse. Take one dose every 15 minutes in the 30x potency until the bleeding is controlled.

Ferrum phosphoricum, a mineral remedy triturated from iron phosphate, is yet another effective remedy in bleeding. Dosage is the same as for Phosphorus and Ipecac in the same indicated potencies.

The skilled homeopathist or the dental practitioner may well employ the

200x potency in all cases of dental hemorrhage, and the highest potencies (to be used only by the licensed health care professional) frequently produce immediate results, stopping hemorrhage literally in seconds.

> ADVISORY WARNING: Should a hemorrhage be profuse, the blood spurting from the socket, and bright red in color, a small artery has probably been nicked or severed. Give any of the indicated remedies as a first-aid measure; pack the socket with a sterile gauze. Even a plug made from facial or toilet tissue will work. If all bleeding has not stopped within 15 minutes, see the dental surgeon immediately, or take the victim to the nearest hospital emergency room.

An adjunct treatment in acute bleeding (because of the trauma to the tissues and the possibility of shock) is Arnica 30x every 15 to 30 minutes until symptoms subside, or 200x once or twice as needed.

TREATING NERVE PAIN

Pain following a dental extraction, cleaning, or frequently a root canal treatment is due to damage done to nerves. Homeopathy's major remedy of great value in nerve pain is **Hypericum.** Hypericum acts as a healer of injured nerve tissue. The remedy acts not like an analgesic to stifle pain (like aspirin or acetominophen) but as a rapid healer of nerves. In other words, Hypericum does not block pain but produces a rapid healing at the site of injury, relieving the pain.

Potency and Dosage: The recommended dosage is 12x or 30x given every 15 minutes for a maximum of six to nine doses if the pain is acute. Give less frequently as the pain lessens. Lower potencies of Hypericum work equally well but more slowly, and bear repetition of the dose over a longer time.

TREATING TOOTHACHE

Toothache is a common dental problem. Most usually it is caused by caries (cavity) left untreated, and the tooth pulp becomes inflamed. There are other causes, however, such as an infection of the maxillary sinus, poor dental occlusion, or an inflamed pocket that has formed below the gum line around a tooth.

The following homeopathic remedies are not cures for toothache. The only cure is proper dental treatment. However, using the best-indicated remedy will greatly lessen the pain and discomfort of toothache until a dentist can be seen.

HOMEOPATHIC TREATMENT
Belladonna
Chamomilla
Hypericum
Plantago Majus Tincture

Belladonna is indicated for any throbbing tooth pain, especially if it occurs on the right side of the mouth, and if the tongue is swollen and red.

Chamomilla in the lower to medium potencies, given internally every 15 minutes, or as needed to control the pain, is of special value in children's toothaches. Great *pain* and irritability in children is a strong indication of this remedy.

Plantago majus tincture is of particular value in toothache caused by local decay. As is true for all the other remedies, it is not a cure. However, applying Plantago majus tincture locally to the decayed tooth, a few drops as required to control pain, is of considerable value until the person can see the dentist.

There are literally dozens of toothache remedies in the homeopathic *Materia Medica*, each remedy showing a specific symptom picture. However, to simplify the discussion for the first-aider and medical self-helper, only the three remedies most often indicated are presented. The homeopathic practitioner may want to consult a good *Material Medica*, such as Boericke's *Materia Medica with Repertory*, under Malic acid, Coffea cruda, Pulsatilla, Antimonium crudum, Magnesium aceticum, Magnesium carbonica, and Mezereum for additional indications.

TREATING DRY SOCKET

A dry socket is a not uncommon complication of tooth extraction. This often quite painful problem results when the blood clot that has formed in the jaw cavity where the tooth had been is dislodged. This usually occurs as a result of rinsing the mouth too vigorously following extraction, or sometimes by drinking hot coffee or tea or by smoking during the first 24 hours.

The homeopathic treatment of choice for a dry socket is **Salvia officinalis** (the sage herb) in tincture form. One teaspoonful of the tincture in a cup of warm water rinsed through the mouth and permitted to flow against the area of the missing tooth is of great value and frequently resolves the condition. Salvia off. has the following Keynote symptoms: tearing pain in jaw bone, sometimes felt in the temple; pain in teeth and gums; *worse* from touch and pressure; *better* from warmth.

If additional medication for pain is required, the first-aider should consider one of the following remedies: Hypericum or Belladonna.

Hypericum's chief characteristic is *excessive pain*. It may be given in the low potencies every 15 minutes for several hours as required to reduce the pain, or less frequently in the higher 30x potency.

Belladonna pain is best described as *throbbing,* and the area immediately surrounding the wound is red and often swollen.

For local application, if Salvia off. is unavailable, *Calendula* in its succus or tincture form may be substituted and used as a mouth rinse. Calendula is an outstanding healing agent in all open wounds and wherever the possibility of infection is present.

ADVISORY WARNING: In some cases it may be necessary to have the dentist repair the dry socket surgically. The homeopathic remedies listed here have proved to be of considerable value in treating this condition and are frequently used by dentists trained in homeopathy. However, should they fail to "hold" after a few hours of use, discontinue them and consult a dentist.

REMOVING THE AFTER-EFFECTS OF NOVOCAINE

Most people are familiar with the lasting numbness of the local anesthetic used in dentistry. There is a puffy feeling, "deadness," and drooling. These side effects may last for hours following dental surgery. To lessen the overall effect of Novocaine, homeopathic *Thuja* in the 12x or 30x potency may be given orally, one dose every hour for 3 to 4 hours until all numbness has worn off. Usually one or two doses are all that are required.

TREATING DENTURE IRRITATION

HOMEOPATHIC TREATMENT
Calendula Tincture or Succus
Salvia Officinalis Tincture

If a sore or localized ulcer has formed from a poorly fitting denture, either *Calendula tincture* or *succus* (the fresh plant extract) or *Salvia officinalis tincture* may be used locally as a mouth rinse. Dosage is 1 teaspoonful to 1 cup of warm water. The mouth should be rinsed thoroughly with this dilution.

ADDITIONAL HOMEOPATHIC REMEDIES
Arnica
Hydrastis Tincture
Nonalcoholic Calendula

If a localized sore has formed beneath the denture, give *Arnica* in any potency, 30x or below, as needed for pain and to promote rapid healing.

Hydrastis tincture (golden seal herb) is also of value, applied locally, to heal denture sores. Hydrastis tincture, because of its alcohol content, will, of course, "burn" or "sting" when applied to an open irritation, but the discomfort is quite temporary and the results are usually rapid.

Nonalcoholic Calendula is an excellent remedy for denture sores; its great advantage is that it heals without pain. Apply the nonalcoholic form locally as often as is required until healing occurs.

TEETHING PAIN IN CHILDREN

In cutting teeth, children frequently experience severe discomfort, as all parents who have passed through this stage of development know well. The symptoms of teething include sensitive, tender, swollen gums, and frequent salivation. These are often accompanied by a low fever, restlessness and crying.

HOMEOPATHIC TREATMENT
Chamomilla
ABC-30

Perhaps no other remedy is of more value in teething troubles than *Chamomilla*. Its chief characteristic is *pain*. Besides pain, Chamomilla's Keynote symptoms are: sensitiveness, irritability, restlessness; child is quarrelsome, whining; child wants things, then refuses them; child is thirsty, feels hot, cannot be quieted or calmed; child is impatient, spiteful, and snappish.

When the child presents these symptoms, parents will quickly discover that a few doses of Chamomilla will rapidly calm and settle him or her.

ABC-30 is a special combination remedy of considerable use in teething troubles. A combination of the three most often indicated remedies in the pain children experience (Aconite, Belladonna, and Chamomilla), ABC-30 covers all the major symptoms of teething discomfort. It is available in special combination "teething tablets" sold in many health food stores carrying homeopathic remedies, or from homeopathic manufacturers such as those listed in Appendix One.

MOUTH ULCERS

To treat mouth ulcers, often called "canker sores," two remedies are especially indicated.

HOMEOPATHIC TREATMENT
Borax
Hydrastis Tincture

Borax in potency, especially 3x or 6x, is of definite value in treating this condition.

Hydrastis tincture, mentioned earlier in treating denture sores, applied locally will rapidly heal a canker sore.

Canker sores (medically called aphthous ulcers) may appear on the tongue, inside the cheeks, and most especially on the inside of the upper or lower lips. They appear as if the outer layer of tissue had been burned away, leaving a red-bordered white patch that is quite painful. Borax internally in potency, or Hydrastis tincture locally, or both in combination, will rapidly heal the condition.

CHAPTER ELEVEN

HOMEOPATHIC TREATMENT
OF GENITOURINARY CONDITIONS

Topics Covered

Diseases of Men:
    Testicular Torsion
    Penile Injuries
    Epididymitis
    Orchitis
    Examination for Cancer
Diseases of Women
    Menorrhagia
    Dysmenorrhea
    Urinary Problems

Testicular Torsion

Testicular torsion occurs in pre-adolescent and teenage boys and, less commonly, in men when the testicle (testis) rotates (twists) along its supporting structures. This condition is a profound medical emergency and must be treated immediately, almost always by surgical intervention, to prevent the loss of a testicle.

Walter M. O'Brien, M.D., and John H. Lynch, M.D., of Georgetown University Hospital in Washington, D.C., describe testicular torsion as "characterized by the sudden onset of testicular pain associated with abdominal pain, nausea and vomiting."[75] There is no effective medical treatment, either allopathic or homeopathic, for this condition outside of surgery. However, as testicular torsion is becoming more common (estimated incidence as high as 1 case in every 160 males),[76] especially in prepubertal and adolescent boys, it is presented here. The condition is most often seen in the sudden development of severe pain in the testicle which radiates into the groin. However, W.C. Sharer, M.D., estimates that as many as 35 to 50 percent of patients present with "a gradual onset of pain."[77] Drs. O'Brien and Lynch recommend that, "In general, men and boys with a presentation strongly suggestive of torsion, such as *sudden onset of testicular pain associated with abdominal pain, nausea and vomiting, absence of fever* [emphasis the author's] should seek immediate medical evaluation."[78]

Penile Injuries

Injuries to the penis, especially bruising injuries, are not uncommon, especially in young boys and teenagers whose activity levels are high. Simple bruising injuries are best treated by *Arnica,* which is noted for its rapid ability to heal bruised tissues and damaged blood vessels.

Potency and Dosage: 6x to 30x, 1 dose every 30 minutes for 3 to 4 doses, then 1 dose every 3 to 4 hours, as needed.

Bellis perennis, which, unfortunately, is not often found in homeopathic first aid kits or the home medicine cabinet, is also an excellent remedy in bruising injuries to the penis. Bellis is best used in its low potencies (3x to 6x).

Potency and Dosage: 3x to 6x, one dose every 30 minutes for 3 to 4 doses, then one dose every 3 to 4 hours, as needed.

If the injury to the penis is, or includes, a minor cut or scrape, *Calendula succus* is recommended as a topical application to prevent inflammation and infection through its bacteriostatic action. The small wound may then be covered by a plastic bandage.

Epididymitis

Epididymitis is an inflammation of the sperm duct located at the top of each testicle and is most often caused by a bacterial infection of the urinary tract. The epididymis is the storage area for maturing sperm. According to Drs. O'Brien and Lynch, epididymitis "is the most common cause of an acute scrotum in postpubertal (teenage and adult) males."[79] In this condition pain develops slowly, perhaps over a period of one to two days. Only rarely does the man exhibit symptoms of nausea or vomiting, and an elevated fever may occur in 50 percent of cases.

HOMEOPATHIC TREATMENT
Belladonna
Clematis
Hamamelis
Pulsatilla

Belladonna shows the Keynote symptoms of: great sensitivity to pressure (as from clothing) and touch; intolerance to pain; pain developing suddenly and often disappearing suddenly; extreme *localization* of pain.

Potency and Dosage: 6x to 30x, one dose every 15 to 30 minutes until pain ceases or is greatly lessened, then one dose every 3 to 4 hours as required.

Clematis demonstrates the Keynote symptoms of: swelling of the epididymis; acute pain from pressure; sensitivity of the testicle (especially the *right* testis which feels drawn up).

Potency and Dosage: 6x to 30x, one dose every 15 to 30 minutes until pain ceases or is greatly lessened, then one dose every 3 to 4 hours as required.

Hamamelis, the homeopathic preparation from the witch hazel plant, is most often a major remedy in inflammation of the epididymis. Its Keynote symptoms are a dull aching pain along the testes and the spermatic chord accompanied by exquisite soreness.

Potency and Dosage: 6x to 30x, one dose every 15 to 30 minutes until pain ceases or is greatly lessened, then one dose every 3 to 4 hours as required.

Pulsatilla, made homeopathically from the wind flower, has a great and well-deserved reputation in epididymitis. Pulsatilla's Keynote symptoms are: pain from the testis shooting *downward* into the thigh; dragging pain along the spermatic chord; the testis feels drawn up; perhaps *the* "Key" symptom is any pain that shoots downward.

Potency and Dosage: 6x to 30x, one dose every 15 to 30 minutes until pain ceases or is greatly lessened, then one dose every 3 to 4 hours as required.

> ADVISORY WARNING: *Any sudden* onset of pain (moderate to severe) which is localized or which radiates into the groin is possibly an indication of *testicular torsion* and requires *immediate* medical evaluation. In testicular torsion, fever is generally present together with swelling and extreme redness of the scrotum. If any of these symptoms are present, the medical self-helper is instructed to take the victim to the nearest hospital emergency room or to call his or her physician and say, "I suspect testicular torsion."

Orchitis

Orchitis is an acute infection that involves only the testicle (testis) itself. An inflammation that involves both the testis and the epididymis together is called *Epididymo-orchitis.*

HOMEOPATHIC TREATMENT
Clematis
Hamamelis
Pulsatilla
Gelsemium

The homeopathic remedies **Clematis, Hamamelis,** and **Pulsatilla** have already been presented under the treatment of epididymitis. If the Keynote symptoms agree, each remedy is an effective treatment for either orchitis or the more common ailment Epididymo-orchitis. Potency selection and dosage repetition are the same.

Gelsemium, the homeopathically prepared remedy from the yellow jasmine flower, is often considered a major and superior remedy in orchitis and epididymo-orchitis. With Gelsemium the condition may develop following exposure to cold dampness.

Potency and Dosage: 6x to 30x, one dose every 15 to 30 minutes until pain ceases or is greatly lessened, then one dose every 3 to 4 hours as required.

Traditional and medically appropriate antibiotic therapy may be required in the treatment of the above-mentioned conditions, especially if they derive from a sexually transmitted disease (STD). However, concomitant treatment with the most-specific homeopathic remedy will not interfere with allopathic treatment. Utilizing homeopathic medicines as adjunctive therapies in these conditions may well prevent these conditions from becoming chronic. Such effectiveness in employing homeopathic remedies has been clearly demonstrated innumerable times in homeopathic practice.

> ADVISORY WARNING: Acute orchitis that develops rapidly and is associated with a high fever and a sudden onset of testicular pain is impossible for the medical self-helper to differentiate from testicular torsion as the general symptoms overlap. *Any pain in the testis that develops suddenly and/or is accompanied by fever, redness of the scrotum, and/or nausea and vomiting must be considered a medical emergency. Take the victim to the nearest hospital emergency room or call a physician immediately.*

Testicular Self-Examination

Due to the prevalance of breast cancer among women in the modern Western world, women are constantly instructed in the vital importance of monthly breast self-examination. Males, however, are seldom instructed in the importance of a monthly testicular self-examination. It is just as important.

John Donahue, M.D., Chairman of the Department of Urology at the Indiana University School of Medicine, stresses that *all* males between the ages of 14–15 to 35 receive a thorough genital examination yearly. As the incidence of malignant tumors of the testicle(s) is increasing, and since perhaps only 20 percent of these tumors produce any outward symptom (such as pain), self-examination between annual examinations in this age group is especially important.

THE 3-MINUTE SELF-EXAMINATION

This simple screening test should be done monthly and requires only 3 minutes. Those 3 minutes can be vital in saving a boy's or man's life.

The testicular self-examination is best done during a shower or bath when the warmth of the water permits the scrotum to relax and the testicles to hang low, making the examination of their structures easier.

In a standing position, begin the examination high up at the top of the testicles. Place the thumb and first two fingers gently on each testis and move the thumbs and fingers over each. The normal testicle is *smooth* and slightly *springy*. Note any bumps, lumps, or any local tenderness. Note any difference in size between the two testicles. Normal testicles are mirror images of one another, identical in size and shape. It is normal for one testis (usually the left) to hang slightly lower than its companion.[80]

ADVISORY WARNING: Any hard lump or local tenderness or any change in the size or shape of a testicle might indicate a malignant tumor and must be brought to the immediate attention of a physician. With early detection and appropriate treatment the survival rate from testicular cancer is significantly high.

For additional information and a simple chart to explain testicular self-examination please write to:

CANCER
Saturday Evening Post Society
Box 567
Indianapolis, Indiana 46206

Menorrhagia

Any excessive, painful, or prolonged uterine bleeding may be caused by any number of factors including contraceptive devices, chronic infections, and blood disorders. Menorrhagia is defined, here, as any excessive menstrual flow, rather than uterine bleeding occurring at a time other than the menstrual cycle.

HOMEOPATHIC TREATMENT
Crocus Sativus
Crotalus Horridus
Ipecacuanha (Ipecac)
Belladonna

Crocus, made from the saffron herb, is considered to be a most important remedy in menorrhagia. In excessive menstruation, the Keynote symptoms of Crocus are: *dark* and *stringy* hemorrhage; thick bleeding, especially characterized by *dark-colored* clots; symptoms are *worse* for lying down, hot weather, warmth; bleeding is more profuse in the morning hours.

Potency and Dosage: 6x–30x, 3 to 5 tablets every 2 to 3 hours until symptoms cease or lessen, as required.

Crotalus horridus is the trituration and potentization of the venom of the rattlesnake. As is true in the homeopathic principle of the Law of Similars, what a full-potency crude drug can cause in a healthy person it can also heal in the potentized micro-dose.

Keynote symptoms of Crotalus include: prolonged menstruation; dark hemorrhage that *forms no clots;* symptoms are *worse* in the morning and evening hours; patient *sleeps into an aggravation of symptoms.*

Perhaps this latter Keynote symptom requires an explanation. As appears true of all snake venoms, the patient goes to bed feeling well and upon awakening finds that he or she has developed symptoms, or the symptoms are far more aggravated. In homeopathy this symptom is called a *periodicity.*

Potency and Dosage: The 6x or 12x potency is preferred, 3 to 5 tablets every 2 to 3 hours until symptoms cease or lessen, as required.

Ipecacuanha is one of the most important homeopathic hemorrhage remedies, Keynote symptoms agreeing. The "Key"-most symptom is *bright-red* and *profuse* hemorrhage; hemorrhage is accompanied by nausea; painful hemorrhage; pain radiating from the navel to the uterus; all symptoms are *worse* periodically ("on-again-off-again") and *worse* from lying down.

Potency and Dosage: 6x to 30x, 3 to 5 tablets every 2 to 3 hours until symptoms cease or lessen. The higher 200x may also be used well in hemorrhage, one (possibly two) doses of 3 to 5 tablets or pellets.

Belladonna, derived from the deadly nightshade, is an excellent remedy for menorrhagia if the Keynote symptoms agree: the menses are *bright red;* menstruation comes on too early and is too profuse; a "Key"-most symptom is *heat;* menses are hot; menses are accompanied by a bearing-down pain; symptoms are *worse* in the afternoon and from lying down.

Potency and Dosage: 6x to 30x, 3 to 5 tablets every 2 to 3 hours until symptoms cease or lessen. The higher 200x may also be used well in hemorrhage, one (possibly two) doses of 3 to 5 tablets or pellets. In especially acute cases repeat the lower potencies frequently (every 15 to 30 minutes) for several doses.

ADVISORY WARNING: Unusually heavy bleeding, or less excessive bleeding that does not respond to the most appropriate homeopathic treatment within 24 to 36 hours requires the attention of a health care professional.

Dysmenorrhea

Dysmenorrhea is defined as painful menstruation where the period is preceded by moderate to severe pains in the lower portion of the abdomen and frequently in the lower back.

While the *Materia Medica* lists numerous remedies for dysmenorrhea, the following are perhaps the most often used, as their Keynote symptoms indicate.

HOMEOPATHIC TREATMENT
Belladonna
Chamomilla
Pulsatilla
Magnesia Phosphorica (*Mag. Phos.*)

Belladonna's Keynote symptoms include: severe pain in the lower back; strong pain which seems to bear downward in the lower abdomen (often described "like the insides are about to fall out"); pain often produces a symptom of an urging to defecate accompanied by ineffective straining; pain is *worse* from touch, pressure, and lying down and *better* from sitting; symptoms are always associated with *heat*.

Potency and Dosage: 6x to 30x, 3 to 5 tablets every 2 to 3 hours until symptoms cease or lessen. The higher 200x repeated for one or two doses has also shown to be effective. In especially acute cases repeat the lower potencies frequently (every 15 to 30 minutes) for several doses.

Chamomilla, from the German chamomile flower, is a marvelous remedy for dysmenorrhea, especially when the "Key"-most symptom of *pain re-*

sembling labor pains is present. Other Keynote symptoms of Chamomilla are: labor-like pains beginning in the lower back; pains extend from the lower back around to the front and lower abdomen often accompanied by a griping pain near the navel; hemorrhage is profuse, blood is *clotted* and *dark;* all symptoms are *worse* from heat and in the evening hours.

Potency and Dosage: 6x to 30x, 3 to 5 tablets every 2 to 3 hours until symptoms cease or lessen.

Pulsatilla, the wind flower, is considered by homeopaths as a preeminent female remedy, especially suited to women whose constitutional temperament is mild, gentle, and passive. However, these symptoms, if absent, need not preclude Pulsatilla. In conditions best addressed by Pulsatilla, the temperament may be changeable and contradictory, one moment mild and the next peevish. *Changability* is a "Key"-most symptom in this remedy. Other Keynote symptoms include: abdominal pain coming in spasms; dark menses coming in clots, or pale blood; dysmenorrhagic pain presses into the abdomen and the lower back, sometimes accompanied by nausea and vomiting; pains migrate (shift from place to place); pains are *worse* from heat and *better* from cold applications.

An interesting symptom of Pulsatilla is often expressed by women who report that the more severe the pains become, the chillier they become.

Potency and Dosage: 6x to 30x, 3 to 5 tablets every 2 to 3 hours until symptoms cease or lessen. Pulsatilla is reported to be especially effective when taken *before* the period. As a preventive measure, Pulsatilla may be taken, one dose of the 30x potency, 3 to 5 tablets, every *fourth* evening, according to Iyer, or the 200x potency, one dose every 2 weeks.[81]

Magnesia phosphorica, homeopathic Mag. phos., is a tissue (sometimes called a cell) salt of great power in spasmodic pains that cramp. The Keynote symptoms are: *cramping* pains of a neuralgic nature that precede the menstrual cycle; pain is relieved by warmth; griping pains in the abdomen often forcing the woman to bend over; "membranous dysmenorrhea"—menses are dark, stringy, and membrane-like; symptoms are *better* from warmth, pressure, and bending over.

Potency and Dosage: 3x to 6x, 15 to 20 1-grain tablets dissolved in *warm* water and drunk. Mag. phos. is one of the few homeopathic remedies that is best taken internally rather than dissolved on or under the tongue and in large doses of 15 to 20 grains. The anti-cramping relief of Mag. phos. appears to be greatly facilitated by dissolving the tablets in a small amount of warm water. Without fear of overdosing, this remedy may be taken every hour as needed. Pain relief is often very rapid.

Urinary Problems

The most common cause of female urinary problems, other than that caused by a sexually transmitted disease, is cystitis, an uncomfortable but non-serious bladder infection. Because the urethra (the outlet from the bladder) in women is only 1 inch in length and because of its proximity to the anus, faulty hygiene is often the culprit in cystitis.

The common symptoms of cystitis are: sudden urging to urinate; frequently urging to urinate (every few minutes); urine passes in only a few drops; painful urination accompanied by *burning* pain; sometimes the urine is mixed with a small amount of blood (pinkish coloration).

HOMEOPATHIC REMEDIES
Cantharis
Mercurius Corrosivus
Nux Vomica

Cantharis in its crude form (an extract of the Spanish beetle) creates a severe disturbance of the urinary and genital organs, establishing a violent and painful inflammation. Because the Keynote symptoms of Cantharis resemble the most common symptoms of cystitis, it is most often considered a near-specific remedy. The Keynote symptoms of Cantharis are: intolerable and persistent urge to urinate; burning pains upon urination; pains occur before, during, and following urination; urine passes in drops; urine is sometimes bloody with small clots visible.

Potency and Dosage: 30x is the preferred potency, 3 to 5 tablets every 2 to 3 hours until symptoms cease or lessen. Repeat the 30x potency only to a maximum of nine doses. The higher 200x potency may also be used giving one to two doses only.

A case history well illustrates the power of Cantharis in cystitis. A lawyer consulted her homeopath for advice with her chronic urinary problems which had occurred at intervals of about every 2 months from mid-adolescence. Each episode sent her to an allopathic physician who prescribed various urinary anti-infectives and analgesics, which cleared up the problem but provided no long-term relief. Upon taking a thorough history, the homeopath prescribed Cantharis in the 30x potency to be taken, as directed above, at the earliest sign of an attack. The attorney noted that she could "always tell when my cystitis was about to begin" and at that first sign she took "two or three doses" of Cantharis. The remedy always cleared the symptoms within a few brief hours and, following only 3 months of treatment, as needed, she returned to inform the homeopath that she had been completely symptom-free for many months. To date the attorney has had no recurrence of cystitis.

An interesting side note that shows the effectiveness of Cantharis in urinary tract disorders occurred in a 15-year-old boy who experienced painful urination, burning, and small clots of blood in his urine following a physical education class. As the boy had no history of sexual activity, and based upon the Keynote symptoms, one dose of Cantharis 200x was prescribed. All pain was relieved within 2 hours and there was no further recurrence of symptoms. As with *all* homeopathic remedies, Cantharis does not mask symptoms of disease through any analgesic power, but works rapidly with the body's own immune-response system to produce a cure.

Mercurius corrosivus is a homeopathic mineral remedy (mercury chloride) that is also useful in cystitis when its Keynote symptoms agree with the overall symptom picture: constant urging to urinate accompanied by intense burning; frequent desire to urinate requiring straining; urine is *hot, scalding,* suppressed, or unable to be passed at all; stabbing, knife-like pain extends up the urethra into the bladder; urine may be mixed with small amounts of blood.

Potency and Dosage: 12x to 30x, 3 to 5 tablets every 2 to 3 hours, until symptoms are relieved or greatly lessened.

Nux vomica, a homeopathic remedy produced from the poison-nut, is often called upon in cases of cystitis. The Keynote symptoms of Nux vomica are: irritable bladder; frequent urge to urinate; only a small quantity of urine is passed at any one time; *itching* in the urethra on urinating accompanied by pain in the neck of the bladder; symptoms are most often *worse* in the morning and *better* in the evening hours.

Potency and Dosage: 6x to 30x, 3 to 5 tablets every 2 to 3 hours as required until symptoms cease or are greatly lessened. *NOTE:* William

Boericke, M.D., states that Nux appears to work most effectively when taken in the evening.[82]

> ADVISORY WARNING: Any severe reduction in the normal amount of urine, or the total inability to urinate, signals danger. These symptoms are indicative of *pyelitis,* an inflammation and blockage of the urinary outlets from the kidneys. Low back pain, burning sensations upon passing a small quantity of urine, fever and chills, may be symptoms of a kidney infection. This is a medical emergency and requires the immediate attention of a physician.

CHAPTER TWELVE

FIRST AID IN CHOKING

Choking on a piece of food, usually a bit of meat that has not been well chewed before swallowing, is one of the most common causes of death in public restaurants and at the family dining table. Often called "cafe coronary," this life-threatening accident often results when someone has consumed too much alcohol, which dulls the senses, making the potential victim less aware of careful chewing before swallowing food.

Late in 1985, the Surgeon General of the United States announced that there is now *only* one way to properly treat a choking victim. *Do not use back blows in an attempt to dislodge the object blocking the throat.* Back blows may lodge the object further in the airway. The most efficient technique is the Heimlich maneuver (named after its inventor, Henry Heimlich, M.D.), which is sometimes called the manual thrust technique. The Heimlich maneuver has saved thousands of lives worldwide and has been used by men, women, and even children. The body size of the rescuer is not important, only the proper knowledge of the technique and the willingness to use it.

The Universal Choking Sign

The universal choking sign, understood worldwide, is to place the hands at the throat. The universal choking sign is used when someone has swallowed an object which completely blocks the airway. The first-aider should always ask the victim, "Can you speak?" If the person is able to breathe at all, to speak, or to cough, *do not use the Heimlich maneuver.* Breathing, speaking, or coughing are all signs that the airway is not completely blocked. The victim's own coughing should be sufficient to remove the object.

The Heimlich Maneuver

Ideally, the choking victim is stood upright. This position enables the rescuer to give a vigorous, thrusting squeeze, which it is hoped will cause the air that is normally remaining in the lungs to force the object blocking the airway out of the throat much like a cork explodes from a champagne bottle.

Proper hand placement is important for success. The rescuer's hands are placed midway on the upper abdomen, above the navel and below the sternum (breast bone) of the chest. The first hand is doubled into a fist and placed against the upper abdomen; the opposite hand is placed over the fist.

The life-saving Heimlich maneuver can also be performed with the victim seated, the rescuer kneeling behind. If the victim has fallen to the floor, the rescuer should kneel on the floor, straddling the victim's hips, and perform the forceful, manual thrust.

A person's lungs are never fully empty of air. What residual air is available in the lungs can be forced against the airway obstruction. More than one thrust may be required to remove the object.

Homeopathic First Aid

If the choking incident happens in the home, give *Arnica* in the 30x or 200x potency as a prophylaxis against shock. Remember: The first-aider expects shock in *all* injuries and accidents, and is prepared to treat it accordingly.

ENDNOTES

1. John M. Barry, ed., *You and Holistic Health* (St. Charles, IL: American Holistic Health Sciences Association, 1983).

2. Lewis Vaughn, "Are Doctors Really Necessary?", *Prevention,* August 1983, p. 76.

3. Vaughn, op cit., p. 77.

4. See K. Steele et al., "Iatrogenic Illness on a General Medical Service at a University Hospital," *New England Journal of Medicine,* 304:638–642, 1981.

5. John M. Barry, ed., *Herald of Holistic Health,* Fall 1983, p. 7.

6. Dana Ullman, M.P.H., "Health, Illness, and Medicine in the 21st Century," *Homeopathy: Medicine for the 21st Century* (Berkeley, CA: North Atlantic Books, 1988), p. xiii.

7. Deborah G. Hirtz et al., "Seizures Following Childhood Immunizations," *The Journal of Pediatrics,* 102:14, 1983.

8. Office of Technology Assessment, *Assessing the Safety and Efficacy of Medical Technology* (Washington, D.C.: U.S. Government Printing Office, September 1978), p. 7.

9. "Medicine: Drug Disease," *Newsweek,* May 2, 1966, pp. 64–65.

10. John M. Barry, ed., "For They Know Not What They Do," *Herald of Holistic Health,* Fall 1983, p. 2.

11. "Medicine: Is the Prescription Right?" *Time,* September 20, 1968.

12. Frank Brodman, M.D., "The Role of Homeopathic Medicine in the National Health Service," *The Lancet,* 1:913, 1968.

13. "Homeopathy—A Neglected Medical Art," *Prevention*, February, 1969. (Reprinted by National Center for Homeopathy, Washington, D.C., 1969.)

14. *Homeopathy: The Scientific Practice of Medicine*, Washington, D.C. (Falls Church, National Center for Homeopathy).

15. Brian Inglis writes in his book, *The Case for Unorthodox Medicine*, briefly on the decline of homeopathy in the United States which began about 1910. "Many of the [orthodox medical] professors were resentful of reformers [primarily the homeopaths and other physicians who held eminence and respectability but who were decidedly unorthodox such as Drs. Benjamin Rush and Oliver Wendell Holmes] threatening them with more exacting work for less money. But gradually the pressures exerted by the AMA and state legislatures began to tell, and schools who were not [AMA] approved were squeezed out of existence. The AMA, though, was not concerned solely with the efficiency and honesty of schools; it was also anxious about what they taught. Homeopathic establishments were instructing students in what by this time—with the Pasteur revolution accomplished—the AMA regarded as wrongheaded as well as being heretical. Accordingly, pressure was put on the homeopathic schools to conform to the accepted national standards." Brian Inglis, *The Case for Unorthodox Medicine* (New York: Berkley Publishing Corporation/G.P. Putnam's Sons, 1965), p. 69. For a complete history of homeopathy (also spelled homoeopathy), the reader is encouraged to consult Harris L. Coulter, Ph.D., *Homoeopathic Medicine* (St. Louis: Formur, Inc., 1975).

16. Technically, homeopathy is a subspecialty of internal medicine, but today, at least in the United States, no medical school includes homeopathy in its curriculum. It is learned in postgraduate studies conducted by several homeopathic organizations. Only schools of naturopathic medicine and nutrimedicine include it as an integral part of the regular curriculum.

17. Helen Mathews Smith, "Special Report: The Rebirth of Homeopathy," *MD Magazine* (New York: MD Publications, Inc.), April 1985, pp. 114, 116, 118, 120, 121.

18. Kathleen Duggan, Executive Editor, "Medical Care Depersonalized," *American Homeopathy*, 1(3):4, 1984.

19. Kathleen Duggan, Executive Editor, "Cultivating Competent Patients," *American Homeopathy: Professional Edition*, 1(6):5, 1984.

20. Antimicrobials are of two types. One, the *antibiotics* such as penicillin and its derivatives, acts by directly attacking the cell wall synthesis so the cell bursts when its cell wall is unable to be fully formed as the bacteria divides, or during the normal chemical reactions within the bacteria. Antimicrobials such as the tetracyclines and sulfonamides are *bacteriostatic* agents that interfere with the normal growth cycle of bacteria, preventing them from producing nutrients such as protein in the mitochondria.

21. *Allopathic* is a term coined by Hahnemann to describe the type of medicine practiced during his lifetime and today. *Allopathy* comes from the Greek words *allos* (different) and *pathos* (disease). Allopathy treats disease by prescribing drugs that oppose the symptoms and is therefore the exact opposite of homeopathy.

22. Antibiotic and bacteriostatic drugs are useful against bacteria-caused infections. They are generally ineffective against diseases caused by viruses, which are both living and nonliving organisms. Antibiotics can be used in certain viral infections to help prevent or treat bacterial superinfections that result from the body's debilitated defenses. There exists also a class of organisms that do not meet the definitions of either viruses or bacteria, being too large or small, or not having appropriate cell wall material or appropriate reproductive methods to be classified as either. Rickettsial diseases (sleeping sickness) and mycoplasma pneumonia are examples. Select antibiologicals are effective. Antibiotics for certain viruses are now available, such as Zovirax for genital herpes.

23. Burroughs Wellcome Company, Research Triangle Park, NC, February 1982.

24. Old first-aid methods called for tilting the head back. The treatment most recommended today by ear, nose, and throat specialists is a mild forward tilt to allow pooling of platelets and proper clotting. A backward tilt pinches the vertebral arteries, producing greater carotid flow and therefore greater blood flow to the nose.

25. Five to 6 days is more common for blood resorption in a subconjunctival hemorrhage. However, a rebleed is not uncommon on the fifth day.

26. Jack E. Craig, ed., *Homeopathic Miscellany* 2(1):3, 1978 (Los Angeles: The Standard Homeopathic Company).

27. The process of trituration permits homeopathy to employ substances which, in their natural state, are deadly poisons. Arsenicum album (arsenic trioxide), Belladonna (the deadly nightshade), and Cantharis (the Spanish beetle) are only a few examples. Triturated into homeopathic potencies of 6x and higher, these substances lose their poisonous nature and become valuable medicines. Even these normally poisonous substances, in homeopathic form, are completely safe, even for use by children. United States law, however, requires that all medications carry the advisory label: "Warning: Keep out of the reach of children."

28. Kathleen Duggan, Executive Editor, "About Potencies," *American Homeopathy,* 2(2):7, 1985.

29. Ibid.

30. Stanley Ries et al., "Triacontanol: A New Naturally Occurring Plant Growth Regulator," *Science,* 195:1339–1341, 1977. See I. Amato, "Molecular Divorce Gives Strange Vibes," *Science News,* Nov. 1, 1986, pp. 277–278. This article reports briefly on a study conducted by chemists in the United States National Bureau

of Standards. Experimentally, these scientists violently agitated the coupled molecules of nitric acid and discovered that rather than the molecular bonds weakening and breaking apart the molecular bonds actually became stronger. This discovery may well be found to reinforce the rediscovery of the homeopathic principle of Dr. Samuel Hahnemann's potentized micro-dose. In the late 18th century, Dr. Hahnemann discovered that by diluting a drug and then violently shaking it (a process called succusion) the resulting drug did not lose its strength through continued dilution and succusion but rather *increased* in strength.

31. In France, where homeopathy is especially popular, French law prohibits even physicians from prescribing remedies above the 30c (60x) potency.

32. Elizabeth Wright-Hubbard, M.D., *A Brief Study Course in Homeopathy* (St. Louis: Formur, Inc., 1977).

33. The homeopathic micro-dose is now often referred to as ultramolecular medicine.

34. "Until recently, [homeopathic] physicians have been unable to explain the mechanism involved in the healing effect of their particular practice. Today's physicist can explain the mechanism of action of both acupuncture and homeopathy. Medicines in homeopathy are often diluted beyond the existence of a single atom of the original substance. The unique energy field of a substance, the magnetic blueprint, maintains its identity in the absence of that substance in a material sense. Indeed, the less of a material substance present, the greater the intensity of the magnetic field and the greater or more profound is the effect upon the body." F. Fuller Royal, M.D., "Accupath 1000: Combining Acupuncture Treatment with Homeopathic Treatment," *Journal of Ultramolecular Medicine,* 1(1):42, 1983 (Provo, UT: Brigham Young University).

35. One dram equals 1.77 grams, or about ⅓ teaspoon.

36. A number of excellent books currently are available from homeopathic book supplier covering homeopathic veterinary care: K. Shepphard, M.D., *Homeopathic Treatment of Cats* (a paperbound guide to complete feline care); K. Shepphard, M.D., *Homeopathic Treatment of Dogs* (a paperbound guide to the comprehensive treatment of canines); G. Macleod, D.V.S.M., *The Treatment of Horses by Homeopathy* (a guide to complete equine care); G. Macleod, *The Treatment of Cattle by Homeopathy.*

37. Jack E. Craig, ed., "Homeopathic Botanicals Are NOT the Same as Herbal Remedies," *Homeopathic Miscellany,* 1(3):1, 1977 (Los Angeles: The Standard Homeopathic Company).

38. The decimal (x) and centesimal (c or CH) potencies have been discussed earlier. While they are not equivalent, they may be substituted one for the other in first-aid treatment without difficulty.

39. A patient consulting a qualified homeopathic physician for treatment and who is taking cortisone may possibly be treated successfully. The physician may attempt to nullify the allopathic cortisone with a high potency of homeopathic cortisone. This, however, is the practice of *medicine* and not first aid. It is the physician's decision. The first-aider, and medical self-helper, must never attempt this.

40. "Homeopathy and Sports Medicine," *American Homeopathy:* Professional Edition, 1(6):5, 1984.

41. Maesimund B. Panos, M.D., "Family Self-Help Using Homeopathy," Lecture III (Falls Church, VA: National Center for Homeopathy, 1974, p. 34).

42. A 99.2% pure Aloe vera extract is available in a spray bottle from many natural health outlets. Aloe vera not only relieves pain quickly, but also establishes a rapid healing of the burned tissue.

43. As some persons are allergic to PABA-containing sunscreen products, check the label. Synthetic non-PABA sunscreens have been developed that offer similar protection.

44. "How a Wound Mends," *Science Digest,* May 1983, p. 86.

45. One of the advantages of some brands of plastic strips (e.g., Band-Aid) is the Teflon coat making it "nonstick." Teflon dressings are relatively expensive compared to sterile gauze, but much more comfortable on removal.

46. Dorothy Shepherd, M.D., *The Magic of the Minimum Dose* (Devon, England: Health Science Press, 1964), p. 156.

47. A #10 scalpel has a deep, nearly half-moon shaped blade which is ideal for removing embedded foreign particles from wounds through a gentle, scraping motion. The narrower #11 blade is inappropriate.

48. The first-aider will have noticed throughout this book that most homeopathic remedies have multiple uses. In the first-aid treatment of wounds, the first-aider should, of course, use that remedy which is *most specific* to the condition being treated. However, in the case of open wounds, if the most effective remedy is out of stock and unavailable, the first-aider may substitute one remedy for another with good effect. Calendula tincture may be used in place of Hypericum tincture, Ledum pal. tincture substituted for either, as well as Echinacea tincture, and vice versa. Even Bellis perennis tincture, in diluted solution, is effective in the treatment of wounds.

49. *The Merck Manual of Diagnosis and Therapy,* 13th edition (Rahway, NJ: Merck Sharp & Dohme Research Laboratories, 1977), p. 1577.

50. Shepherd, *The Magic of the Minimum Dose,* op. cit., p. 161.

51. When the pupils of the eyes are unequal and dilated or do not react to direct, bright-light stimulus as from a penlight flashlight, this is a sign of extremely serious

brain injury and requires the prompt care of a qualified physician. Arrange for the rapid transport of the victim to the nearest medical facility.

52. Andy Moss, "On Combination Homeopathy," *BHI Roundtable* 3:3, 1988 (Albuquerque, NM: Biological Homeopathic Industries).

53. Dana Ullman, M.P.H., "In Support of the Limited Use of Combination Homeopathic Medicines," *Homeopathy Today* January 1984, p. 6 (Washington, D.C.: National Center for Homeopathy).

54. J. B. Chapman, M.D., and Edward L. Perry, M.D., *The Biochemic Handbook: How to Get Well and Keep Fit with Biochemic Tissue Salts* (St. Louis: Formur, Inc., 1973), p. 14.

55. In order to determine the condition of the eardrum, it is necessary to use an instrument by which the external auditory meatus and the tympanic membrane can be examined. Health care professionals employ an instrument called an *otoscope,* which includes attachable specula of assorted sizes, a brilliant illuminator, rotary light control, and a powerful magnification lens. Specialized training is required in the use of the otoscope for diagnostic purposes. Another instrument is available to the first-aider and medical self-helper which is far less expensive and simpler to operate. Called the orotoscope, it is essentially a penlight flashlight with an attachable fiberoptic speculum that allows the user to examine the external ear canal and the eardrum, but does not permit the speculum attachment to be inserted into the canal beyond a safe distance. The orotoscope may be a useful piece of first-aid equipment. It is available from the Piper Brace Sales Corporation, 811 Wyandotte, P.O. Box 807, Kansas City, MO 64141. It comes with detailed instructions for use.

56. Shepherd, *The Magic of the Minimum Dose,* pp. 47–48.

57. Ledum pal. appears to be especially effective in the 6c or 12x potency.

58. W. A. Dewey, M.D., *Practical Homoeopathic Therapeutics,* 3rd ed. (New Delhi: Jain Publishing Company, 1981), p. 150.

59. Dewey, *Practical Homoeopathic Therapeutics,* op. cit., p. 155.

60. James H. Stephenson, M.D., *A Doctor's Guide to Helping Yourself with Homeopathic Remedies* (West Nyack, NY: Parker Publishing Company, Inc., 1976), p. 55.

61. M. L. Tyler, M.D., *Homoeopathic Drug Pictures* (Devon, England: Bradford, Holsworthy, 1952), p. 196.

62. Tyler, *Homoeopathic Drug Pictures,* op. cit., p. 714.

63. "In Reply to Your Recent Inquiry . . . ," *Homeopathic Miscellany* 2(1):3, 1978 (Los Angeles: Standard Homeopathic Company).

64. Serge Duckett, M.D., "Plaintain Leaf for Poison Ivy," *New England Journal of Medicine* 303:583, 1980.

65. Stephenson, *A Doctor's Guide to Helping Yourself with Homeopathic Remedies,* op. cit., p. 87.

66. Kerry Pechter, "How to Handle Summertime Emergencies," *Prevention,* June 1983, p. 58.

67. Enteric-coated salt tablets are available, which dissolve in the small intestine and do not cause stomach erosion or distress.

68. Three excellent books are available on the nature and use of the 12 "tissue (or cell) salts" first isolated by W. H. Schuessler, M.D., in 1873. Also called "biochemical cell salts," they are not drugs, but mineral preparations, natural components of the body. The tissue salts are homeopathically triturated in potencies of 3x, 6x, 12x, 30x, and 200x, and in England they are available in a mixed 3x/200x potency. They are extremely useful in treating various illnesses and disorders and, like all remedies compounded homeopathically, are completely safe, non-habit-forming, and rapid acting. The three books are: (1) *The Biochemic Handbook* (St. Louis: Formur, Inc., 1973), (2) *Biochemic Prescriber,* Eric F. W. Powell, N.D., Ph.D. (Devon, England: Health Science Press, 1960), and (3) *How to Use the 12 Tissue Salts: A Guide to the Biochemic Treatment of Pain and Disease,* Esther Chapman (New York: Pyramid Books, 1971).

69. In their book *Homeopathic Medicine at Home* (Los Angeles: J. P. Tarcher, 1980, p. 109), M. B. Panos, M.D., and Jane Heimlich, R.N., state that the death rate under allopathic care during the 2 years of the pandemic ranged from 30 to 40 percent, whereas under homeopathic care, less than 1% of the cases treated proved fatal.

70. Shepherd, *The Magic of the Minimum Dose,* op. cit., p. 14.

71. "Flu: There's A Lot You Can Do About It!" (Wilmington, DE: Du Pont Pharmaceuticals, Biochemical Department, E.I. du Pont de Nemours & Company, Inc., 1983).

72. Other skin affections, such as boils, carbuncles, and vesicular eruptions (poison ivy, poison oak, and poison sumac) have been presented earlier. Consult the listing of contents for appropriate chapters.

73. P. R. Dodds and T. Chi, "Balanitis as a Fixed Drug Reaction to Tetracycline," *Journal of Urology* 113:1044, 1985. "Balanitis is a frequent form of fixed drug eruption for the antibiotic, possibly starting within an hour after taking the drug. Severe pain, swelling, and hemorrhagic ulcerations may persist for several days after drug stoppage."

74. Lewis Thomas, M.D., *The Medusa and the Snail* (New York: The Viking Press, 1979), p. 76.

75. Walter M. O'Brien and John H. Lynch, "The Acute Scrotum," *American Family Physician*, March 1988, p. 239.

76. B. E. Haynes, H. A. Bessen, and V. Haynes, "The Diagnosis of Testicular Torsion," *Journal of the American Medical Association* 249:2522–2527, 1983.

77. W. C. Sharer, "Acute Scrotal Pathology," *Surgical Clinic of North America* 62:955–970, 1982.

78. O'Brien and Lynch, op. cit., p. 246.

79. O'Brien and Lynch, op. cit., p. 242.

80. The author is indebted to Kenneth R. Sladkin, M.D., for information on testicular examination contained in his article, "Examination of the Genitalia in Male Adolescents," *Medical Aspects of Human Sexuality*, June 1987, pp. 56–79.

81. T. S. Iyer, *Beginners Guide to Homoeopathy* (New Delhi: B. Jain Publishers, 1981), p. 251.

82. William Boericke, M.D., *Pocket Manual of Homoeopathic Materia Medica*, 9th ed. (Calcutta: Sett Dey & Company, 1976), p. 478.

APPENDIX ONE

SUPPLIERS OF
HOMEOPATHIC REMEDIES

Annadale Apothecary
7023 Little River Turnpike
Annadale, VA 22003

Biological Homeopathic Industries
11600 Cochiti, S.E.
Albuquerque, NM 87123
(800–621–7644)
(Health professionals only)

*Boericke and Tafel, Inc.
1011 Arch Street
Philadelphia, PA 19107
(215–922–2967)

*Boiron-Borneman, Inc.
1208 Amosland Road
Box 54
Norwood, PA 19074

*Ehrhart & Karl, Inc.
33 North Wabash Avenue
Chicago, IL 60602
(312–332–1046)

Homeopathic Educational Services
2124 Kittredge Street
Berkeley, CA 94704
(415–653–9270)

Horton & Converse
621 West Pico Blvd.
Los Angeles, CA 90015

Dolisos America, Inc.
3014 Rigel Ave.
Las Vegas, NV 89102
(800–365–4767)
(702–871–7153 in Nevada)

*Humphries Pharmacal Company
63 Meadow Road
Rutherford, NJ 07070

Keihl Pharmacy, Inc.
109 Third Avenue
New York, NY 10003

*Luyties Pharmacal Company
4200 Laclede Avenue
P.O. Box 8080
St. Louis, MO 63156–8080
(800–325–8080 outside MO)

Nutri-Dyn
717 South Bristol Avenue
Los Angeles, CA 90049

Santa Monica Drug
1513 Fourth Street
Santa Monica, CA 90401

*Standard Homeopathic Company
P.O. Box 61067
Los Angeles, CA 90061
(213–321–4284)

D. L. Thompson Homeopathic Supplies
844 Yonge Street
Toronto 5, Ontario, Canada M4W 2H1

*Washington Homeopathic Pharmacy
4914 Delray Avenue
Bethesda, MD 20014
(301–656–1695)

*Weleda, Inc.
P.O. Box 769-H
Spring Valley, NY 10977
(Health professionals only)

*Regular Members, American Association of Homeopathic Pharmacists.

APPENDIX TWO

IMPORTANT BOOKS ON HOMEOPATHY

The following books, while not an exhaustive list, are recommended to the interested lay person and to the health care professional interested in the history, theory, philosophy, and practice of homeotherapeutics.

Harris L. Coulter, Ph.D., *Homeopathic Medicine* (St. Louis: Formur, Inc., 1975). A comprehensive presentation of the history and theory of homeopathic medicine written by the leading American historian of homeopathy.

Colin B. Lessell, M.B., B.D.S., *Homeopathy for Physicians: A Practical Introduction to Prescribing* (Wellingborough, Northamptonshire, England: Thorsons Publishers, Ltd., 1983). A short text written for physicians who desire a basic understanding of homeopathic medicine and apply it to their practice. This book is recommended to anyone in the health care professions.

Noel Puddephatt, *Puddephatt's Primers* (N. Devon, England: Health Science Press, 1976). This book is actually three volumes in one and provides an excellent basic introduction to homeopathy.

Keith A. Scott, M.D., and Linda A. McCourt, M.A., *Homeopathy: The Potent Force of the Minimum Dose* (Wellingborough, Northamptonshire, England: Thorsons Publishers, Ltd., 1982). An outstanding presentation on the history and foundation of homeopathic medicine, presenting homeopathy as a viable alternative to orthodox medicine.

Trevor Smith, M.D., *Homeopathic Medicine: A Doctor's Guide to Remedies for Common Ailments* (Rochester, VT: Healing Arts Press, 1982). A practical book and detailed self-help guide to homeopathic treatment entailing the practice of homeopathy in childhood, adolescence, middle age, through geriatric care.

George Vithoulkas, *Homeopathy: Medicine of the New Man* (New York: Arco Publishing, Inc., 1979). Written by the world's leading classical homeopathic theorist, the book is readable and provides a complete introduction to the homeopathic system of medicine.

Elizabeth Wright-Hubbard, M.D., *A Brief Study Course in Homeopathy* (St. Louis: Formur, Inc., 1977). Written by one of America's foremost homeopathic physicians, this book provides an invaluable introduction to the science of homeopathic medicine. Recommended for lay people as well as for the professional health care provider.

Lyle W. Morgan II, H.M.D., Ph.D., *Homeopathic Treatment of Sports Injuries* (Rochester, VT: Healing Arts Press, 1988). A thorough discussion of homeopathic therapies and first-aid procedures appropriate for treating common and uncommon athletic injuries and attending illnesses. "The most detailed book available on how to treat common problems of the serious or occasional athlete" (Dana Ullman).

Margery G. Blackie, M.D., *The Patient, Not the Cure* (London, England: Macdonald and Jane's, Macdonald and Company, 1976). Written by the late physician to Her Majesty, Queen Elizabeth II, this is one of the finest introductions to the concepts of homeopathy. The book includes homeopathic history, discussions on case taking, remedies, *Materia Medica,* and numerous case histories of successful homeopathic treatment in common and rare illnesses.

Stephen Cummings, F.N.P., and Dana Ullman, M.P.H., *Everybody's Guide to Homeopathic Medicines* (Los Angeles: Jeremy P. Tarcher, Inc., 1984). An accurate and very readable guide to medical self-help through homeopathy for acute conditions, written by a family nurse practitioner and a master of public health. Ideal for physicians and adjunct health care providers as well as the general public.

Dana Ullman, M.P.H., *Homeopathy: Medicine for the 21st Century* (Berkeley, CA: North Atlantic Books, 1988). An extremely well-written book that clearly and readably presents the art and science of homeopathy from a modern point of view. Includes homeopathic approaches to problems in pregnancy and delivery, pediatrics, women's health, infectious diseases, psychological disorders, and dentistry.

APPENDIX THREE

SOURCES OF HOMEOPATHIC BOOKS

Book catalogs are available from the following suppliers, usually upon request:

Boericke and Tafel, Inc.
1011 Arch Street
Philadelphia, PA 19107

Boericke and Tafel, Inc.
2381 Circadian Way
Santa Rosa, CA 95407

Boiron-Borneman, Inc.
1208 Amosland Road
Box 54
Norwood, PA 19074

Dolisos America, Inc.
3014 Rigel Avenue
Las Vegas, NV 89102

Ehrhart & Karl, Inc.
33 North Wabash Avenue
Chicago, IL 60602

Formur, Inc.
4200 Laclede Avenue
P.O. Box 8080
St. Louis, MO 63156

Homeopathic Educational Services
2124 Kittredge Street
Berkeley, CA 94704

National Center for Homeopathy
1500 Massachusetts Avenue, N.W.
Suite 41
Washington, DC 20005

Standard Homeopathic Company
P.O. Box 61067
Los Angeles, CA 90061

Yes! Inc. Bookshop
1035 31st Street, N.W.
Washington, D.C. 20007

APPENDIX FOUR

HOMEOPATHIC ORGANIZATIONS

Each of the following organizations was founded to promote the study and practice of homeopathy in the United States. These groups, comprised of physicians, adjunct health care professionals, and lay people, provide beginning, intermediate, and advanced training in homeopathy to lay people and health professionals; publish monthly or quarterly newsletters or journals; and provide many other valuable services and information.

Foundation for Homeopathic Education and Research
5916 Chabot Crest
Oakland, CA 94618
415–649–8930

Homeopathic Educational Services
2124 Kittredge Street
Berkeley, CA 94704

International Foundation for Homeopathy
2236 Eastlake Avenue E. #301
Seattle, WA 98102
206–324–8230

National Center for Homeopathy
1500 Massachusetts Avenue, N.W.
Suite 41
Washington, DC 20005
202–223–6182

INDEX